Amy quickly turned around and searched the murky darkness for the owner of the low voice, her hackles spiking.

"Who's there?" she whispered.

A tall figure emerged from behind the behemoth domed roof. He had wide shoulders and a smooth gait as he slowly approached her, his footfalls quiet.

She maneuvered away from the stranger. "Do I know you?"

"No, but I know you . . . Zarsitti."

She stiffened. "I am not the dancer."

"You are the dancer," he insisted, his voice smoldering. "Your eyes give you away."

"How would you like to lose *your* eyes, you wretched cur!"

She bumped into the building's edge with her heel and teetered. A desperate shout escaped her lungs before a set of thick, hard arms gripped her waist and pulled her against a sturdy chest.

The man's dark, thick, wavy locks grazed her temple as he murmured into her ear, "I would have followed you over the edge for one sweet kiss."

She shuddered at the heat, the softness in his breath; it tickled her ear, caressed her senses like a silk kerchief, and she suddenly yearned for the scoundrel to keep his scandalous word and kiss her . . .

Romances by **Alexandra Benedict**

THE NOTORIOUS SCOUNDREL
MISTRESS OF PARADISE
THE INFAMOUS ROGUE
TOO DANGEROUS TO DESIRE
TOO SCANDALOUS TO WED
TOO GREAT A TEMPTATION
A FORBIDDEN LOVE

The Notorious Scoundrel

ALEXANDRA BENEDICT

AVON

An Imprint of HarperCollinsPublishers

This is a work of fiction. Names, characters, places, and incidents are products of the author's imagination or are used fictitiously and are not to be construed as real. Any resemblance to actual events, locales, organizations, or persons, living or dead, is entirely coincidental.

AVON BOOKS
An Imprint of HarperCollins*Publishers*
10 East 53rd Street
New York, New York 10022-5299

Copyright © 2010 by Alexandra Benedikt
ISBN 978-0-06-168932-1
www.avonromance.com

First Avon Books paperback printing: May 2010

Avon Trademark Reg. U.S. Pat. Off. and in Other Countries, Marca Registrada, Hecho en U.S.A.
HarperCollins® is a registered trademark of HarperCollins Publishers.

Printed in the U.S.A.

10 9 8 7 6 5 4 3 2 1

To Tommy

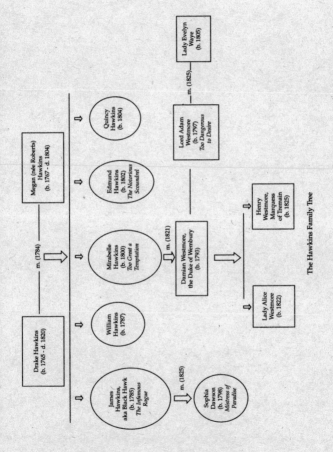

The Hawkins Family Tree

- Drake Hawkins (b. 1765 - d. 1820)
- m. (1784)
- Megan (née Roberts) Hawkins (b. 1767 - d. 1804)

- James Hawkins, aka Black Hawk (b. 1785) *The Infamous Rogue*
  - m. (1825)
  - Sophia Dawson (b. 1798) *Mistress of Paradise*
- William Hawkins (b. 1787)
- Mirabelle Hawkins (b. 1800) *Too Great a Temptation*
  - m. (1821)
  - Damian Westmore, the Duke of Wembury (b. 1793)
    - Lady Alice Westmore (b. 1822)
    - Henry Westmore, Marquess of Tremain (b. 1825)
- Edmund Hawkins (b. 1802) *The Notorious Scoundrel*
- Quincy Hawkins (b. 1804)

- Lord Adam Westmore (b. 1797) *Too Dangerous to Desire*
  - m. (1825)
  - Lady Evelyn Waye (b. 1805)

The Notorious Scoundrel

Chapter 1

London, 1826

"**I** think he wants to stab us, Eddie."

Edmund Hawkins set down the glass of gin and eyed the ne'er-do-well with a baleful expression. The bearded ruffian puffed out his chest in anticipation of a brawl; however, he quickly slunk off under the younger seaman's glare.

Edmund might be four-and-twenty years of age, but he had lived a life as hard and dangerous as any cracksman or murderer in the flash house, and his deadly stare—and meaty fists—proved it.

"He won't stab us," Edmund said with quiet confidence. "He's changed his mind."

Quincy chortled. He rubbed his eyes, red and swollen with fatigue. "We must be getting old. There was a time we would have *started* a scuffle with a brute twice our size."

"Aye, I remember." Edmund studied his brother, two years his junior. Quincy's mussed, curly black hair and dark blue eyes matched Edmund's own visage, yet the men's temperaments differed considerably. "Perhaps we're wiser now."

Quincy humphed and tapped his thumb in an impatient manner across the grimy tabletop.

"You're restless," said Edmund.

"Aren't you?"

He shrugged. "I'm home now."

Edmund had entered the notorious public house, filled with all sorts of scheming criminals, putting the stresses at sea behind him. It was in the notorious public house he was most contented, for there was no hypocrisy within the establishment, just life in gruesome detail. It was where he belonged.

"What's there to be restless about?" he wondered.

"Everything." Quincy rubbed his tanned chin. He glanced at the table, then back at his kin. "Do you think we've made a mistake?"

Edmund understood his brother's meaning, for he had wondered the same thought himself for many months now.

"I dunno. Maybe."

Quincy sighed. "It's not how I imagined it to be."

Six months patrolling the coast of West Africa as privateers in the Royal Navy's African Squadron had not produced the desired results for adventures. The endless, uneventful patrols stripped a mariner of all enthusiasm and spirit. The heavy rains and tremendous heat maintained the body in a constant state of discomfort. And when a ship was spotted, heavy in the water with her human cargo, there was often nothing they could do about it, even with a letter of marque authorizing them to stop any vessel suspected of slaving, for most British ships traveled under foreign papers and raised foreign flags, preventing the seamen from legally boarding them and confiscating the slaves.

Edmund swigged the gin. He remembered the first time he had sighted a British slaver. He remembered the thrill of the battle as the enemy vessel had put up a valiant fight to keep her precious cargo. She had lost, however. Edmund, Quincy, and a few other tars had boarded the ship as the prize crew, and had prepared to sail her into Freetown, where an Admiralty Prize Court had been established to deal with the illegal trade . . . but when he'd first entered the slave decks to release the shackled captives, he had been overwhelmed by the gruesome images: images that haunted him still.

"It can't be guns and glory all the time, I suppose." Edmund moved the glass across the table in an absent-minded fashion. "We should enjoy the respite. We'll have to set sail again in a few weeks."

"I can't sit here anymore." Quincy lifted from his chair. "I'm off to my favorite haunt. Care to join me?"

"No."

"Suit yourself."

Quincy departed from the flash house in quick strides.

Edmund frowned. He was worried about his younger brother. Quincy's favorite haunt was the opium den, and ever since he had tasted the seductive smoke from the Orient, about a year ago, he had grown more and more attached to the substance.

Edmund downed the rest of the gin and wiped his mouth with the back of his hand. The door opened and the room soon filled with other nefarious characters.

He watched the spry figures order a round of spirits from the barkeep. The level of noise inside the public house increased dramatically, and it wasn't difficult to overhear the men's boisterous exchanges:

"A den o' sin, ye say?"

"The most wi'ed in London."

"Where is it?"

"Cove'ent Garden. There's a coat o' arms wiv a bull's head above the door."

"Well, what's it li'e inside the club, ye ol' bugger?"

"How the bleedin' 'ell should I know?" He pointed at his coarse features. "Can't ye see me blag eye?"

"Oh, it's fer gen'lm'n."

"Aye, the gatekeeper thought me a mudlark and trounced me."

A barmaid delivered the ordered drinks then.

"Fanny 'ere will get ye a cold fish to put o'er that blag eye, 'iggins."

Higgins snorted. "I'll just get me wife to sit on it."

The men guffawed.

The jaded Edmund half listened to the gossip, for there were many such establishments within the city, and all boasted similar lurid entertainments. However, the clubs tended to exaggerate their sinful amusements in the hopes of luring rich, young, and bored aristocrats within their walls. A fancy whorehouse might be a "den o' sin," but the most wicked in London? Edmund doubted the claim. And yet his brother had deserted him for more insalubrious pursuits, and he had little else to occupy his time.

With an air of ennui, Edmund hoisted his big frame from the rickety chair and departed the flash house amid the curious stares and penetrating looks of the shifty patrons. He entered the dark and impoverished Buckeridge Street, making his way toward Drury Lane and then on to Covent Garden, where the notorious club was allegedly located.

A thick, greenish fog choked the soiled thoroughfare even more as Edmund moved through the squalid, seedy part of the city. He passed the late-night muffin seller and baked-potato vendor, the cheesemonger and child prostitute. He passed their worn and cheerless faces, guarding his pockets and his throat.

As he neared Covent Garden, gas lamps illuminated his path, but the district at night was no less unsavory than the rookeries, for it was close to the river Thames and inspired all sorts of illicit activity under the cloak of darkness.

It was an odd configuration that the rich and the poor abided next to one another in such close proximity, that one sordid street lay beside its affluent counterpart. Edmund had always marveled at the juxtaposition. It made his own segue from the underworld into respectable society all the more comfortable, and thus all the more deceitful.

Edmund moved through the district, a marketplace during the day, brimming with vendors, and a haunt in the evening for the demimonde, who prowled the famous Royal Opera House steps in search of coin and companionship.

He observed the surrounding structures, seeking the insignia that marked the site of the secret club, and soon located the blazon. He stopped at the foot of the clean-swept steps and gazed at the tall edifice. The architecture was classical in style, the windows masked with heavy drapery, permitting thin beams of light to pierce the glass.

Edmund listened for any sound of revelry coming from inside the building, but the spring night was still. He shrugged and mounted the three stone steps that directed patrons to an imposing front door of paneled wood, flanked by Doric columns. He gripped the chilled brass knocker and pounded on the wood.

A minute passed before the heavy door peeled open on its sturdy hinges and a robust figure appeared in silhouette. The gatekeeper took one look at Edmund's homely attire and promptly shut the door with a resounding smack.

Edmund's fingers twitched and he thumped on the door once more with greater vigor.

The same surly gatekeeper parted the wood.

Edmund announced in his most officious tone: "Edmund Hawkins."

The gatekeeper lifted a brow. It was clear the ornery sentry had recognized the young seaman's familial name, so Edmund refrained from listing his relations with any further pomp, which he loathed to do.

The gatekeeper stepped aside and mutely extended his arm, welcoming Edmund inside the high-end establishment.

As soon as Edmund set foot within the "den o' sin," he concluded his first assumption had been correct: it was not the most wicked establishment in London. He followed the silent sentry through the quiet passageway and entered the foyer with its sweeping high ceiling, the roof capped with a domed and painted fresco.

He scaled the winding steps after his guide, the carpet a rich red fabric. The balustrade was composed of polished wood and intricate wrought iron. The walls were papered in fine yellow print and interspersed with silky, raspberry red panels. At the top of the stairs were a series of elaborate columns and daring artwork.

Edmund passed through the tunnel. The interior was a feast for the senses. The ornate furnishings gleamed under the resplendent chandeliers, making the environment scintillate. It was meant to bedazzle the wits and to strip a wealthy rake from his blunt. It was no more scandalous or provocative than any of the other establishments Edmund had ventured into during the past five years he had lived in the city.

The gatekeeper paused beside a set of white double doors with gold trim.

Edmund listened to the merriment seeping through the slim space between the wood. He almost yawned at the tedium of another conventional gentlemen's club.

He even considered turning away from the doors and leaving the sentry flummoxed, for it inspired more amusement in his reflections than the thought of a "den o' sin." However, he shrugged off the lethargy and allowed the gatekeeper to part the double doors with a measure of fanfare.

The room teemed with cigar smoke and masculine energy, instrumental music and exotic incense. There were tables scattered everywhere, filled with jolly patrons, and the pretty serving girls kept the spirits flowing. Layer upon layer of brilliant silk fabrics swooped from the ceiling and cascaded along the walls and onto the thick-carpeted floor. The room was peppered with palms and other tropical flowers. Satin cushions purled with gold thread bedecked the seats and divans and even the floor. The decor smacked of a desert harem from a storybook. The only odd feature in the vast space was the stage at the front of the room, cloaked with sensuous red velvet drapes.

"Good evening . . . sir."

A woman paused and looked him over with a critical eye, clearly convinced the gatekeeper was being remiss in his duty to keep out the riffraff.

"Mr. Hawkins," he returned stiffly.

Her beautiful, dark brown eyes mellowed and she even offered him a smile. "I am your hostess, Madame Rafaramanjaka."

She was about five-and-thirty years of age, with a relatively smooth complexion and fine features. She had darker skin, and her accent placed her from a faraway part of the world. Her name might be an elaborate pseudonym . . . or perhaps it was her real name, for she radiated with pride, and he suspected she took great pleasure in her noble appellation, even if it was unfamiliar to his ear.

"Welcome to the Pleasure Palace."

He almost rolled his eyes at the tawdry epithet.

"I'll have one of my serving girls take your order." She slipped her hand through his arm and gently guided him deeper into the establishment. "We have the finest selection of spirits in Town."

"Thank you."

She smiled. It was an amorous smile. She wasn't out to seduce him; he sensed that intuitively. She was out to caress and lull his better judgment, though, with her artful ministrations, to make him more pliable to her desire: the surrender of his blunt.

"I hope to see you here often, Mr. Hawkins." She stroked his elbow. "Enjoy the entertainment. We aim to please our guests."

A piquant perfume rested heavily in the air as she departed from him, her flowing skirts swishing seductively with each measured step.

It was the feeling of squander that made Edmund's nose pucker, though: the squander of time, money, and even good sense. Yet what else was there for a wealthy gentleman to do with his time? He stood inside the familiar void and resigned himself to a few hours of squander.

"Have you come looking for salvation?"

Edmund slowly turned around and spotted the stranger seated amid the shadows in the corner of the room. There was a low-burning candle on the table; it illuminated his cheeks and brow, leaving only the recesses of his eyes in darkness.

Edmund frowned at the cryptic question.

The stranger expounded with "From your tired life?" A cloud of smoke hovered above his head as he sucked on a cigar. He gestured to an empty chair.

Edmund settled into the padded seat. "What makes you think I'm seeking salvation?"

"You've not come into the club with the same jovial step as the other young bucks; your eyes are empty."

Edmund wasn't bothered by the gloomy observation. He ordered a glass of gin from a passing serving girl before he returned his attention to his mysterious companion.

The stranger was about forty years of age. He sported soft brown hair smattered with slim silver streaks. He was dressed in swanky attire, top-quality fabrics, and polished brass buttons, but he had unfastened his cuff links and relaxed his cravat, telling Edmund he didn't give a jot about his public appearance.

There was only one part of him that remained in secret: his eyes. Edmund could not see his eyes, even from his new vantage point at the round table, for the shadows masked the deep-set pools. He sensed the man's penetrating gaze, though.

"Is that why you've come here?" wondered Edmund.

"There is no salvation for me."

Edmund withheld a snort at the melodramatic retort.

He rubbed his chin, convinced the nob was searching for a saphead to listen to his groans about life—like his valet's failure to polish his boots. Edmund wasn't willing to offer him an ear, though.

"Then why have you come to the club?" said Edmund.

"For the same reason you've come to the club . . . to forget."

"And does being here make you forget?"

"No."

Edmund thought as much. He looked around the room for another place to sit, but the serving girl returned with the beverage then, and he wasn't inclined to move away from his seat now that he'd a drink in hand. He paid her a coin.

"It won't help you, you know."

Edmund took a swig of the gin. "What won't help me?"

"The drink." He nursed the cigar in his bejeweled hand. "It won't help you to forget."

"It's all worthless, is it?" He chuckled at the theatrics. "The club? The drink? Is there no escape from one's 'tired' life?"

"There is escape."

"Oh?"

"In death."

Edmund snorted at the smattering.

"You laugh at death?"

He peered at the stranger with a sardonic expression. "I laugh at men who speak with courage about death, but who have never faced it."

"Hmm . . . and you've faced death?"

"I have."

Edmund downed the rest of the gin and smacked the empty glass on the table, but the spirits had yet to stifle the dark memories in his head.

"And how does it feel to confront death?"

"Do you want me to philosophize?" He shrugged. "I can't say, in truth. It's only after the danger has passed that I even realize I've come close to death, and then I feel triumphant."

"Because you've bested death?"

"That's right."

"I see."

Edmund waited for the stranger to break the silence with another odd question or puzzling remark, but the shadowy figure refrained from further comment, drawing on his cigar.

Edmund didn't mind the quiet; he was a man of few words himself. He was also accustomed to more peculiar companions, his history at sea so varied and colorful; yet, at present, he wasn't in the mood for any more blathering.

He looked at the stage. "What is the show about?"

"I don't know. This is my first visit to the club, too."

Edmund sighed, weary. Soon the gin took effect and he sensed his muscles loosen. The sensual music and rich colors and low mood lighting in the room started to make him drowsy . . . but then the sudden clash of instruments pierced his skull and jostled his wits.

He blinked and glanced around the room, bemused.

"I think the show's about to start," said the stranger in an offhand manner, clearly uninterested in the whole proceeding.

Edmund stretched out his long legs and yawned. He was prepared to sleep through the insipid performance, which he assumed was a bawdy comedic act or a recital from a half-rate singer, but the soft clash of cymbals and tambourines, the rhythmic slaps of a hand drum roused his dormant senses.

He remembered sailing to North Africa, stopping in Morocco for supplies before continuing toward the continent's western shores and bustling slave waters. He remembered similar sounds and lush melodies coming from the foreign port, filling the night air, which was already sweet with spices and tangy fruits.

Edmund opened his eyes and observed the stage as the red velvet curtains parted. The room hushed but for a few patrons, who whispered the word "Zarsitti" with excitement.

A figure soon appeared, scantily attired in white silk. The coquette had a long flowing skirt, beaded with crystals, and a hip scarf bejeweled with gold coins. A matching top crisscrossed over her lush breasts, but her arms and belly were nude.

The dancer's artful movements, a captivating pattern of hip rolls and twirls, stirred Edmund from his listlessness, bewitched him—and every other male member of the club. She gyrated and shuffled and swayed, hypnotizing him like a snake charmer with music.

He noted a birthmark shaped like a kiss just below

the center part of her breasts. He wasn't sure if it was an actual mark or makeup designed to enhance her sensual allure. A veil concealed her nose and lips, and an elaborate coin headdress crowned her lengthy, wavy blond locks. There was only a set of piercing and painted eyes that peered at the crowd through the silk mask.

The blood in his veins warmed as she undulated and swooped in step to the pulsing instruments. He stared in both admiration and longing at the woman's lean figure, her smooth, muscular midriff. Every tendon stretched, seeking glory and applause, and inwardly he offered her that very ovation, for even his bones throbbed in appreciation.

He relished the savory sensations that welled inside him. He had drifted across the sea of idleness for far too long, and the dancer's mesmerizing appearance was like an anchor staking him to the seabed. She beckoned him back onto land, to feel again. And he was dizzy with the woman's heady call. He felt like a tar on firm ground after months at sea; the earth was motionless yet he still swayed with the movement of the waves.

The unsteadiness in his soul had him grappling for security. He sensed there was only one way to calm the storm in his heart: he had to see the woman without her mask. He had to touch her, learn her name. He had to know she was real.

The sensual dance ended after a few minutes. The room erupted in a cacophony of applause and cheers.

Edmund glanced at his enigmatic companion, prepared to excuse himself from the table. However, the man's chair was empty; he had slipped away during the course of the performance.

Good. Edmund needn't bother with pleasantries. He lifted from his seat and headed for the double doors, avoiding the stage area. As he passed through the room, he heard the enamored compliments and similar sentiments of longing to meet the mysterious dancer coming from the other patrons.

He was not the only charmed soul who wanted a private audience with the beautiful Zarsitti, but unlike the other hopeful men at the club, who were doomed to dream about the dancer, for the gatekeepers refused to permit them behind the stage, Edmund had quickly realized the exotic dancer was a highly guarded commodity—and he had already formulated another plan to meet her.

Chapter 2

Amy Peel sat on the cushioned stool and scrubbed her features with the moist towel. The cosmetic ink was smeared across her cheeks like black tears. She peered into the large mirror and polished the stains away, removing the painted mask of Zarsitti, the Gold Lady.

Soon the door to her dressing room opened. She stiffened, as she was wont to do whenever Her Highness, Queen Rafaramanjaka, entered the small space. The former monarch from the island of Madagascar was regal in poise and appearance. She carried herself with the utmost pride, draped her limbs in the finest fabrics, doused her flesh in the most expensive perfume. She towered over Amy, not in stature, but in class and education, and she was keen to make Amy aware of the difference between their stations in life, even if no one else was privy to the truth of her royal heritage.

"You danced well tonight, my dear."

"Thank you."

Amy spied the woman's crisp movements through

the looking glass. She crossed the room and paused beside the wardrobe, fingered the brash costumes, inspecting their condition.

"I think I shall have the seamstress fashion you a new outfit. I want our customers to see you in the most unique attires, especially our regular visitors."

Amy was silent. She set the moist towel aside, smudged with cosmetic ink, and picked up the bone-handled comb, running it through her tousled locks.

"I think we should vary your performances, as well."

There was a small oil lamp on the vanity next to the mirror. Amy watched, tight-lipped, as the voluptuous woman approached her from the shadows and stepped into the pool of light. She set her soft hands, lathered with cream, on Amy's shoulders.

"I can teach you a few more dance steps."

Amy shivered and set down the comb.

"Is something the matter, my dear?"

"No." She pinched the woolly wrapper at her bust. "I've a chill, is all."

"Take care you don't fall ill." She stroked Amy's fair hair with a sentiment suspiciously akin to spite. "Your fame grows every night. There are more patrons than ever before, and soon I will have to turn gentlemen away at the door."

She sounded pleased at the thought of turning respectable gentlemen away from the club's door, triumphant even. She had lost her royal rank and prestige. No one bowed or saluted her with appropriate veneration anymore—except for the besotted patrons. It was her only means of recapturing the past, Amy supposed, though she dared not pity the wretched woman.

The queen's icy fingers moved across her protégée's cheeks. "Were I still as beautiful as you."

Amy suppressed the darkness that threatened to overtake her senses. If she mused about her predicament for too long, she might surrender to the despair, and give the cold queen the last vestige of her soul and independence.

"Take care to hide your face as you leave the club." She peered at Amy through the glass with her dark eyes. "If your identity is revealed, the allure of your mysterious character will vanish. Poof!" She snapped her fingers. "I'll have no need of your services anymore."

The blood in Amy's veins swelled, her heart thumped with greater vigor. "Yes, Madame Rafaramanjaka."

She smiled with scorn at the unjust appellation. "You are still young, my dear." She traced her plump fingers across Amy's stiff brow. "No lines. No marks. There is nothing to blight your youth or beauty." She smirked. "But as soon as the signs of age appear, as soon as youth and beauty are lost, the threat of death casts its grotesque presence, and no man wants to admire a woman who reminds him of his own mortality. I'm afraid you will have to fall to that other, less noble profession then."

Amy breathed hard and heavy through her nose. She was only about nineteen years of age, for she didn't know the exact date of her birth, and yet the horror of poverty and destitution strangled her even now. She was convinced, at the first glimmer of her maturity, she would be cast back out into the streets . . . and she didn't think she could survive the hardships again.

"Here, my dear." The woman removed a small satchel pinned at her waist. "Your earnings."

She dropped the purse onto the vanity; it made a soft, muffled thump.

Amy remained motionless, staring fixedly at the glass, until the queen departed from the dressing room. As soon as the door closed, she bowed her head and shut her eyes, tamping down the wild urge to clout her tormentor soundly between the devilish eyes.

She took in a few measured breaths before she stared at the black purse. She had come to loathe the sight of that purse. It contained her hard-earned wages, enough money to keep her alive for a week, and a little surplus for her savings chest; however, it also imprisoned her, kept her chained to the mad queen's side like an obedient dog.

Amy emptied the purse into her palm, still quivering with rage, for she had to leave the cursed satchel on the table inside the room; it would be used again for her next pay date.

The coins burned her flesh, and she glared at the wicked pieces of minted metal before she slipped the blunt back inside the black bag.

She contemplated escaping her life as the notorious dancer, and dropped the purse on the vanity. She removed her wrapper; rushed to gather her regular clothing, pulling on the garments in haste.

As soon as she was fully attired in a white top and brown skirt, stockings and brown-leather ankle boots, she twisted a patterned, fringed shawl around her shoulders and departed from the dressing room, seeking fresh air.

She wasn't likely to find fresh air in a sooty city like London, but she was eager to be away from her dressing room for just a few minutes to think about her life as Zarsitti, and she scaled the back entrance steps, ascending toward the roof.

She opened the door that led topside. The roof's domed architecture ballooned behind her like a bubble in the water. She approached the building's edge and gazed through the misty fog at the dark, towering silhouettes.

The city's looming structures surrounded the club, guarding the Pleasure Palace like ominous sentries, keeping her trapped inside the establishment.

She shuddered and rubbed her arms, warming her chilled limbs, reflecting on the past. She had once called the streets and flash houses home. She had once lived among the shadows in the rookeries. But then the runaway queen had found her, praised her for her beauty, buried under a protective mask of soot and grime.

"You're a pretty thing," she had said, rubbing her thumb across Amy's insolent chin, removing the dirt. "Very pretty. Come with me. I will take you away from here. I will give you a new, wonderful life, my dear."

Amy had resisted the temptation at first, too suspicious to accept the strange woman's invitation, but loneliness and despair had changed her mind, and at the age of sixteen, she had followed Madame Rafaramanjaka into a gilded cage.

Amy wanted freedom from her life of near servitude, but as she stared at the familiar, unforgiving city landscape, she realized she couldn't go back to her life on the streets of London; that it was an even greater hell.

"Good evening."

Amy quickly turned around and searched the murky darkness for the owner of the low voice, her hackles spiking.

"Who's there?" she whispered.

A tall figure emerged from behind the behemoth domed roof. He had wide shoulders and a smooth gait as he slowly approached her, his footfalls muffled.

He possessed stealth. The silence was ominous. As he neared her, her pulses quickened, for she sensed the brawn teeming inside him with each swaggered step, the animal strength.

"What do you want?" she demanded, words clipped.

"I want to know you." He paused, then: "I didn't expect to find you here. I thought I would have to climb down to meet you."

Amy maneuvered away from the stranger. "Do I know you?"

"No, but I know you . . . Zarsitti."

She stiffened. "I am not the dancer."

Thoughts of destitution swelled in her head. If the vicious queen discovered her secret identity had been revealed, Amy would be replaced as the club's main attraction. She would be homeless again.

"I'm just a serving wench," she said brusquely.

"You are the dancer," he insisted, his voice smoldering. "Your eyes give you away."

"How would you like to lose *your* eyes, you wretched cur!"

The shadow stilled. "I didn't expect such language from a lady."

She detected the humor in his gruff voice and huffed. He was foxed. And like all besotted fools, he was filled with bravado and had come looking for her, the legendary Gold Lady.

"What do you want?" she repeated.

"What is your name?"

He moved to block the door and she had to retreat to the building's edge once more. "Why don't you just give me whatever name you think suits me best, and be gone."

"I'd rather know your real name . . . I'd rather know you."

"Why?"

"You move me," he said softly. "You make me feel—"

"I know what I make you feel," she snapped.

A line of white teeth flashed in the darkness. "That, too."

Amy gnashed her own teeth.

"I mean," he said, "you make me want to stay on land."

"What?"

She bumped into the building's edge with her heel and teetered. A desperate shout escaped her lungs before a set of thick, hard arms gripped her waist and pulled her against a sturdy chest.

Breathless, Amy grabbed the shadowed figure in a fierce hold, her heart in her throat, her limbs quivering with tension after the near mishap. She glanced over her shoulder and shivered at the thought of the three-story fall to her doom.

"Thank . . ."

She looked into the stranger's dark eyes, his deep-hooded brow masking the pools, and was struck by the storm of feeling she saw reflected in the glossy orbs, a storm that threatened to come upon her and consume her. She almost welcomed the tempestuous storm into her heart. It was a fleeting yet alarming impulse, and she trembled at the thought of being so reckless.

"Are you all right?" he whispered.

He moved his warm palm across her spine. He had a large hand; it spanned most of her lower backside. He stroked her trembling muscles, the lazy, sensual movements so soothing, comforting.

"I'm fine."

She quieted her uneven breathing. She was pressed so tight against him, she sensed his pulsing heartbeat, stunned at the intimacy.

"I wasn't sure I would catch you in time." The man's dark, thick, wavy locks grazed her temple as he murmured into her ear, "I would have followed you over the edge for one sweet kiss."

She shuddered at the heat, the softness in his breath; it tickled her ear, caressed her senses like a silk kerchief, making her toes cross.

Amy closed her eyes, lulled. She listened to his raspy breathing, stiffened as his fingers strummed the knobs of bone along her spine. He fingered the hollow at her lower back in wispy strokes, teasing her.

She suddenly yearned for the scoundrel to keep his scandalous word and kiss her . . . and then she blinked and gathered her disoriented thoughts, mindful of the trouble she was already in up to her flushed ears.

"Let me go." She squirmed in his strong arms. "You very nearly killed me!"

He frowned, clearly confused by the abrupt shift in her demeanor. "*I* very nearly killed you?"

The young man's glower contorted his otherwise handsome features. His lush bottom lip puckered and his brow dropped even lower, pinching the flesh between his brooding eyes.

He dragged her away from the building's edge. "I saved you."

"You cornered me, you mean." She twisted her arm. "Let me go!"

The man's frown darkened. "I think I liked you better onstage—beautiful and silent."

She humphed. "I am *not* the dancer."

"You're lying."

"Oh, bullocks!"

Amy curled her fingers into a firm fist and walloped him right in the jaw with her free hand.

The scoundrel staggered back, bewildered. He rubbed his chin, scowling.

"I suppose I deserved that," he said dryly.

Amy humphed and hiked up her long skirt before she dashed toward the door in the roof, making her way back to her dressing room in haste.

She was still trembling with a maelstrom of feeling when she entered her private quarters, seeking her wages. She wanted to take her earnings, to quickly get out of the club—but she was confronted by two unfamiliar figures inside the room, rifling through her wardrobe.

"Out!" she demanded.

The blood in her veins burned as her temper roiled even more. How many wastrels were lurking inside the club, looking to meet Zarsitti? And where were the blasted guards to keep them *away* from her dressing room?

But Amy hadn't a moment more to fulminate. She was dragged inside the dressing room and wrestled to the ground.

A savage energy gripped her bones, and she kicked and thrashed in panic. A hand clamped over her mouth, preventing her screams. She mumbled frantically instead, rolled with the attacking bodies in an attempt to break free of their holds.

The blood in her head pulsed until her skull ached with the thumping pressure. She struggled with her fists, scratching, punching, unmindful of the pressure on her limbs as she resisted the brutal assault.

A fiend soon restrained her wrists with cord, curtailing her outburst. He grunted and sighed as he toiled, winding the coarse rope, his cohort keeping her pinned to the ground.

The door opened.

"I fear I must apologize for my—" The stranger from the roof paused and stared at the spectacle on the floor. "What the devil . . . ?"

Amy mumbled wildly for help. An attacker charged toward the handsome scoundrel. The men butted fists, and Amy's heart filled with vigorous hope as she anxiously watched the contenders. At length, the second assailant was pressed into battle or he risked watching his comrade smashed to bits.

He released Amy's wrists. She swiftly disengaged the still loose cord from her arms and jumped to her feet. She snatched the stool beside the vanity and whacked a ruffian over the head. He staggered, disoriented, before he collapsed. The stranger from the roof brawled with the other, ill-matched challenger . . . until the handsome devil was pushed into the looking glass.

Amy gasped.

The mirror shattered and the weakened would-be hero winced, but it took little effort to take down the other breathless assailant, and with one last jab between the eyes, the stranger ended the violent quarrel, victorious.

It was a short-lived victory, though. He clutched his bleeding head and slumped forward, landing on his knees with a loud thud.

"Your other admirers, I presume?"

Amy scowled. She gathered her shaky breath and quickly hunkered beside the stranger. "Let me see the wound."

He parted his fingers and she spotted the bloody gash, pressing her lips firmly together in distress.

"That bad, eh?"

Amy contemplated the situation. She considered dashing from the dressing room before any more danger presented itself, but she quickly rejected the cowardly instinct. The stranger had saved her reputation, if not her life. She would do what was right—and fret about the consequences later.

She grabbed the coin purse off the table. "Can you walk?"

"I think so."

He staggered to his feet and wavered. "We should summon the authorities."

"No!"

It wasn't uncommon for wealthy, ambitious bandits to want to see her privately, to learn her true identity. But Madame Rafaramanjaka was strict: she insisted Amy keep her dancer's anonymity, for it enhanced the mystery, the excitement of her performances. The fantasy would be ruined if the patrons discovered she wasn't an exiled princess but an orphan from the city's rookeries, and Amy would be tossed back out into the streets. She couldn't risk summoning the authorities; she couldn't risk her identity being revealed.

"The club's guards will take care of the attackers," she said.

"Where *are* the guards?"

Amy wrapped her arm around his midriff in support. "Don't worry about them. What's your name?"

"I . . . I don't know."

She sighed. He was too woozy to answer her questions, and she had to move with him quickly—and discreetly—through the club, so she suspended further inquiries.

"I trust you'll behave yourself," she said stiffly after a short pause, "if I take you back to my lodgings to rest."

"I don't know if I can promise that."

Amy almost dropped him in a fit of pique, but she regained her temperament, concluding the scoundrel was likely too light-headed to ponder his scandalous remark.

Stealthily she steered him toward the back entranceway, all the while hoping she hadn't misplaced her charitable inclinations.

Chapter 3

He opened his eyes.

A soft glow illuminated the narrow, unfamiliar space, and he squinted, searching through the haziness, trying to make out the colored splotches in the darkened room.

He lighted upon a figure, wrapped in a coverlet. She rested in a chair at the end of the bedstead, dozing.

He rolled onto his side, parted his lips to call out to her . . . then grimaced at the shooting pain in his head.

The figure stirred and murmured sleepily, "You're awake."

He wished to the blazes he wasn't awake. He couldn't make out the woman's figure clearly, for his vision was blurred and the room was in shadow. The vigorous pulsing in his head muddled his senses, too, and his jaw was tender.

He groaned and clutched his bandaged skull. "What happened?"

She slipped away from the chair, stepped into the faint candlelight, and knelt beside the bedstead. It was

then he was able to observe her features more plainly—
and she was lovely. Long, fine hair framed her winsome
face, the fair tresses wavy and sparkling in the misty
light. She possessed a milky complexion, with well-
defined lips and a small, straight nose, the rounded tip
upturned slightly.

She might be considered haughty with such a proud
façade; however, there was a much more agreeable side
to her countenance: a passionate, sensual side. It was
there in her eyes. Sharp, almost exotic green eyes that
pierced a poor fellow with their haunting beauty. He
remembered those eyes from . . .

"What happened?"

Had he asked her that question already? he wondered. Had she responded? He didn't remember.

"You were injured in a fight," she said in a sweet-
sounding voice that matched her charming visage.

He traced a finger across his bandaged brow, searching through the murky memories in his head. "Did I
win the fight?"

She frowned. "Is that all you care about? There's a
gash at the back of your head."

The woman's petulant expression marred her pretty
features. He thought about smoothing her down-
turned lips into a smile with his fingers. He sensed she
wouldn't appreciate the teasing gesture, though, and
said instead:

"Where am I?"

"At lodgings in St. Giles."

He closed his eyes, searching for a memory, a recollection, but a pleasant thought soon entered his drowsy mind, and he wondered:

"Are we married?"

"What? No!"

He rubbed the sore muscles across his midriff. "Then why am I naked in your bed?"

"You're half naked," she clarified, blushing. "I removed your shirt and coat because the garments were stained with blood. I've washed the linens and they're drying in the other room."

That didn't sound too scandalous, he thought glumly. "Are you my sweetheart, then?"

"No!"

She looked as if she wanted to clout him. Very unromantic.

"Don't you remember anything?" she said.

He paused, thoughts spinning. "No."

She peered at him suspiciously. "You really don't know who I am?"

"I don't even know who I am."

She seemed oddly pleased by his confession, for she smiled slightly. "My name is Amy. I was attacked. You offered me assistance."

"That was very noble of me."

She quickly made a moue. "Yes, very noble."

"Who am I? Where am I from?"

"I don't know," she admitted with a sigh. "I don't know anything about you."

That sounded dire, and yet he wasn't all that perturbed. Perhaps the head injury was making him mellow. It didn't seem right that he should be so calm at the prospect of amnesia.

Or perhaps it was the lovely Amy who was making him feel so tranquil. She had a magical, bewitching appeal about her. It suited him just fine if he forever stayed in her bed and admired her.

Had she sensed his intimate thoughts? If so, the lass didn't share his wistful sentiment, for she moved away from the bedstead then, and approached a small dressing table in the corner of the room.

"I found this on your person when I removed your coat."

She handed him a small coin purse. He fingered the fine leather satchel and glanced at the embroidered initials.

"E.H.," he drawled.

"It might be your name," she suggested.

The letters didn't stir his memory, however. "What sorts of names begin with the letter E?"

She shrugged. "I don't know."

He mused, "There's Eric or Elmer."

"Elmer?"

He glanced at her dubious expression. "I don't look like an Elmer, do I?"

She shook her head.

"There's Edward," he said.

"Edward's nice."

He shrugged and set the purse aside. "Edward it is

then. I don't think the initials are mine, though. I think I stole the purse."

"*Why* do you think that?"

"It's embroidered with gold thread. Look here." He lifted it again, stretching it toward the candlelight. The stitching was luminous. "It's too fancy, something a bloody nob would sport, not a . . ." He frowned. "Well, whoever I am, I'm *not* a nob. I'm sure of that."

"Wonderful," she said dryly. "I'm harboring a thief."

"Ah, but a thief who saved your life."

She snorted. "That would explain your foul manners at—"

"My foul manners?"

"Never mind."

He persisted: "At . . . ?"

"Never mind!" She sighed. "I think you're a sailor." She murmured, "When you're not thieving."

He tossed the purse aside. "Why do you think that?"

"You have a tattoo on your back."

"I do?"

"An anchor on your right shoulder. There are some more letters there, too."

He fingered his shoulder. "What do they say?"

She looked away. "I can't read."

He observed her embarrassed mannerisms, her averted eyes. He didn't want to make her feel even more uncomfortable, so he said to comfort her:

"I might not be able to read, either."

"But you know the name Edward starts with an E?"

"Good point." He wrestled with his dizziness, and with great effort settled into a precarious sitting position. "Do you have a mirror?"

She eyed him warily. "You're pale."

He had sensed the blood drain from his face as soon as he'd righted himself. The pounding in his head was ferocious, too. "I'll rest soon, I promise. The mirror?"

She sighed and skirted across the room once more. She collected two small mirrors from the dressing table, for she had anticipated his intention.

"Here." She handed him a looking glass with a white bone handle. "I'll hold the other one."

He gazed into the reflective material, then slowly lifted the other small mirror, angling it over his right shoulder.

He spotted the inked anchor and the penmanship. "Bonny Meg."

"I suppose *she's* your sweetheart." She snatched the mirror away from him. "I'm sure you have one in every port."

Amy sounded . . . jealous, and that pleased him immensely, warming his belly. She ordered him to rest again. He obliged her; his head was throbbing.

"I guess I can read."

He sighed as he lowered his head onto the feather pillow.

"I guess you can," she returned stiffly, setting the mirrors onto the dressing table. "An educated thief. I'm impressed."

Was she still brooding over the bonny Meg? he thought wolfishly.

Who was Meg?

His sweetheart? His wife? No . . . not his wife. He had no memory, but he had a feeling, an instinct the lass was not his spouse. The woman was dear to him, though, that much was for sure. He wouldn't have inked her name on his back otherwise . . . unless he'd been foxed at the time. Perhaps she was just a pretty wench he'd tried to impress with the tattoo?

He was thinking too much; his head pounded with vim.

"Are you married, Amy?"

She whirled around. "I told you, we're *not* married!"

"To someone else, I mean?"

"No." She placed her arms akimbo. "I live alone."

"What do you do for livelihood?"

She hesitated. There was obvious uncertainty in her handsome green eyes.

"Don't trust an educated thief, do you?"

"No," she said flatly.

"I wouldn't, either."

She screwed up her lips. "I suppose it's no secret . . . I'm a barmaid at a gentlemen's club. I serve drinks—and that's all I do!"

"You've said that to me before, haven't you?" He frowned. "It sounds like you're repeating yourself."

"I am." She glowered at him. "You were both foxed—and bold—tonight."

"At the club? Where we met?"

"That's right."

"I'm sorry."

She bobbed her head. "You're forgiven."

He might still be woozy and disoriented, but something didn't seem quite right about her cajoling him into an apology.

"Didn't I save your life?"

She pointed at him with accusation. "You *do* remember!"

"No," he said, drawing out the word. "You told me I saved your life, remember?"

She looked flustered. He admired the color in her cheeks. It suited her pale complexion well.

"Yes, you offered me assistance," she confirmed. "And?"

"Well, where's my thank-you?"

She eyed him with suspicion. "Thank you."

"That wasn't very sincere."

She scowled at him. "What do you want from me?"

"A kiss."

She pressed her pretty lips together until the rosy flesh turned white. "You're teasing me. You do remember everything about tonight, don't you?"

Had he kissed her at the club? What a miserable quirk of fate that he shouldn't remember the sensual experience. It made the agony in his head all the more acute, for he rummaged through the foggy shadows in his mind, searching for the sweet memory.

A series of knocks resounded at the door in the other room.

Edward winced at the cacophony in his skull.

"Let me in, Amy!"

"Oh no!" The lass whitened even more. "It's Madame Rafaramanjaka."

The unusual name rolled around in his head. "Who?"

"Stay here!"

She sprinted from the room and soon returned with his shirt and coat. She tossed both garments, still moist, onto the bed.

"Don't leave the room, please! If she finds you here, she'll have me tossed into the street!"

The look of horror in Amy's eyes sobered Edward. Madame Raf . . . whatever her name was . . . must be the eccentric landlady who frowned on any immoral activity taking place under her roof—like an unmarried girl entertaining a bachelor in her bedchamber. He certainly didn't want to see the lass destitute. However, staying in the room wasn't going to protect Amy, not if the landlady was determined to search the quarters.

He gathered his clothes as soon as Amy had closed the door, kicked his boots, sitting on the floor, under the bed, then slowly made his way to the tall, decorative screen at the other end of the bedchamber.

He was dizzy and a bit confused by the need for a room divider in such a small space, but he slipped behind it, unwilling to dwell too much on the oddity

. . . or the collection of ladies' mirrors that rested on the dressing table. There had to be at least a dozen!

Amy was a vain minx, wasn't she?

Amy frantically searched the sitting room with her eyes for any sign of Edward's presence. She had removed his shirt and coat from the hearth. She observed no other indicator that there was a man staying in her lodgings: a man who might know her secret identity as Zarsitti.

More pounding at the door.

What was the queen doing at her apartment so late at night?

Amy glanced at the mantel clock. It was after midnight. With a deep breath and trembling fingers, she unfastened the bolt at the door.

"Madame?"

The surly queen elbowed her way inside the apartment. "What is the meaning of this?" She produced a piece of shattered glass and shoved it in Amy's face as if she might cut her. "The dressing room is in shambles: broken glass, furniture. What did you do?"

Amy veered her head to one side to avoid the lacerated edge. "I didn't do anything."

"Liar!"

"I'm not lying," she insisted in an even voice, heart swelling. "I was attacked."

The queen pinched her brows together. "By whom?"

"Whom do you think?" The wicked woman was

privy to the overexcited patrons at the club, and Amy gathered her courage to demand: "Where were the guards to protect me?"

Madame Rafaramanjaka set the piece of glass aside. She eyed the dancer with venom. "I saw no one inside the dressing room."

The men must have regained their senses and escaped before the queen and guards had spotted them, Amy thought, but she refrained from making the claim aloud, for she was sure the cruel woman would not believe her.

"I *was* attacked," Amy insisted.

"You look fine to me." She grabbed her chin and roughly pushed it from side to side, inspecting the flesh. "Not a scratch."

Amy wriggled away from her icy claws, shivering at the woman's vile touch. "That's because I had help. One of the patrons came to my aid, but he doesn't my true—"

"Who?" Her black eyes flashed. "Your lover?"

"I don't have a lover."

"Is he here?"

The queen glanced around the room as if she had not heard the assertion, her cheeks filling with blood. She headed for the bedroom door.

"There's no one here!" cried Amy.

But it was too late. The wretched woman entered the bedchamber and Amy sensed her heart pause in trepidation, sweat gather between her brows . . . and then she sighed, the room empty.

Where the devil had he gone?

The queen marched out of the bedchamber in a haughty manner. "Why are the bedsheets rumpled?"

Amy blinked, casting aside her bewilderment. "I was asleep," she fibbed.

"In your clothes?" She sneered. "He was just here, wasn't he?"

"Who?"

"Your lover, you stupid slut!"

Amy clenched her fingers into fists. "I *don't* have a lover." She pinched her tongue between her teeth, but, oh, there was so much more she wanted to impart to the miserable, insufferable witch. "And if I had a lover who'd just departed, wouldn't I be in my *under*clothes?"

"Whore!" The queen was unmoved, erratic. She approached Amy, fingers quivering. "There are other girls employed at the club to service the needs of the patrons."

Yes, and it was Amy's duty to arouse the patrons into fits of ecstasy, encourage them to seek out the "other girls," thus plumping the queen's purse.

She shuddered.

"What if you become enceinte?" demanded the queen. "Do you think men will want to admire a woman with a fat belly?"

"I'm not pregnant!"

"At the first sign of a babe"—she moved her forefinger across her throat—"I'm cutting you off."

Amy gasped for breath, her fingers quivering. It was as if she wasn't even in the room, for the self-centered queen had already tried and condemned her for her imaginary folly.

Amy eyed the iron poker next to the coal hearth and imagined . . .

She soon smothered the gruesome thought.

Madame Rafaramanjaka looked around the sitting room with scorn. "What is the meaning of so many trinkets?"

An instinct to protect the so-called trinkets welled in Amy's breast. She had diligently saved her pennies to afford more luxurious items, like the damask window treatments with decorative finials, the bright patterned rug, the brass candlestick holders, the cranberry glass vase.

"Is this why you're whoring?" The queen fingered an expensive, handmade oak chair with disdain. "To supplement your income?" She snickered. "What are you trying to do? Become a lady?"

Amy trembled with vexation. The desire to spit at and wipe the witch's fingerprints from the furniture stirred her blood. She bit out stiffly, "I don't have to explain my reasons to you."

"I pay you too much." She huffed. "I'm cutting your salary in half until you pay off the damage to the dressing room."

Amy parted her lips to protest; the damage inside the dressing room was *not* her fault.

"Don't tempt me, girl," warned the witch, anticipating the objection. "One more troubling word from you and I'll terminate your services at the club—entirely!"

Amy pinched her lips together, her resistance dashed.

"I want the coin purse, too," she snapped. "You sallied off with it tonight. Do you think I'm going to fashion you a new one every week?"

"Yes, Madame Rafaramanjaka."

Amy returned to her bedroom. As she entered the cramped space, she looked for Edward. Was he under the bed? She eyed the narrow gap between the furniture and the flooring; she concluded the man was too big to fit there.

Where are you?

There was a chest in the corner of the room, next to the bedstead. The sturdy piece of furniture was locked. She removed the key from her bosom and retrieved the cursed satchel. As she departed from the room, she noticed bare toes shuffling under the fashionable screen.

Amy sighed and returned to the sitting room, where the petulant queen was still waiting. She removed her earrings from the little black bag before she returned the purse to the wicked woman.

The witch opened her hand for more.

"What?" demanded Amy.

"I want half your wages now."

Amy's heart pulsed. She squeezed the cold, hard-earned metal between her fingers. "No."

"You can give me half the money now or forfeit *all* your wages next week."

Amy gnashed her teeth, trembling, as she counted the coins, halving the much-needed salary.

"Here," she said crisply.

The queen humphed before she snatched the blunt and removed her white, short gloves from her reticule. She slipped on the pair, then bustled from the room.

Amy was rooted to the spot, her breathing deep and heavy, her thoughts whirling in her head. She waited a few more seconds before she cautiously opened the door and peeped into the passageway. It was empty. She closed the barrier and secured the bolt.

As soon as the iron lock was in place, she sighed. She was stiff, every muscle taut, every nerve thrumming. The queen had an unfortunate knack for unsettling her good sense, for taking away every vestige of hope she possessed.

She moved away from the front entrance and gathered her breath, her thoughts. She glanced at the bedchamber through the opened door. "Come out, Edward."

She entered the room just as the man's tall figure emerged from behind the burnished divider. He had removed the bandages, and his low brow and smoldering blue eyes met hers with poignant regard.

He was clutching his shirt and coat. He set the garments on the bed. "She isn't the landlady, is she?"

Amy shivered at the low timbre of his voice. It was rough, but not harsh. It was such a soothing contrast to the queen's shrill tone that she yearned to keep him talking even though she knew it was better for him if he rested again.

"No," she admitted cheerlessly. "She's my employer."

He reached for his coin purse, tangled in the white bed linen. As he stretched his long limbs, his muscles moved and flexed, and she was suddenly aware of his robust figure.

She blushed at the thought that she *was* aware of his robust figure. A warm sensation quickly rushed from her head to her toes, making her quiver.

He approached her. In the dim candlelight, she observed the smooth stretch of skin that covered his chest, his strapping form: a seaman's form. He had an athletic build; it teemed with strength. Healed cuts marked his ribs, the scarred flesh paler than the rest of his tanned physique. He had been injured before, it seemed.

He followed her gaze with his eyes and glanced at his torso, rubbing the wounds. He said nothing, however. What was there to say? He had no memory . . . or so he claimed. She was still dubious about his bout with amnesia.

"I want you to take the money, Amy."

He offered her the coin purse.

"No, it's all the money you have in the world."

She wanted to smother the stirring sensations in her belly, and she stepped away from him . . . but his dark blue eyes still fired her senses.

"I'll be fine," he assured her in a cool, confident manner. "If I don't remember my name soon, I'll join a ship's crew and earn my keep."

"I don't want your money."

"The room at the club was damaged in the fight, wasn't it?" He looked at her with a sharp glare. "I damaged it."

"Helping me," she clarified.

He had listened to the entire exchange between her and the queen. For a moment, she had forgotten about the wretched witch. She was soon filled with anxiety, though, as she rehashed the quarrel in her mind, wondering if she had inadvertently revealed any details about her secret identity as the dancer. In the end, she concluded she had not offered any insight into Zarsitti's existence.

"I still want you to take the money." He placed the purse on the dressing table since she still refused to take it. "I'll leave it here whether you like it or not. Do what you want with it."

An honorable thief?

Amy munched on her bottom lip. He wasn't acting like an obnoxious lout anymore; he was behaving like a gentleman. It had to be the forgetfulness, she thought, making him so chivalrous. If he regained his memory, she was sure he wouldn't be so gallant . . . that he'd return to his scoundrellike ways.

Slowly he grappled with his shirt and slipped it over his head, grimacing at the clearly difficult movements.

"What are you doing?" she demanded.

"I'm leaving."

"But your clothes are still wet."

"It isn't right for me to be here."

That much was true, but the man was injured. He had risked his own well-being to protect her from the attackers. She couldn't just let him wander the streets at night in a daze. Where would he go?

"Stay here for the night," she insisted. "You have to rest."

"No."

He reached for his coat, and she grabbed the garment away from him. "You're staying for the night whether you like it or not." She tossed the coat onto the dressing table, then pointed at his chest. "Your shirt."

There was a mulish gleam in his eyes. "I can't stay here."

"You have to heal."

She stepped toward him with determination and tugged at his shirt. He lifted a black brow at her brazenness, but she ignored the impropriety of the gesture, for she was much more concerned with his unreasonable state of mind.

He sighed at last. With effort, he pulled the moist fabric off his back. She sensed it as he struggled with his breath, his steps wavering, and she quickly grabbed his arms to support him. He yanked the shirt over his head—caging her between his arms and the garment that still hung from his wrists.

Amy's heart pattered at the hard, warm feel of his sinewy body. The masculine musk from his skin teased her senses, too, and the deep glow in his eyes melted her hardheartedness. She listened to the rugged sound of his breathing, impervious to the more reasonable shouts of danger that crowded in her head.

"Amy."

"Yes," she whispered.

"I think I'm going to black out."

Eyes wide, Amy quickly slipped away from his strong embrace. She escorted him back to the bedstead, where he dropped with a hard sigh before, as threatened, he fainted.

She chastised herself for her folly. She removed the shirt from his wrists, gathered the coat from the dressing table, and headed back into the sitting room, stretching the garments across the chairs and pushing them nearer the warm hearth.

Chapter 4

<div align="center">~~~⟨⟩⟨⟩~~~</div>

The Westminster Bridge was swarming with Sunday afternoon merrymakers, all seeking amusement. The flowing Thames was congested with boat traffic, coal and passenger barges, and Edward stopped to observe the atmosphere, searching for a familiar face or ship.

A warm body pressed beside him, and he smiled to feel the woman's comforting presence.

"Well?" said Amy. "Do you remember anything?"

She had accompanied him on the excursion, journeyed with him along the river's shoreline as he'd explored the various docks and wharfs. The robust hike hadn't exhausted her, though. She was fit, hearty. And he enjoyed her company. In a strange environment, she was a welcome companion.

"No," he admitted. "I don't remember anything."

He rested, for he sensed the dull throbbing at the back of his head. He gazed across the polluted waters and spotted the far-off and cheering crowd at Searle's yard in Stangate. The Leander's Club was preparing for their popular weekly race. The quays were jammed with eager, betting spectators of every age and both genders. Minstrels offered musical entertainment, while vendors hustled tobacco. At two o'clock sharp a pistol fired. The sculls set off toward the bridge amid a hail of shouts and waving kerchiefs.

Edward watched the thrilling race . . . feeling at home.

"What's the matter?" said Amy in an anxious voice. "You look . . . sick."

"I just feel like I belong here."

"Ah, you're sick with longing." She looked out across the water. "Do you want to take a closer look at the south side of the Thames?"

He shook his head. There was no reason to prolong their travels. The water was home, that much he was sure about, but there was no spot along the Thames that was familiar to him. He would have to figure out some other way to regain his memories . . . or he would have to learn to live without them.

Edward glanced over his shoulder at the loud peddler woman, making her way across the long, bustling bridge.

"I'd rather have a glass of ale." He looked at Amy with disappointment. "I gave you all my money, though."

Amy wrinkled her pert lips and narrowed her brilliant green eyes on him before she sighed. She flagged the peddler woman with her wheeled barrel and purchased the half-penny malt.

Edward courteously offered Amy the refreshment first. She had walked a far distance, and she had to be equally as parched.

Amy swigged the frothing malt.

He downed the rest of the cool ale and returned the glass to the peddler woman, who recommenced her sales pitch and merged with the masses.

Amy looked at him sharply. "Now what?"

"Now I take you home."

He steered her across the bridge in the direction of the Palace of Westminster, keeping her safe from the crushing horde.

"What will you do, Edward?"

He shrugged. "My memory might still return."

"And if it doesn't?"

"I'll join the navy, I guess." He admired her down-turned lips. "You don't need to worry about taking care of me, Amy."

She looked away from him. "I'm not worried about that."

"What's troubling you then?"

She twirled the cords of her reticule, the purse tucked up her sleeve, wrapped the laces around her fingers until the flesh turned white. "Aren't you frightened?"

Edward glowered at the street urchin, who had spotted the dangling cords from Amy's sleeve. The young chap quickly reconsidered purloining the purse, however, for he scampered away, Edward's stare ominous.

"I would've boxed his ears, you know." She pointed at the grubby urchin. "I don't need you to protect me from him."

Edward scratched his head. "Very well then. Am I frightened about what?"

"Your future. It's so . . . bleak."

He snorted with laughter at her "comforting" words.

"I mean, you can't even remember your past. You might have a family, a livelihood. Are you just going to wander the seven seas without bearing?"

"I'm not going to join the navy today, Amy. I've still more of the city to search. I'm sure I'll remember something soon." He stroked the back of his head. "I'm feeling stronger."

She stared at her feet. "But what if you *don't* remember your past? Can you accept your former life as lost?"

"You're determined to see the worst in my situation, aren't you?"

She shrugged. "I've spent most of my years thinking about the worst in every situation—and how to avoid it."

"Ah, so this is your way of making sure I avoid the pits? I'm touched."

She pinkened. "About the worst . . . ?"

He chuckled at her hedging retort. "If I don't regain my memory, I suppose I'll make a new life."

"Really?"

"I won't have any other choice, Amy."

She murmured, "I don't think I would be so calm about the prospect if I were in your place."

"I'm not too keen to worry about tomorrow." He circled her trim waist and steered her aside as a hackney coach thundered across the pebbled road. "I'm only concerned with today."

Edward puckered his brow in curiosity. He sensed the woman's hard muscles under her woolly shawl and crisp, linen shirt—and was aroused by the sensual thought of parting her clothes and running his fingers along the rigid flesh.

She pushed his hand away from her midriff . . . but not before she'd shuddered.

"I can't live like that," she said.

"On Fate's whims?"

She nodded. "I need to know what will happen to me tomorrow—and the next day."

"So what will happen to you tomorrow?" he wondered.

"I will serve drinks at the club where I'm employed, while you'll search the city for clues to your past."

"You can't control everything, Amy."

"I can try."

Edward looked at his scuffed boots before he eyed the mudlarks in the foul river, scavenging for bits of metal and rope to sell at market. Their haggard faces boasted a level of misery that seemed uneasily familiar to him. One woman's gaunt cheeks and soulless eyes pierced his head with such intensity, he staggered.

"What's the matter?" said Amy, clutching his sleeve.

He grabbed his skull, his brain spinning with murky thoughts: howls and putrid scents. "I . . . remember."

"What?" She assisted him to the street's edge. "What do you remember?"

But after a few deep breaths, the images in his head blessedly faded away again. "Perhaps it's best if I don't remember."

He sighed and righted himself again, combing his fingers through his mussed hair.

Amy gazed at him with concern. "What happened, Edward?"

"I had an impression . . . but it's gone now."

She frowned and looped her arm through his in a sturdy hold. Did she mean to guide him back to St. Giles? He found her attention amusing . . . endearing.

"I guess some memories aren't worth remembering," she said in a wistful manner.

"And others are worth forgetting about." He speculated about her deep reflections: "Like last night's quarrel with your employer?"

"The witch." She spat. "I hope she chokes on the shattered glass."

Edward lifted a brow at her vicious curse, even more amused. The feisty barmaid had a duplicity about her that piqued his interest: she was considerate in one moment and venomous in the next.

"Why do you work for her?" he asked. "I'm sure there are plenty of other clubs that'll employ such a pretty face."

Amy's long, blond hair was twisted into a braid, revealing her dignified profile . . . and flushing features. The bright glow spread across her high cheekbones, while her thick lashes lowered in a demure manner.

She wasn't accustomed to compliments? He considered that too unusual. In her line of work as a barmaid, she surely received hundreds of flattering remarks— a night! Then again, a besotted patron drooling over her probably wasn't so very flattering. Edward's praise was sincere—and he was sober. Perhaps it was that she wasn't accustomed to?

She tried to pull her arm away from him in a skittish manner, and he quickly squeezed her hand between his ribs and biceps, caging her firmly. His muscles bristled at the thought of parting from her. He wasn't ready to let her go, to lose the heat generated between her warm fingers. Blood moved steadily through his veins at her touch, his heart beat with vigor. She stirred his senses to perceptive life. He ached to hold on to her for a little longer.

"I might faint," he jested.

She eased her grip at the justification, and together the couple strolled through the lively thoroughfare.

"I told you it was too soon for you to be roaming about the city," she chastised.

After a short lull, Edward returned the conversation to the previous matter: "Well? Why don't you seek employment at another club?"

"I'd have to do more than serve drinks at another club," she returned bitterly. "I'm not a whore."

"Ah, yes, you've told me that more than once now."
He glanced at her sheepishly. "I should teach you how
to protect yourself from patrons . . . like me."

She snorted. "I can protect myself—well, most of
the time—just fine. I had no trouble defending myself
against you, after all."

She tapped her chin.

Edward reached for his bruised mandible. "*You*
struck me?" He fingered the tender bone, bemused.
"And after I'd rescued you from the attackers?"

"Before," she clarified with a boastful smile.

"I'm not sure what to say." He eyed her warily. "I
can't remember being such a scoundrel."

"Forget about it. I'm used to overbearing characters."

He frowned. He didn't like the sound of that. How
many other patrons had approached her in a foxed state
of mind? How many had she clouted?

The dark thoughts in his head rankled his temper,
and soon another "overbearing character" entered his
mind.

"Like Madame Raf . . . ?"

"Rafaramanjaka? Yes, there's her."

"She *is* a character." He conducted Amy around a
heap of horse dung. "What a stage name."

"It's her real name, I think."

"Is it?"

She nodded. "She's from the island of Madagascar."

"Off the southern tip of Africa."

"Yes." She looked at him with surprise. "Have you
been there?"

He shrugged. "I don't—"

"Remember, right." She looked back at the congested road. "Well, she was once a queen."

"I can believe that," he said dryly. "She certainly acts like one."

"She was one of the twelve royal wives of King Radama, but she fled from the kingdom about three years ago."

"Why?"

"Her sister-monarch, Queen Ranavalona, was apparently plotting to poison the king, assume the throne—and behead all the rival wives."

"I think I understand the other queen's motives."

Amy chortled. "She came to England as 'Madame' Rafaramanjaka to hide from the other queen's wrath."

"Do you believe her tale?"

"As you said, she certainly acts like a queen."

"Hmm . . . and how did you find your way into her hands?"

"She found me, in truth." Amy's voice dropped in pitch. "I was living in the streets at the time."

"You're an orphan?"

She stiffened. "Yes." After a brief pause, she resumed: "I was living in a foundling asylum until about the age of twelve. After that, I was sent to work in a household as a serving girl. I stayed there for a few years . . . until the master of the house troubled me."

Edward bristled. "Did he hurt you?"

"He wanted to, I think." She shrugged. "I left my

employment and went back into the streets. That's where Madame Rafaramanjaka happened upon me. She took me away."

"To work at the club," he surmised, appreciating Amy's wretched upbringing. "You don't sound like you come from the streets, though."

"Ye mean, I donna 'ave a cockney tongue?" she said, like a common wench from the rookeries. "Madame schooled me in society, polished away my rough manners . . . well, most of them. She refused to be surrounded by anyone without good breeding—or at least the appearance of it."

"You have more good breeding than that vicious queen," he said passionately. "Don't let her convince you otherwise."

Amy bowed her head.

He recalled the items in her apartment: the mirrors, the fancy furnishings. She yearned to be a lady. Did she think if she surrounded herself with posh knickknacks, she would be a woman of standing?

In Edward's eyes, she was already such a woman.

"Why didn't the queen teach you to read?" he said. "Or the asylum's mistress, for that matter?"

"I was schooled in the foundling asylum for a short time, but I was then sent off to work. I wasn't allowed to touch my employer's books, so I soon forgot my letters. And Madame doesn't like me knowing *too* much, I think."

"So she can better control you," he said darkly.

"What's the matter, Edward? Why are you scowling?"

"There's something about that word . . . control." He smoothed his features. "It's nothing, Amy. Shall we dine?"

After a modest supper at a local pub, the couple returned to Amy's lodgings, exhausted.

"Do you have to work at the club tonight?"

"No," she said. "The club is closed on Sundays."

"No sin on Sundays, eh?"

She scoffed slightly.

He shut and locked the front door before he admired her sprite figure as it darted across the sitting room, stoked the coal hearth, then lighted a few candles with the Lucifer matches.

The space brightened, and Edward settled into an oak chair, content to observe her bustling movements, which he suspected routine. She had an agile form, quite bewitching, even dancerlike, and in the misty candlelight, she was a tempting sight.

She soon glanced at him, starting.

"What's the matter, Amy?"

"Why are you looking at me like that?"

"Like what?"

She returned the matches to the tin box on top of the mantel. "Never mind. It must be the shadows in the room. I'm tired."

She averted her eyes, and the soft orange glow from the small flames caressed her high cheekbones, making him wonder what it would feel like, smell like to nuzzle her there.

He folded his arms over his chest, more mindful of the "look" he had offered her just a moment ago. "I'll sleep out here."

"In the sitting room?"

"Sure." He shrugged. "I think I'm used to less comfortable surroundings."

She nodded. "I'll get you a blanket."

She slipped inside the bedchamber, and he listened with interest as she rummaged through a series of unidentifiable articles in a chest, looking for the blanket, he supposed. What sorts of treasures had she buried in there? he wondered.

A minute later, she returned.

She offered him a white embroidered quilt and matching bolster. "It'll keep you warm."

"Thank you."

He touched her slender fingers as he reached for the linens, and she quickly dropped the bedding into his lap, skirting away as if he had burned her.

"Good night, Edward."

She closed the bedchamber door.

He remained in the chair for a minute more, looking at the sealed barrier. He hadn't intended to make her feel uncomfortable; however, it was hard for him to suppress the intense feelings she evoked in him.

Edward unraveled the linens and settled on the round, woolly hearth rug. He placed the bolster under his head and covered himself with the blanket, staring at the ceiling.

He sensed the wood floor under his bones, even with the plush carpet. He tossed from one side to the other before he settled on his back once more and sighed, weaving his fingers together and placing them behind his head.

He soon noticed a dark figure standing, watching him from the bedroom door, clearly cross. She had opened the barrier without making a peep.

"What's wrong?" she said.

Was he making too much noise? He found that unlikely, for the sounds coming from the other tenants were far more boisterous.

He sighed. "I don't think I'm accustomed to going to bed so early in the evening."

He had walked a far distance today. He should be ready for sleep. He was restless, though. It was only about ten o'clock, he guessed.

"You'd rather be out chasing skirts and getting tattoos?" she quipped.

He grinned at that. "I think so."

She snorted. "Don't let me stop you."

Truth be told, he'd rather be in the apartment with her. He'd rather be close to her . . . touching her.

"What do you do for fun, Amy?"

"I don't have fun."

He cocked a brow, gazing up at her from the floor. "At all?"

"I work six days a week and I only get one day off to rest."

"So what do you do for fun?"

Amy made a wry face and returned to the bedchamber, shutting the door quietly.

She was an odd lass, wasn't she?

Edward was nestled beside the coal hearth, the spring nights still chilly, staring at the shadows on the ceiling, when Amy slowly opened the bedroom door once more.

"I like to play croquet," she confessed quietly.

The genteel sport suited her temperament. She wasn't one to enjoy the rat pits, he reckoned.

"I even purchased a croquet set."

Edward pulled the blanket away and jumped to his feet. "Let's play then."

He folded the embroidered linen and set it and the bolster, aside.

"Here?" she said, puzzled. "Now?"

He started stacking the chairs in the corner of the room. "Why not?"

"I'm tired," she said lamely.

"You don't look tired."

She was hardy, like him. And if he wasn't all that fatigued, she wasn't, either, he suspected. She was only putting up pretenses, for she was . . . odd.

"Do you play?" she wondered, folding her arms across her bust.

"Perhaps." He pushed the round table into the other corner and rolled up the rug. "And if I don't know the rules, you'll teach them to me."

She wavered.

"What's the matter, Amy? You like to play the sport and I'm restless."

She sighed at that. "Wait here."

She vanished back inside the small bedroom, and again he heard the shuffling and knocking as she groped through the mysterious items she had buried in the sturdy wood chest.

She returned to the sitting room with a long leather case, and set it carefully on the floor, unfastening the belted straps.

"It looks new," he observed.

"It is." She opened the container. "I've yet to use it."

Slowly she removed the wickets, balls, and mallets.

He hunkered across from her and collected the pieces. "Don't you play with your friends?"

She scoffed. "I don't have friends."

"Why not?"

"I don't like the people who live in the building . . . or in the area at large."

He eyed her intently before he arranged the thick wood wickets around the room in a pattern, keeping the arches steady, as he wasn't able to stake them into the soil, as the game required.

"I guess you do know how to play croquet." She nodded at the figure-eight arrangement. "You've placed the wickets in the proper order."

He looked around the room and shrugged. "I suppose I do."

Amy handed him the mallet with a blue stripe. "Why don't you start?"

He picked up the corresponding blue ball and readied himself at the starting point. The space was cramped, but he managed to gauge the wicket and send the ball rolling through the arch.

He stepped aside, and allowed Amy the next play with her red mallet and ball.

"Don't you ever get lonely, Amy?"

She knocked the ball through the first wicket. "No, I like my company."

"I like your company, too," he admitted, observing her blush. His belly warmed, rumbled with pleasure even, at the charming sight. "But what's the use in having a croquet set if you can't play the game with others?"

He struck her red ball with his blue ball, earning himself another point and a bonus play.

"I don't keep the croquet set so I can play with it," she returned tersely, waiting for him to make another attempt.

He frowned as he took his bonus turn. "Why?" What was the purpose of amassing so many "treasures," then? To engage in make-believe?

But she remained quiet.

"What about a beau, Amy?"

She stiffened. "I don't have a beau." She eyed the red ball and knocked it through the next wicket, bumping his blue ball. "You heard Madame Rafaramanjaka. I'm not to keep a beau."

"I heard she doesn't want you to have a lover . . . but that doesn't mean you have to listen to her."

She bowed her head, her beautiful long locks loose from the braid and hiding her features. "If I want to keep my employment at the club, then, yes, I do."

"But who will keep your bed warm?"

She glared at him, missing her bonus shot. "Are you trying to distract me from the game?"

"No." He took up his turn. "I'm just curious."

She huffed. "I keep my own bed warm."

"There can't be any fun in that," he said seriously.

"I told you, I don't have fun."

He had rounded the figure-eight course and was making his way back to the starting point. "And yet here we are, playing croquet."

She was quiet for the rest of the game—and appeared piqued to lose as he struck the blue ball back through the starting wicket, ending the play.

"I've won, Amy."

Her pert lips twisted and he smiled.

"Don't be peevish. I've clearly played more often than you."

She humphed and snatched the mallet from him.

He nuzzled her soft cheek, scented with lemon soap. "This is why you should play with friends, Amy . . . you might lose every time if you don't practice."

She bristled, rooted to the spot. He listened to the sound of her breathing, so heavy and irregular, and blood hastened through his veins as he sensed her growing arousal.

"How about a kiss for the victor?" he whispered.

She glanced at him sidelong: a sharp, wicked glance, for she then let her right fist swing in the direction of his jaw.

He ducked this time, avoiding the blow, and chuckled. It had been worth the effort, he thought roguishly.

Amy gathered the equipment and secured it in the leather case before she returned to her bedchamber. "Good night, Edward."

She shut the door with a sharp snap.

Chapter 5

Amy was seated at the dressing table, combing her hair. She twisted her long locks into a queue and secured the tresses with a white ribbon, observing her reflection in the vanity glass. She rarely fashioned her locks outside the club, but today she decided to adjust her routine.

She stood and smoothed her skirts before she opened the bedchamber door. Her heart pattered at the imposing sight of Edward. He was standing beside the window, gazing out into the street below, a meditative expression across his low brow. He offered no indication that he was even aware of her presence, so she took the quiet, discreet moment to observe him in greater detail.

He was dressed in a slightly rumpled shirt and creased trousers, his coat draped casually over an oak chair. The man's dark locks were mussed, his otherwise piercing blue eyes still somnolent. He was in such a bedraggled state that he stirred her blood. It was almost dreamlike, the impression he made upon her. He filled the room with his energy, and she welcomed the comforting company. For the first time in many years she had someone else in the home to talk to after waking up in the morning.

"You can stay here as long as you'd like," she blurted out.

Slowly he looked away from the pane of glass and stared at her. He gazed at her quietly for a lengthy time, the silent observation making her bones quiver.

She was quick to impart: "As you search the city for your home, I mean."

He returned his attention to the window without commenting, and she busied herself in the room, collecting the blanket and bolster and returning them to the chest in her bedchamber.

"You have no money, after all." She next moved into the small kitchenette and gathered the pewter dishes, set two bowls on the table in the sitting room. "You might as well stay here until your memory returns."

"Are you trying to keep me around, Amy?"

"Of course not."

She fastened an apron around her waist before she stuffed kindling into the iron stove in the kitchenette. She started a fire with the matches, then set a copper pot over the range and filled it with water from a pitcher that was sitting on the shelf.

"But what will you do for funds?" she said. "Shelter?"

"I'm resourceful," he assured her with confidence. "Don't worry about me."

She opened a ceramic jar and scooped a handful of oats from the container, stirring the contents into the pot. She wiped her fingers in her apron, careful to keep her back turned toward Edward. "You mean, you'll steal."

"I'm sure it won't come to that. I'm sure my memory will return soon."

She twisted her lips at his annoying tranquillity. Did nothing ruffle the man's feathers? How could he act with such coolheadedness? Was it all just bravado? Or was the man really unperturbed at the prospect of starting over?

She whisked the oatmeal in the steaming pot with a wooden spoon before she ventured a glance at Edward again. He was still standing beside the window.

"What are you looking at so intently?" she demanded, sounded unintentionally peevish.

"The two suspicious-looking fellows who keep pacing the street."

Amy frowned and crossed the sitting room. She paused beside Edward and peered through the damask drapery at the bustling crowd.

"What two—?"

She quickly stepped away from the window, her heart pounding.

"What's the matter, Amy? Do you know them?"

Unfortunately, she thought grimly. It was the same two assailants from the Pleasure Palace. The men had looked confused, prowling the street as if searching for the right building. Perhaps someone at the club had confessed she lived in St. Giles? But who? The guards staunchly shielded her true identity. The queen paid them handsomely for their silence . . . and yet the thugs had infiltrated her dressing room the other night. There was a snitcher at the club.

Edward had quickly guessed her thoughts about the thugs, for his eyes darkened and he suddenly stormed from the room.

"Edward, wait!"

But he was gone. She looked out the window again and watched him with bated breath as he moved through the throng in the direction of the assailants. He disappeared from view and she wrung her fingers.

"Oh, bullocks."

She snatched her shawl, wrapped it around her shoulders, and descended into the congested street. She passed the lemonade vendor, the lavender seller. She circumvented the young girls and boys fencing stolen goods from the previous night.

Amy pushed her way through the pressing crowd, looking for Edward. He was a skilled pugilist, she thought. He had already trounced the attackers, but he had injured himself in the fight, too. He was still recovering from his head wound. If he ended up in another scuffle so soon, he'd likely come out the loser . . . bloody . . . broken.

As the images in her head grew more gruesome, she hastened her steps and broadened her search, making her way toward the river. She followed the natural flow of heavy traffic into Billingsgate Fish Market on Lower

Thames Street. The costermongers hawked herrings, stockfish, oysters. The robust shouts and pungent smells filled the wharf. She peered over myriad heads, searching for Edward's tall figure. He wasn't at the market, though. She had lost him.

Amy cursed under her breath. She treaded back toward her lodgings, determined to wait for the scoundrel there. As she traversed the narrow lanes, she passed the charity school for female foundlings.

The gloomy structure chilled her. She had survived her girlhood in a similar asylum. She preferred not to reflect upon those wretched days, though, and she skirted past the building . . . when lyrical laughter arrested her rushed movements.

Amy stilled, muscles pinched. She slowly looked over her shoulder at the charity school and spotted the back of a well-dressed lady as she entered a regal-looking vehicle. A white-gloved hand waved through the parted window at the children. The girls wished their benefactor cheerful good days in return before the carriage set off.

The warm figure soon approached her and knelt, and Amy sensed a pair of gloved hands squeeze and tickle her midriff.

She squealed with delight.

Amy stared after the vehicle, feeling dizzy. She sorted through the shadowed figures, the muddled sounds in her head . . .

"Watch it, girl!"

She stumbled as a bounder bumped into her backside, pitching her into another pedestrian, the missteps causing a calamity.

"Troublemaker!"

"Rioter!"

Amy girded her muscles, befuddled. "It was an accident."

But the swelling mob wasn't so sympathetic, their expressions black. She fisted her fingers in anticipation of a brawl, but a hard hand gripped her wrist and jerked her roughly away from the rankled crowd.

"What the devil do you think you're doing, Amy?"

She was rattled, breathless. "I-I was looking for you."

Edward frowned. "Why?"

"I wanted to make sure you were all right."

"I don't need you to protect me," he said firmly. "*You*, on the other hand, need protecting." He ushered her toward her lodgings. "You almost started a rampage."

"It wasn't my intent," she snapped. "I saw . . ."

"What did you see?"

The vehicle. The laughter. The gloved hand. She had remembered . . . but the vision vanished.

Amy mumbled, "Never mind."

The moment they entered the apartment again, she wondered, "What happened with the thugs?"

"I lost sight of them in the crowd," he returned in a surly manner.

She sighed. "Damn fools! Why won't they give over and trouble some other, more *sociable* barmaid?"

"I doubt there's any as pretty as you."

The man's gruff voice had softened at the expression, making her cheeks warm. She looked at the floor and observed his booted feet approaching her. The muscles in her midriff tightened, and she sensed the blood pulse in her ears.

"I think you're right, Amy."

He tipped her chin up with his forefinger, meeting her gaze . . . that smoldering gaze; it singed her flesh, unsettled her nerves.

"I think I should stay with you for a little while more—until my memory returns."

He was staying to protect her. It was there in his eyes, the gentlemanly impulse. Funny he should be such a gentleman now, without his memory. If the scoundrel ever regained his thoughts and former bad habits . . .

In truth, she didn't mind him staying awhile longer at the apartment with her, and so long as he stayed away from the club and the vicious queen, there wasn't any harm in keeping him for a short time more, she supposed.

Edward sniffed . . . then sniffed again.

Indignant, she took a step back, glowering, but she quickly smelled the burning oats and kicked up her heels. "Oh no!"

"Everything all right in there?"

She removed the bubbling pot from the stove, the oatmeal ruined. She would have to begin anew, though she hoped the wasted grains weren't an ill omen, that she wasn't making a mistake in letting the seaman reside with her.

* * *

The coal fire in the hearth warmed Edward's toes as he sat, slumped, in an oak chair, arms folded across his chest, frowning. He peered at Amy through the parted bedchamber door. She was seated on a stool at her dressing table, oblivious to his darkening mood. He observed her with growing impatience as she brushed her lengthy locks, dolling herself up for an evening shift at the gentlemen's club, where she'd have to gratify another party of overbearing patrons. And thanks to him, she'd get half her usual earnings for her trouble.

"Well, I'm off." She grabbed a shawl and draped it over her head and shoulders as she entered the sitting room, and looked at him pointedly with her sharp green eyes. "I'll be home late, so I suggest you get some rest."

Rest? He snorted. He lifted out of the seat and approached the front entrance.

"Where are you going, Edward?"

"I'm escorting you to the club."

Amy's eyes swelled. "No."

He ignored the woman's brusque retort and opened the door. "You were attacked two nights ago."

She sighed. "I appreciate your concern, but I don't need an escort."

"I think you do," he returned evenly.

"I have been going to the club alone every night for almost three years, and there's no reason for me to change my habits now. Besides, when you regain your memory and return home, I'll still be working at the club. You can't protect me all the time—and I don't want to depend on you."

He eyed her mulishly. "I can protect you tonight."

"I'll be fine, really." She pried his fingers off the door's latch. "Madame Rafaramanjaka knows about the attack. She'll make sure the guards are more vigilant."

Edward took her hand and squeezed her warm fingers, sensing her rapid pulse. "Do you really think I'm going to sit here idly, while you walk the streets alone at night?"

"Are you daft?" She glowered at him. "I just told you, I've been walking the streets alone at night for almost three years. I've yet to meet my Maker." She wrested her fingers away, lips pinched. "You'll never get inside the club, anyway."

"I got inside two nights ago."

She looked him over in a quick, keen manner. "How *did* you get inside the club?" She waved her fingers in a dismissive gesture. "Perhaps you sneaked inside the establishment."

"You see? You have poor security at the club if *I* was permitted within its walls."

"You have to stay here and rest, Edward."

"I can at least escort you to the club's door."

"No!" She flounced off and entered the passageway. "If Madame Rafaramanjaka thinks I have a beau, she'll dismiss me from the club. Stay here, Edward. Please!"

She skirted through the darkened hall.

He stared after her bustling figure, the blood in his veins pounding. He took one step back inside the apartment, reached around the door to locate the iron key on the hook, then shut and locked the entrance, skulking in the shadows after Amy.

Edward followed her to the impressive establishment in Covent Garden. There he waited for her in the streets for more than an hour, restless. He waited for her to come out again, so he could walk her home, but as he witnessed more and more posh gentlemen flood the club's premises, the irritability in his blood strengthened, and he itched with the profound need to smash their aquiline noses into the pavement.

Edward crossed the street with wide strides. He had sneaked inside the club the other night. How hard would it be for him to sneak inside again?

Slowly he climbed the three stone steps leading to the front door and stealthily attempted to part the main entranceway. The thick door was secured.

No, it wouldn't be so easy, he supposed. He headed down the steps and decided to make his way around to the back of the building. Perhaps there was another door there? The sound of heavy iron hinges rooted him to the paved walkway, though.

He glanced over his shoulder at the surly-looking guard peering at him suspiciously through the slightly parted door. He must have detected Edward's endeavors to steal inside the club. Edward anticipated a rude remark and a threatening show of fists . . . he wasn't prepared for the gatekeeper's welcoming gesture.

The gruff sentry opened the door fully and bowed. "Good evening, sir."

Edward hesitated for a second before he composed himself and scaled the steps again, walking into the sensuous club with confidence. Had he impersonated a gentleman the other night? Was that how he'd entered the club? Was that why the gatekeeper was being so welcoming now?

It was the only logical conclusion, and keeping the thought in his mind, he headed through the elaborate passageway and up the flight of winding steps with aplomb. He intended to keep a close watch over Amy. He would remain in the shadows; he wouldn't give off the impression that he was her "beau," and risk her losing her livelihood. However, he would safeguard her well-being . . . for tonight.

Chapter 6

Amy danced under the brilliant white limelight. She performed the scandalous choreography with ease, having memorized the steps. She shuffled sideways, rolling her hips and moving her hands to the rhythmic music. Twisting and undulating in her red silk skirt and coin belt, she maintained her eyes on the crowd.

She didn't meet the patrons' gazes, though, or focus on one side of the room for too long. She loathed connecting intimately with the visitors, however briefly. She loathed the way they looked at her, salivated over her.

Amy moved across the stage with methodical grace. As she dropped, then rolled her right hip, she spotted a tall figure approaching the stage with uncharacteristic urgency. The limelight in her eyes, she wasn't able to see the man's face clearly . . . until he neared the platform.

She gasped.

Heart cramped, she stumbled, but quickly regained her footing as she stared into Edward's bewildered blue eyes. He looked confused—and furious. She was wearing a veil that concealed her lips, but he had plainly recognized her painted eyes.

She wanted to dash off the stage. An uncomfortable heat scorched her cheeks, her belly. She wanted to hide behind the curtains and evade his critical glare, for a deep shame welled in her breast. He had discovered her true, sinful occupation at the club—again! That he might reveal her identity right then didn't trouble her; that *he* looked at her with such disapproval disturbed her beyond words.

The drumbeats ended and Amy shuffled off the stage in a maladroit fashion. She quickly peeled the veil off her features, feeling stifled even under the loose silk scarf.

"What must he think of me?" she said in a panic.

She rushed through the dimly lit passageway, glancing over her shoulder to see if he was following her. There were guards posted at every door, and yet she sensed the "resourceful" seaman would find some way of getting past them.

She entered her dressing room and with fingers trembling removed the exotic costume and headpiece. She swiftly donned her usual, unassuming attire and grabbed her shawl, leaving the charcoal paint around her eyes. She would remove the makeup at home. She was anxious to flee the Pleasure Palace.

Amy skirted through the empty passageway again,

hazily illuminated with innovative gas lighting. The hissing flames burned in her ears, like malicious hecklers.

She burst through the back entranceway—right into the sturdy arms of a vagabond . . . two vagabonds, for she spotted another shadow rounding the corner. The same two devils who had accosted her the other evening!

"You two do *not* give up, do you?" she cried in frustration.

One devil grinned. "I get one hundred pounds if I deliver you to my master."

She firmed her lips and nailed him right in the nose with her knuckles. "Tell your master to go to hell!"

Swiftly Amy slipped back inside the club and bolted the door. The vagabonds banged on the door and rattled the latch, cursing up a storm.

"Trouble, Amy?"

She whirled around and spotted Edward's muscular figure stalking through the ghostly passageway, charging her. The brooding fellow grabbed her arms and pierced her soul with his glare, making her shiver.

"How did you get back here, Edward?"

He ignored her query and demanded, "Why did you lie to me?"

Amy was overwhelmed by the man's biting words and rough manner. She tamped the indignity she was feeling into the very tips of her toes, letting loose her frustration and fury instead.

"I don't have to tell you anything about me!" She struggled in his arms and swatted at his chest. "Let me go!"

She was prepared to kick him in the leg, when the vagabonds slammed their shoulders into the sturdy door in an attempt to break it.

Edward curtailed their row with a brief scowl before he yanked her arm and dragged her through the rear of the club. "We'll finish this at your apartment."

"Arrgh!" She punched him in the arm. "You promised me you wouldn't come to the club."

"I did no such thing," he returned stiffly, steering her toward an alternate exit.

He smuggled her away from the establishment undetected, and pulled her alongside him. She quarreled with him all the way back to her lodgings.

"You lied to me, Amy."

He unlocked the apartment and pushed her inside the sitting room. Two candles sheltered in glass lamps still burned on the table.

"You told me you were a barmaid." He pointed at her eyes and flicked his finger. "But you're . . . you're . . . I don't even know who you are."

She tossed the shawl aside, the blood burning in her veins. She scooped up a candle and strutted through the sitting room. She entered her bedroom, where she set the candle aside and poured clear water from an earthenware pitcher into a basin.

"I don't need a lecture from *you* about honesty." She grabbed a small white towel and immersed it in the basin before she scrubbed the black ink off her eyes. "You're an admitted thief!"

She peered into the mirror on the dressing table as she removed the cosmetic paint. She then observed the man's wide, shadowy figure as he stood under the door frame, glowering at her.

"How can you prance on stage, arousing so many men? I thought you said you weren't a whore?"

"I'm not, you blackguard!" She dunked the towel into the basin again, the water turning grimy. "But I need the money."

"Aye, so you can purchase more mirrors," he returned dryly. "Such vanity, Amy. I'm disappointed in you."

"How dare you!" She scrubbed her skin with more vigor, the black makeup clinging to her flesh like baked filth. "The mirrors have nothing to do with vanity."

"Then why collect them?"

Amy peered even deeper into the dark glass. The candlelight in the bedchamber danced, casting rippled waves of fire across the shiny surface.

Amy picked up the small mirror with an ivory handle and gazed at her features. The soft swooshing sound of petticoats flirted with her ears as the older woman moved lightly about the room, fluffing her carefully pressed curls and pinning her glittering earrings.

The warm figure soon approached her and knelt, and Amy sensed a pair of gloved hands squeeze and tickle her midriff.

She squealed with delight.

"Never mind about the mirrors." She took in a deep, shuddering breath. "And keep your voice down or you'll disturb the other tenants."

"Oh? Do you mean the couple fighting on one side of the wall? Or the couple shagging on the other?"

She flushed. The level of noise from the other residents was troubling. She had one set of neighbors who bickered every night, their rows often ending in vicious blows. A prostitute regularly entertained her clients in the other apartment, leaving Amy boxed in between all the commotion.

"I suspect the other tenants won't mind our quarreling," he said with wry humor.

"We are not quarreling; *you* are quarreling. Unjustly, I might add." She dropped the dirty towel into the basin, the water splashing. "I don't owe you an explanation regarding my life or my choices."

She picked up the candlestick and glass orb, the flame flickering, and brushed past him into the other room.

He followed her.

"You have to quit the club, Amy."

She placed the candle on the table in the sitting room, fingers quivering. "No."

A strong hand grasped her wrist, and she pivoted.

"You can't work at the club anymore." Hard, steely eyes pegged her. "It's too dangerous."

Amy gazed into the dark pools, reflecting the glimmering light like mirrors. However, unlike the glass, she didn't see herself cast back in the glossy orbs. She looked deep into the obdurate man's soul and witnessed a bevy of emotions that both alarmed and strangely thrilled her. Being so close to Edward teased her senses, muddled her thoughts. Every word and breath was more acute, every touch more sensitive.

"I can handle the situation at the club," she insisted in a low voice.

"You've been attacked *twice* in two nights."

The man's sharp, warm breath stirred the fine hairs at her temples, making her shiver. "I was attacked once," she clarified tersely. "I protected myself tonight."

She wriggled her wrist loose and stepped away from him, her heart thumping in her chest with greater vigor.

"And who will protect you tomorrow night?" He glared at her. "There's one lazy guard who can't get off his arse and quit napping during the performances."

So that's how Edward had finagled his way into the rear of the club, she mused.

"I'll protect myself," she said with confidence.

"Amy," he drawled in a deadly tone, "the attackers have been offered one hundred pounds to kidnap you. I heard them before the door closed."

"I heard them, too," she said indignantly. "I'm not deaf."

"Do you think such men will quit coming after you? Forfeit the fortune?"

She gritted, "I can't quit the club."

"It might be the queen who wants you dead." Slowly he approached her. "She might have hired the attackers to kill you. The woman hates you, you know."

Amy snorted. "Madame Rafaramanjaka would never waste one hundred pounds on me. If she wanted me dead, she'd strangle me herself."

Amy stepped away from the nearing scoundrel. He roused her blood, her pulse in such an alarming manner, she felt safer at a distance from the brooding fellow.

"Look," he said more softly, stilling his steps. "I know you're frightened about the unknown future, but you can't risk your life at the club."

She shook her head vehemently.

"You need to find another form of livelihood," he persisted in an even voice.

"No. No!" She skirted around the table to evade his darkening expression. "I refuse to live like one of them!" She pointed at the two opposite walls. "I refuse to be poor and desperate."

"Amy," he said sharply, eyes aglow, "you have to be reasonable. You're being hunted."

"I am being reasonable," she retorted sourly. "As soon as my youth is gone, Madame Rafaramanjaka will dismiss me from the club and hire a replacement." She jabbed her forefinger into her bust. "But I will have saved enough funds by then to live out the rest of my days in comfort." She looked daggers at him. "What do you want me to do? Be a seamstress? A governess? I can't even read! I'll make a pittance each year toiling under some other ruthless employer. I make more than sixty pounds each annum working for the queen!"

"You slave for the queen," he corrected darkly. "And it isn't worth your life."

"You want to see me living in the streets! How is that any better?"

"I want to see you work in a less dangerous profession."

She scoffed and rubbed her hands together, pacing the room. "You want me to work under the direction of some other boor for a meager amount. And then, one day, when I'm too old to work, and I've no money saved because I've spent every penny on food and rent, I'll be destitute. Thank you," she said sarcastically, "however, I don't like your plan for my future."

"Well, do you have some money saved? Or have you spent it all on mirrors?"

"Why do you think I live in this wretched place?" She glowered at him. "I want to save every penny, but I still don't have enough."

"You can get married. A husband will look after your needs."

He offered the alternative as if it was an obvious solution to her troubles, and she looked at him with scorn.

"A husband will only drink away my hard-earned pennies. I see what it's really like out there." She pointed at the window. "I see the wives with their drunken curs for spouses. Just listen!" She outstretched her arms as if to take in all the vile noises stemming from every side of the room. "I won't live like them."

She crossed the room and collected her shawl, fingers trembling, heart pounding. "I've survived on my own since I was a babe, and I'll continue to survive on my own just fine."

She hustled from the room, impervious to Edward's shouts. She made her way through the building and reached the ground level, where she quickly skirted across the muddy street, rehashing the quarrel with Edward in her mind.

It burned her blood to even think about forsaking her profession, as scandalous as it was, and working in a shop or a factory like a miserable horse for scraps. She would keep her livelihood as a dancer and confront the risks, as she had done—successfully—in the past.

Insensible to her surroundings, Amy rounded the dark corner and rammed a towering figure.

She murmured, distracted, "Pardon me," and side-stepped the ruffian with his two gruff companions, but a firm hand arrested her movements and a deep voice stirred her hackles.

"You must be Amy."

Amy's heart palpitated as she gazed into the ruffian's sinister eyes, and the danger Edward had warned her against flitted through her head, for the shaggy barbarian, with his long hair secured in a queue, was the most menacing fellow she had ever set eyes on.

"She looks just like he described her," said another ruffian.

He was almost as tall as the devil holding her, though not nearly as ominous. Still, Amy's chest cramped as her heart beat wild and sweat formed across her brow.

"Aye, she's as lovely as a rainbow," praised the third shadow. He even smiled in the dark, for his teeth gleamed like moonbeams.

She didn't recognize the three assailants. How many were out there searching for her? As Edward had expressed, there was a one-hundred-pound bounty on her head. Who would forfeit such a fortune?

"Oh, bullocks!" she cried.

Amy struggled with her captor. In vain. The man shoved her against the nearest slimy wall with one hand, and glowered at her.

"Where is he?"

"Who?" she whispered.

"Edmund."

"I don't know anyone named Ed—"

Amy's thoughts scampered like dry leaves in a windstorm. Did he mean Edward? What did *he* want with Edward? No, Edmund. Had Edmund robbed him of his coin purse? Was that why he was after him?

She imagined the ruffian's meaty fist slamming into Edmund's handsome head, and she shuddered, pinching her lips.

"I see you do know who I'm talking about." Dark eyes flashed. "Now tell me where he is, wench."

However, she refused to betray Edmund's location. It was so uncivilized, to be a snitcher. She wasn't so dishonorable. She wouldn't let them have the man who had saved her life, even if he was a thief.

"I don't know where he is," she returned stiffly, her heart in her throat.

"A guard at the Pleasure Palace told us he saw you run off with him."

She paled. "A g-guard told you that?"

The same lazy one who had napped during her performance, allowing Edmund to sneak into the rear of the establishment?

"Hmm . . . he was very forthcoming. He needed a little encouragement before making the confession, though. Will you need encouragement, wench?"

She ignored the threat, filled with one haunting thought: she was ruined. If a guard at the gentlemen's club had witnessed her dash off with Edmund earlier in the night . . . then Madame Rafaramanjaka would hear about it eventually, as well. She would know Amy had lied, that she had a "lover," that her true identity had been revealed, and Amy would be dismissed from the establishment for good.

Hot tears filled her eyes. "Damn him!"

She railed at Edmund. She had told him *not* to follow her to the club, but he had been stubborn; he had refused to listen. He had ruined her.

She should confess the scoundrel's whereabouts, that he was staying at her apartment. She should let the three bounders trounce him soundly for upsetting her life in such a cruel fashion!

Edmund rounded the corner then. He glanced at Amy, pinned between the barbarian and the wall—and started swinging.

"Get away from her!"

He knocked the other two ruffians aside, amid hails of protests, with little effort, he was so incensed. He tackled the barbarian with precision next, but the ominous fellow had enough brute strength to pin the deft pugilist against the wall, curtailing the fisticuffs.

He shoved his elbow under Edmund's chin, and growled. "Where have you been?"

Slowly Amy slunk along the wall, hoping to skirt away; however, one of the other beasts, who had recovered from the earlier assault, grabbed her arm, and she sighed in defeat. The young buck offered her a flirtatious wink in consolation, though, and she frowned.

"What the devil is wrong with you, Edmund?"

Edmund stopped struggling at the sound of his name, looking confused. "Ed . . . what?"

"Do you think you can just run off and hide with a ladybird, without letting us know where you are?"

Amy bristled. "I'm not his ladybird."

He already had a bonny Meg stashed away in some port, she thought tartly.

"Belle's been worried sick," the ruffian charged.

Amy rolled her eyes. Edmund had another sweetheart weeping for him in port? Was that why the men had come looking for him? To drag him back home to his family, his wife? Hell, he might even *be* one of those drunken curs she had denounced just a few minutes ago.

Amy's temper rankled as she stewed in her own folly. She had forsaken her livelihood to care for and protect *him*, the wretch!

Edmund narrowed his eyes. "J-James?"

"Are you drunk?" the barbarian demanded.

"With love," said the flirty ruffian, grinning at her.

Amy twisted her arm in a bid to escape his clutches, but he maintained a firm grip.

She huffed. "He's not drunk—with love or otherwise." She looked pointedly at her cheeky captor, then: "He hit his head and can't remember his name."

James relaxed his hold. "Is that true, Eddie?"

"You can't remember us?" said the third ruffian. "Your own brothers?"

Amy glanced from one face to the other, and quickly assessed the claim was true: the men were his brothers. It was there in their rugged features and dark hair, the shapes of their eyes, and even their manners of expression.

Edmund grabbed his skull as he was wont to do whenever a memory came upon him. "My head hurts."

"Let's get him indoors," suggested Amy. "He needs to rest. I live just around the corner."

She yanked her arm away from the young upstart, who chuckled at her curt manner, and guided the brothers back to her lodgings.

Inside the apartment, the four men filled the room, making it seem so much smaller than it really was.

"Sit," ordered James.

"No."

Edmund moved toward the window and stood beside the glass, pensive. The other three ruffians settled into the oak chairs, the wood joints creaking.

Amy looked at each of the big fellows crowding her small apartment. Within a few days, she had witnessed her life sink even deeper into turmoil. Distressed, she remained beside the door, lips pinched.

"I'm Quincy," said the scamp who'd guarded her in the street, clearly sensing her unrest. "That's William." He pointed to the third, quiet ruffian. "And James you know."

The barbarian. He and William were about twenty years older than Edmund and Quincy, for she observed the smattering of silver at their temples.

Edmund still gazed out the window, wondering: "How did you find me?"

"We retraced your steps from the flash house in Buckeridge Street," William informed him.

"We had a drink there before parting ways," said Quincy. "Remember?"

"I remember."

"Why don't we take you home so you can rest, Eddie." James shifted from the chair and approached his brother at the window. "You hit your head?"

"Aye." Edmund ruffled his hair. "But I can't go home yet. I have to talk with Amy." He crossed the room, eyes alight, and took her by the hand. "Alone."

He dragged her into the bedchamber and shut the door.

Edmund had regained his memory, that much Amy was sure about, for he had looked at her with such fire in his eyes, it was clear he had recollected their first unfriendly meeting.

The small room was dark. Moonlight moved softly through the space, illuminating the man's wide form as he sat down on the edge of the bedstead.

She remained standing beside the closed door and folded her arms across her chest. "Who are you?"

"My name is Edmund Hawkins," he said with some uncertainty.

"Are you a thief? Or a seaman?"

He was silent.

"Ugh!"

"I didn't steal the purse," he returned with quiet conviction. "It's mine. The initials are mine."

"What are *you* doing with such a fancy pouch?"

"It was a gift from my sister, Belle . . . I think."

Aha! Belle wasn't a sweetheart he had abandoned, then. For some obscure reason, she was relieved to hear that. Although it didn't explain the identity of the mysterious bonny Meg he had tattooed on his back.

"I would never keep the purse otherwise," he said dryly.

She approached the locked chest in the corner of the room and removed a key secured on a chain from around her neck. She opened the chest and rummaged through the contents for the pouch. The coins still secured within the leather, she tossed him the purse.

He captured the small satchel with one hand.

"The tattoo on your back?"

He rubbed his shoulder. "The bonny Meg?"

"Yes, her."

Amy tried to keep the tartness out of her voice, but she had failed to do so, and the scoundrel had noticed her tone, for he murmured softly, "Are you jealous?"

She snorted at the absurd suggestion.

"I thought I would ask." He shrugged. "The *Bonny Meg* is a schooner. She was my late father's ship, named after my late mother, Megan." He said with reverence, "I sailed aboard her for many years."

The stiffness in Amy's shoulders eased. "I see."

"Amy."

"What?"

He lifted off the bed and stepped toward her. "I want you to come home with me."

"As your ladybird?" she snapped, pulse fluttering.

"I can help you find another line of work." He pressed his hands against the door, trapping her. "You can't work at the club anymore."

He was too bloody close, the proximity making her senses dance with awareness. A hard set of eyes stared at her, offset by a pair of lush, well-formed lips that seemed balmily tempting to taste.

"Did you hear me, Amy?"

"Hmm?"

"You can't work at the Pleasure Palace anymore."

"I know."

"You do?"

He sounded unconvinced, surprised even, that she had acquiesced, and after resisting the suggestion so ardently earlier in the night.

"Yes, thanks to your brothers, I've learned one of the sentries at the club witnessed us leaving together." She said tightly, "The wretched queen will soon find out my identity is revealed."

"As Zarsitti?" he whispered.

The man's lips moved with captivating sensuality, leaving Amy grasping for her wits, and even her breath.

"She'll dismiss me, I'm sure," she said, voice shaky.

"I remember the first night I saw you on stage—the very first night." He peered at her intently, as if conjuring the images in his head. He then glanced hotly at her belly. "You have a mark between your breasts."

She shivered, senses ravaged, for he stared at her midriff, peeling away the layers of her garments in his mind, she was sure. And the thought that he was thinking about her without her attire properly secured made her heart beat with ferocious swiftness.

"A kiss," he murmured. "You have a kiss between your breasts, I remember."

He sounded like *he* wanted to kiss her right between the breasts, the man's voice was so low, hardly audible . . . and the thought was so wickedly tempting, moisture gathered between her breasts.

"Is it real, Amy? The mark?"

She licked her lips. "I-I was born with the birthmark."

"Hmm . . . It's a good thing you can't return to the club." He lifted his eyes and gazed at her with mesmerizing intensity. "Come home with me and I will find you a new profession."

It was hot inside the room. The scoundrel's heated words warmed her even more, making the blood pump through her veins with greater vigor.

"As what?" she said hoarsely.

"How about a lady's maid? No one knows your identity as the dancer, for you always concealed your features with a veil and paint. And Madame Rafaramanjaka will never move in high society, so she will never cross your path at a social function; she will never betray your past."

Amy dismissed the heady effect he had on her for a moment, and glowered at him as if he were daft. "A lady's maid?"

"You want money *and* a comfortable life. I can see to it that you get both things."

"How? You're just a sailor . . . aren't you?"

After another perturbing pause, she cried:

"Oh no! You *are* a gentleman? The fancy purse. The

gentlemen's club. *That's* how you got inside the Pleasure Palace!"

Thoughts whirling, Amy pushed away from the man's warm embrace and crossed the room. *He* was a bloody gentleman? *He* could . . . help her?

She rubbed her flushed cheeks. "Why are you dressed like a vagabond?"

"So I won't be robbed at the pub," he returned sensibly.

Yes, of course. That meant the other men in the adjoining room were gentlemen, too, all dressed down so as not to attract criminal notice in the city's poor district.

"I pegged you a thief. A sailor," she said in an excited fashion. "But I never considered you a gentleman."

"I wasn't born a gentleman," he said to appease her, not sounding the least bit insulted by her rude remarks. "Come back to St. James with me, Amy."

"St. James!"

The bachelor quarters of London? One of the richest parts of London? He wanted her to live *there*?

"I can't live with you openly in St. James!"

"Not openly, of course. I'll soon find you a position as a lady's maid or companion."

She was still confused, flustered. "Why are you doing this?"

"I can't leave you destitute," he said firmly.

She glowered at him. "This *is* all your fault."

"Then let me make it right."

A series of objections entered her head: the

impropriety, the danger of the situation. If she was discovered living in the bachelor district with Edmund, she would never become a lady's maid or companion . . . and yet the proposition, the opportunity for social advancement, was too tempting to resist. Besides, what other choice did she have but to go with the scoundrel? She would be dismissed from the club tomorrow. She would survive off her savings for a short while, and then what would she do?

Amy gathered a deep, fortifying breath. "My things?"

He smiled, a triumphant gleam in his eyes. "Take what you can tonight. Quincy and I will round up the rest of your belongings the next day."

She looked around the room, fretting. "I want everything, including the curtains."

"We'll collect the curtains."

"And the rods and finials."

"And the rods and finials, I promise."

Amy sighed. "All right."

He nodded. "I'll tell my brothers."

Edmund left the room to converse with the other ruffians about their newly formed arrangement.

Amy stood in the small chamber, her home for the last three years, without a measure of regret. She wouldn't have to listen to the endless squabbles from the other tenants or the hoarse, distasteful couplings. She wouldn't have to squat in such ignominious lodgings anymore. Refinement. Breeding. Respect. She'd be surrounded by the elegance, the sophistication of life.

As joy swelled in her breast, she grabbed a carrying bag from the chest and started to gather her clothing and toiletries . . . but one niggling question still hounded her: How she was going to live with the sensual scoundrel now that he had regained his memory?

Chapter 7

"**T**he Duchess of Wembury?"

Amy's ears tingled at the sound of the grand title. She glanced at Edmund, seated beside her in the hackney coach. He was bedraggled and surly-looking. To think, *he* was related to the Duchess of Wembury!

She eyed Quincy again; he was positioned opposite her on the cushioned squabs. There wasn't enough room in the coach for five occupants, so the two eldest brothers traveled behind them in a second vehicle.

"How did your sister meet the duke?"

As a seafaring family, the Hawkinses hadn't the social connections to mix with the aristocracy, so Amy was keen to know how they'd worked their way into the tightly guarded circles of the upper crust.

Quincy grinned. "She stowed away aboard the *Bonny Meg*."

"Why?"

"She's rebellious," said Edmund in a terse manner.

"It's more like James is hardheaded. He wouldn't let her sail the *Bonny Meg*, so she stowed away. The duke was traveling with us at the time, and, well, trapped aboard ship together . . ."

"I see," she said knowingly. "Is it a happy match?"

"I think so, but the rest of my brothers don't like the duke."

"Oh?"

"He was—"

"Is," interposed Edmund.

"—a rogue."

Amy raised a brow at the hypocritical grump seated beside her, who continually disrupted her discourse with Quincy.

Edmund frowned. "What?"

"Never mind," she said.

She looked back at Quincy. A good thing he was a gossip, for she'd learn little about their unique family dynamic from the surly Edmund. For instance, she'd discovered there was a significant age difference between the brothers, stemming from the fact that their father had been away at sea for more than a decade, pressed into naval service. Upon his return, the family had expanded, and so had their maritime ventures with the acquisition of the *Bonny Meg*, their ancestral ship.

At the age of one-and-forty, James Hawkins now commanded the merchant schooner, whereas his brother, William, at age nine-and-thirty, captained the *Nemesis* as a privateer in the Royal Navy's African

Squadron. At one time, the fledglings had served aboard the *Bonny Meg*, but about six months ago they had joined William's crew in search of more "adventure," according to Quincy.

The scamp chuckled. "James almost had an apoplexy when our sister married the 'Duke of Rogues.' "

"The duchess must be a brave woman."

He shrugged. "The duke's a good fellow."

What about her brother, the barbarian? she thought. He wasn't such a good fellow. The duchess had gumption if she'd crossed his will . . . but, then again, to be a respected duchess, Amy would've thwarted the man's will, too.

She glanced at Edmund again. His seaman's upbringing explained his rough manners, and his rise to the rank of gentleman was the direct result of his only sister's marriage to the Duke of Wembury. However, Amy was still perplexed by Edmund's sudden, uncharacteristic sullenness. Wasn't he happy to be reunited with his brothers? Wasn't he happy *not* to be adrift in the city without home or family?

The hackney coach slowed to a halt before the well-groomed town house. Amy peered through the glass in wonder at the three-story edifice, its sleek white façade a brilliant, towering monument, even in the dull darkness.

Quincy hopped out first and maintained the door open for her as she exited the vehicle. Edmund followed, carrying some of her possessions.

She examined her unfamiliar surroundings with

scrutiny, muscles tight. If she was going to become a lady's maid or companion, she had to preserve her respectability. It was late, though, the street deserted, so she relaxed her stiff spine.

James and William approached them as one coach rattled off into the night, while the other one remained stationed, and the entire party quickly entered the prestigious address, illuminated with oil lamps. The decor was decidedly masculine in flavor, with dark wood furnishings and accent colors of deep brown and red with hints of gold. There was some scandalous artwork on the walls, appropriate for a bachelor residence. Amy wasn't put off by the familiar nude figures, which had adorned the Pleasure Palace, too.

Once inside the dwelling, James said, "I'll visit with you tomorrow, to make sure you've recovered."

Edmund nodded. He didn't say a word to his older brother, which didn't seem to disturb the captain, for he next turned to William and murmured a few discreet words, perhaps advising the man to keep a close eye on her, for she might murder them all in their sleep and purloin their riches.

Amy pinched her lips and looked at Edmund for clarification. Wasn't the captain staying at the house, too? The scoundrel remained quiet, though.

She looked at Quincy for illumination instead. "I thought you said you lived with your brothers?" she hissed.

He smiled at her in a charming fashion. "James lives in Mayfair with his newlywed wife, Sophia."

Someone married the barbarian? Amy thought, stunned.

"We're all still reeling over it, too," the scamp whispered into her ear, having clearly guessed her inappropriate thoughts.

Amy blushed.

Edmund frowned, his dark glare fixed on Quincy, who shrugged and quietly stepped away from her.

Their coterie disbanded, James wondered aloud, "How's Sophia?"

"She's fine," William returned dryly. "I do so appreciate you leaving her in my charge."

Amy furrowed her brow. Wasn't James's wife named Sophia? She looked at Quincy again.

"The snake," he mouthed silently.

Snake?!

Quincy made a curt hand gesture, a cutting movement, telling her to end the conversation, that he would inform her about the unusual details at a later, more appropriate time.

How fitting that the intimidating brood should keep a snake as a pet, she mused wryly. Was the serpent caged? If not, it would find its head crushed under her heel. Amy wasn't going to share her accommodations with a pest. She'd lived with enough vermin over the years.

James bid his brothers farewell before he stepped across from Amy. He was silent, yet his penetrating stare was abysmally clear: *Behave yourself at the house or you will have to deal with* me.

She shivered.

James seemed satisfied with the physical indicator of her compliance. "Good evening, Miss Amy."

He offered her a brisk nod before he swaggered out the door and headed for the waiting hackney coach.

Amy was especially pleased to see him leave.

"Why don't you show our guest to James's old room?" suggested William in an even tone.

Edmund nodded in accord and placed his sturdy hand at her backside, making her muscles jump, and nudged her toward the steps at the end of the great hall.

"Good night, Amy," from Quincy. The scamp even winked at her. "Sweet dreams."

Amy muttered under her breath in discord as she mounted the regal staircase. At the top of the second level, she paused, awaiting Edmund's guidance.

"This way, Amy."

He steered her through the darkened passageway. As she traversed the imposing structure, she thought about being secured within its great walls with Edmund—the professed gentleman. She had met "the gentleman" once before at the club. Now she was going to reside with him.

She waited for him to say something more, to assure her she was safe at the house, perhaps even inquire if she needed anything. It would be the gentlemanly thing to do, she presumed.

But he remained silent.

Her heart throbbed at the stretching quiet, and she

sighed—loudly—in a bid to attract the man's attention, but he remained dedicated to the task at hand: escorting her to her temporary lodgings.

At the end of the long tunnel was a set of double doors, the wood engraved in a lovely jungle motif. She thrummed her fingers in appreciation across the well-crafted relief as Edmund removed a candle from the wall sconce.

"Where's your room?" she wondered.

He lifted a brow, eyes smoldering in the misty candlelight.

"In case I need your assistance," she was quick to explain.

He nodded toward the third door at the end of the tunnel. "I should warn you, though, I like to sleep in the nude." He looked at her pointedly. "Knock first."

He ushered her inside the darkened bedchamber as she twisted her lips and frowned . . . and yet her heart thumped with energy at the thought of him naked in his bed.

Amy dismissed the titillating reflection from her mind and examined her sensuous surroundings. It was a large bedchamber. The bed itself was enormous, with a six-foot-high headboard that dwarfed the rest of the elegant furnishings. The simple bed linens, pristine white, complemented the lavish woodwork in a subdued manner. She'd anticipated an embellished coverlet stitched with sparkling gold thread, but the plain and minimal design of the bedding was strangely comforting—unlike its former occupant.

She suddenly glowered at the bed, dropped onto her knees, and peered under the looming structure.

The low light flickered across the glossed flooring as boots treaded toward her, pausing at her head.

"What are you doing, Amy?"

She peered into the dark nooks. "Looking for Sophia."

He said with a measure of amusement, "We keep her caged in William's room."

"Good."

She scrambled to her feet, smoothing her skirts, her hair—and stilled as soon as she sensed the man's knuckles skim her cheek.

He murmured, "You don't need to fear snakes or mad queens or attackers here."

His intimate touch warmed her blood, locked her breath in her lungs. At length, he stepped away from her, ensconced the tallow candlestick into a glass orb before he made his way over to the fireplace, preparing a flame with the kindling and candlelight.

Slowly she released her breath. "What about scoundrels?"

Guardedly she sat down on the edge of the bed, as if it would swallow her the way James's dark eyes had swallowed her, and watched Edmund's hunched figure.

"Now scoundrels you should fear . . . fortunately, there are no scoundrels within these walls."

She humphed.

As the stillness stretched between them, she wrung her fingers in her lap. She waited for him to look at her again, but he seemed engrossed by the fire, blowing into the fragile flames, so she tapped her foot in rapid strokes, releasing the tension that had welled inside her. At length, he turned his head to look at her, lifting a single dark brow.

"Is something the matter?" he inquired in a drawl.

"I was meaning to ask you the same question."

He lifted off his haunches and approached the bed in laggardly strides. She admired his fit figure, his long legs and wide shoulders. She quickly shifted from the bed, gaining height, so he didn't loom above her like a towering ogre . . . he brooded like a towering ogre, though.

"Nothing's the matter," he returned gruffly.

She was even more convinced something was dreadfully amiss after *that* curt remark. Had he reconsidered his offer of assistance? Did he now think it was too great an effort to see her settled as a lady's maid or companion? Did he resent her for putting the burden on him?

"Are you angry with me?" she snapped.

He frowned. "No." He cupped her chin between his thumb and forefinger. "Why do you think that?"

Amy was strapped for words as she delved deep into his haunting eyes. The soulful expression bewitched her. She listened to the gentle crackle of the burning wood, and sensed the heat crackling in her belly as well, for the warm, strong feel of his touch on her skin chased away all her uneasiness, stirring other, more pleasant feelings.

"You've been so reserved," she said in a near whisper. "I thought something was wrong."

He stared at her intently, as he was wont to do, brushing his thumb across her chin in feathery strokes, making her bones quiver in the slowly warming room.

"I'm not angry with you, Amy." He pressed his thumb against her lips and she started at the intimate contact. "Not with you."

Then with whom? she wondered. His brothers? It was obvious that the brood cared for one another. After all, they had searched for Edmund during his absence. And the eldest brute was keen to keep them all safe, even from the likes of her. Yet she was too engrossed by the scoundrel's close proximity, his sensuous touch, and soon the questions flittered from her mind, and she concentrated on just him.

Edmund.

As his thumb smoothed her jawline, she struggled to keep her breathing steady, but each heartbeat was erratic and her lungs shuddered at the scoundrel's gentle caresses.

Amy suspected a seduction. She suspected the man was lulling her senses for some nefarious purpose, yet she still remained rooted to the spot, unaccustomed to the ginger taps of his fingertips . . . and yearning for them even more. She wondered what it would feel like if he kissed her right then, pressed his hot mouth over her lips . . .

"Good night, Amy."

He dropped his hand away from her face in an abrupt manner, leaving her dazzled. She stared at him, confused, as he lazily moved through the room and departed, shutting the doors softly behind him.

Amy folded her arms across her bust and scowled.

Chapter 8

❦

"**H**ere it is!"

Quincy entered the sitting room with a thick book in his hands. He seated himself in a brown leather chair next to Amy, and smiled.

Edmund frowned. It was his responsibility to look after Amy's needs, to see her well established, and yet he had been usurped of the duty by his cheeky younger sibling.

"What is it?" said Amy, leaning closer to Quincy as she peered at the tome with curiosity, arousing Edmund's hackles.

Quincy lifted the green leather binding and blew away the layer of dust, the particles swirling in the air. "*The Book of Etiquette*. My sister, Belle, gifted it to me about five years ago when I first entered society."

"It appears new."

"It is. Look." He turned the spine. "Not a crack in the binding. I've never even opened it."

Edmund snorted.

Quincy glanced at his brother with a mischievous expression. "I don't need a book to teach me about proper manners and charm. You, on the other hand . . ."

Amy disarmed the darkening temperaments when she gathered the heavy tome into her hands and set it in her lap, leafing through the pages in an idle fashion.

Edmund followed her artful movements with keen interest, dismissing his brother from his thoughts. He watched her as she caressed each corner page, genuinely engrossed by the words on the sheets of paper . . . that she couldn't read. It must be so unsatisfying for her, he mused, to have the knowledge literally at her fingertips, and yet be unable to access the information.

Amy carefully closed the book and returned it to a puzzled Quincy.

"You'll need to read it," he said, "if you intend to be a lady's maid or companion."

Edmund gauged the direction of the conversation, and curtailed it with a sharp "Amy is fine. There's nothing the matter with her manners or charm."

In truth, she already acted with too many airs.

Quincy looked horrified. "I didn't mean to suggest there was anything wrong with her, but there are so many finicky rules she needs to remember."

"I can't read," she confessed stiffly.

Amy next offered Edmund a cutting glance as if she was vexed that he had made such a fuss about her illiteracy. He glowered back at her, slighted. He had only wanted to spare her any embarrassment. He folded his arms across his chest and vowed to sit quietly in the plush chair beside the window, and refrain from uttering another word.

"Oh . . . well . . . we'll teach you letters some other time." Quincy opened the book. "I'll just read the passages to you now and we can practice the mannerisms and movements."

Amy looked back at him and nodded, smiling slightly. "I'm good at memorization."

"Splendid!" He flipped through the pages. "Let's begin with conversation. The book is divided between the sexes, for there are different tenets for men and women. Ladies 'must exhibit sensibility and tact. Be sure to inquire about your partner's interests, for one always loves to comment about one's affairs.' Now"— he closed the book—"we're seated together at supper. How will you begin the conversation?"

Amy straightened her spine and folded her hands in her lap. "I . . ." She slumped her shoulders in defeat. "I don't know."

"Well, what do you know about me?"

"You're a sailor and a gentleman."

He chuckled. "I'm not so sure about the latter."

She made a wry face.

"Let's keep to the topic of sailing, shall we? How will you exhibit tact and sensibility, while inquiring about my interests?"

She sighed and primped herself for another attempt at polite conversation. "Good evening, Mr. Hawkins."

"Good evening, Miss . . ." He frowned. "I'm afraid I don't know your last name."

Edmund mulled that over, too, concluding he wasn't familiar with her surname, either. There was still so much he didn't know about the lovely Amy. He found it surprising that he was eager to learn more about her, for he wasn't the sort to fret about details . . . especially when he was already privy to the woman's most salacious secret.

"It's Peel," she whispered, as if Quincy had made a genuine social blunder.

Quincy grinned. "Good evening, Miss Peel."

"I understand you are just arrived from a long tour at sea?"

"That's right, Miss Peel. I've spent the last six months off the coast of Africa."

"Africa, really? Have you ever been to Madagascar?"

Edmund suspected Amy had suddenly overlooked her lessons in favor of a more earnest, even sensational interest in the wicked queen's sordid past. He observed her arched spine as she leaned more closely toward Quincy, seeking answers.

"I've been there once," he admitted.

"What was it like?"

The couple prattled on for a few more minutes before Quincy grinned, bringing the conversation to an end.

"Well done, Amy," he praised. "You maintained the conversation in a pleasant manner and demonstrated true intelligence with your questions."

She beamed—and it squelched Edmund's heart to know Quincy had made her feel proud of herself, and he had not.

"I don't see what any of this has to do with being a lady's maid or companion," Edmund groused, breaking his vow of silence. "Amy needs to know how to look after her future mistress, is all."

"A woman expects her companion to be a proper young lady." Quincy eyed his brother in a critical manner. "Amy needs to meet her employer's expectations or she won't make much headway in the field."

Edmund quieted at that sound reasoning, however much it irked him.

Amy, meanwhile, narrowed her scintillating green eyes on him again, clearly cross, before she looked away. "I appreciate your help, Quincy."

"Not a'tall." He smiled. "Someone should get some use out of this book."

"At least you're willing to offer me assistance," she said to the scamp, though she looked pointedly at Edmund once more.

"Don't mind Eddie." He chuckled. "He was born with a frown. It's like pulling teeth to get him to say a few meaningful words."

"What do you mean?" Amy appeared confused, her eyes still fixed firmly on Edmund. "He talked *too* much when he stayed with me."

"He did?" Quincy looked at his brother. "You did?"

"Piss off," returned Edmund.

Amy gasped.

"I was talking to Quincy," he snapped.

"Lesson number two." Quincy lifted two fingers in the air. "A lady doesn't curse, nor does she keep company with men who do."

Amy humphed in compliance, and returned her attention to Quincy and their slowly developing lessons.

After another half hour of mock conversation, Quincy shut the book. "Let's learn about something more fun . . . like ballroom etiquette. Do you dance, Miss Peel?"

The provocative images stormed Edmund's brain: a firm, supple body spinning across the stage, hips rolling, silky fabrics swooshing, gold coins softly clashing as the veiled figure gyrated and twirled in erotic splendor.

Edmund eyed the lovely Amy from across the sitting room, the blood in his veins pounding. He observed the woman's deep flush, sensed her warming flesh. She was seated with poise, yet a wild, exotic creature dwelled secretly within her heart . . . and he ached deep in his bones to lock limbs and dance with the beautiful, sensual Zarsitti.

"Aye, she dances," said Edmund in a quiet yet assured voice, still staring at Amy.

She glanced at him with fire in her eyes. "I don't know the most current, fashionable steps, though."

Swishing her round hips and undulating her tight belly was rather scandalous, he reflected with growing carnal hunger. It was a private dance: one reserved for a lover.

"Like the waltz?" wondered Quincy.

"Yes, that's right," she said in a rushed manner, twisting her fingers together in her lap as if she might tamp down her dark secret, send it into oblivion. But only Edmund was privy to her true nature as a dancer. His brothers assumed her a barmaid from the club.

Quincy placed the book aside and bounded to his feet. "Well, I'll teach you that."

"No," barked Edmund, drawing the couple's prompt attention. He wasn't about to let his flirtatious brother touch Amy in an intimate manner. He'd break all of Quincy's fingers first.

He said with less bite: "I'll teach her the waltz."

Quincy shrugged and returned to the chair. "She still needs to practice good manners in public." He snapped his fingers. "I know! We can take her to the fete at Chiswick on Friday."

Edmund cocked a brow. "We?"

"You'll need a chaperone," he said with a boyish smile.

"I don't think you qualify as the chaperone," Edmund remarked in a dry tone.

"Fine. I'll ask Belle—no, she's too busy with the children." He stroked his chin. "How about James and Sophia?"

Amy visibly shuddered at the mention of his brother James; the notorious captain often elicited that sort of response from women.

"I'll pen Sophia a note right now." Quincy was back

on his feet and heading for the door. "I know she'll consent to their being chaperones."

"James will be here later today," said Edmund. "He's coming to 'visit' with me, remember? Why don't you just ask him about the fete when he arrives?"

The scamp flicked his fingers in a dismissive gesture. "If I ask James, he'll say no. However, Sophia will be much more agreeable." He winked. "She likes me, after all. Oh, and I'll inquire about a new wardrobe for Miss Peel. She needs to look the part of a lady, too."

Quincy departed from the room, leaving Edmund alone with a scowling Amy in the spacious chamber.

"Ignore Quincy's last remark," he said. "He didn't mean to insult you. He's too forthright at times."

He watched her in silence for a short time. Perhaps it was a long time. He'd neglected to observe the mantel clock or listen to its chiming bells. There was one thing he had not neglected, however: feeling the sensual pull Amy had over his senses.

"Alone at last, Miss Peel."

She ignored him as he slowly crossed the room and settled into Quincy's former seat. He picked up *The Book of Etiquette* and randomly turned the pages. "I wonder what the book says about a young, unmarried lady sitting alone in a room with a scoundrel?"

She eyed him sidelong with the characteristic glare that so often amused him, even aroused him.

"I thought you said no scoundrels lived in the house."

He smiled at her.

She said stiffly, "I'm not to talk with gentlemen who curse."

"And if I promise not to behave like a gentleman?"

She pinched her lips together, but she also took in a deep, audible breath through her nose. The slight blush that stained her cheeks was endearing . . . and ever so alluring. The impulse to whisper hot words into her delicate ear, and make her blush even more, gripped him with a savage hold. He had to curl his fingers more tightly around the book just to keep his wits in place and his hands away from her sweet skin.

The silence stretched between them. At length, she snapped, "Aren't you going to teach me how to dance?"

"Do you really need lessons, Zarsitti?" She made a moue as he put the book aside and lifted from the chair, extending his hand. "Shall we dance?"

Amy firmed her lips again and accepted his offered hand, her warm fingers slipping across his palm. He grasped her hand with vigor, muscles stiffening, and he sensed the strong shiver that rippled through her extremities as he escorted her to the center of the room.

He released her hand and pressed the front length of his body against her. She was wearing a simple white day dress with thin bronze lines running all the way down her frame, making her figure look even more elongated. He glanced at her slippered toes, then studiously admired her lanky limbs and well-formed hips before he lighted upon her piercing green eyes. Heart-beats boomed deep in his breast as she pegged him with such might, such vim. She stirred the gloom in his belly until it swirled away.

He circled her waist and cupped her other palm, the blood in his veins slowly heating at their close proximity. It was so right to hold her, he thought with zeal. It was so bloody right to keep her in his arms . . . tight in his arms.

"Should we be standing so close together?" she demanded, flustered.

It wasn't proper, no. However, he wasn't thinking about being proper right then. He was thinking about Amy's lush body secured in his arms, her artful, supple body.

"Place your hand on my shoulder," he instructed gruffly.

She obeyed the direction, licking her bottom lip. He shuddered at the teasing gesture. She hadn't meant to be a flirt; he sensed that intrinsically. But she'd captured his imagination nonetheless.

He was half a head taller than she, so he inhaled the rich scent of her gold locks, twisted and pinned in a loose chignon. He matched her rapid breathing, her quick pulse.

"Now follow my lead."

He stepped to the right. He next took a step back before sliding his left foot to the left side of the room. Taking a step forward, he completed the quadrangle.

Amy eyed his movements with obvious scrutiny, and

quickly learned the four basic steps. "Do we move in a square like this forever?"

"No, we can dance across the room, too, keeping the same rhythm and steps. I just wanted you to become accustomed to the movements first."

"I think I've memorized them," she said tartly, clearly underwhelmed by the simplicity of the waltz, which paled in comparison to the lavish dances she was wont to memorize and perform, he surmised.

"I like watching you dance," he remarked in a soft voice as he whisked her across the wide room, avoiding the furnishings, keeping her secured in his embrace.

She loosened her grip on his hand as soon as he'd made the intimate confession, but he held her fast despite the resistance. He wasn't ready to let her go just yet.

"You keep a pet snake in the house, do you?"

The flutter in her voice betrayed her unsettled disposition. He smiled inwardly, knowing he'd struck a powerful chord within her, so much so that she prattled about more mundane topics in order to keep from thinking about his touch, his presence.

"Aye, a Jamaican yellow boa. She belonged to my brother James. But his wife wouldn't permit the snake inside their house after the wedding."

Amy snorted. "I understand her sentiments. And *why* is the snake named after the woman?"

"Spite." Edmund shrugged. "James and Sophia have a long history. She abandoned him once, and he was furious. He found the snake in Jamaica, where he and

Sophia—the real Sophia—had first met, and so he named the serpent after her."

Amy twisted her lips into a grimace, clearly not appreciating the dark humor in the situation. "Have you been to the Caribbean?"

"I've sailed most of the world." He danced with her with such gusto, he bumped his leg against a side table. The brief spurt of pain had him wondering curtly, "Are you practicing being a lady with me?"

Were all the questions about his family, his past, idle chitchat to pass the time and practice her mannerisms? Did she really care to know anything about him or his life?

"Well, that's why I'm here, isn't it?" she said suspiciously. "It is why you've brought me to St. James? To become a lady?"

He was quiet at that, staring at her intently, even irritably. He had brought her to St. James to protect her and see her settled in a new profession, aye. However, he had thought to know her better, too . . . to seduce her.

Well, kiss her, in truth. He wouldn't tarnish her chances at a respectable profession with a scandalous affair. But he had yet to get past her deft right hook. And now that his memory had returned, he realized he hadn't the delight of knowing the taste of her sweet lips. He intended to correct that injustice before they parted ways.

The woman's eyes narrowed on him in turn, prompting a response from him.

"Yes, of course, that's why I brought you here, Miss Peel."

She glared at him, dubious. "I don't understand you, *Mr.* Hawkins."

He frowned. Mr. Hawkins, was he? That didn't suit the intimate, passionate nature of his desire for the lass. "How so?"

"Quincy insists you never say a word, yet I know that isn't true." She looked deep into his eyes with scrutiny. "Why are you so reserved now that you're at home?"

"Would you prefer to see me unreserved?"

She gritted, "I'm curious, is all."

He shrugged again. "I've nothing much to say when I'm at home."

What was there to say when he was with his brothers? Quincy was too outspoken, enough for the both of them, and James and William preferred to rule the roost. The two eldest siblings brooked no argument that they were in charge of *all* their lives. Edmund found no reason to contest their tyranny, and so refrained from speaking at home unless there was something particularly worthwhile to impart.

Amy scowled at his unforthcoming answer, he supposed. She looked over his shoulder as they danced and spotted something that clearly captured her interest.

"Is that your late father's ship?" she said, and nudged her chin forward, gesturing toward the model schooner on the long side table.

"Aye, the *Bonny Meg*."

A pirate ship.

Edmund wondered with wolfish delight what the diffident Miss Peel would think to know she was residing with a band of former pirates: the most infamous pirates to ever ravage the high seas.

He smiled at the scandalous thought.

"What is so amusing?" she demanded, words clipped.

"You have your secrets," he said in a coy manner, "and I have mine."

It was their father, Drake Hawkins, who had first pirated, and then, after a bout with an incurable illness, he had transferred command of the *Bonny Meg* to James. All four brothers had served aboard the schooner as buccaneers. Even their sister, Mirabelle, had at one time joined the crew—as a stowaway! But after she had married the Duke of Wembury, it was too dangerous for them to maintain their wicked pursuits. If word ever spread that the duchess was related to pirates, her reputation would be ruined, and they all loved her far too much to ever let that fate befall her. And so they'd "retired" from piracy, though not from the sea.

"What secrets?" Amy demanded, but at his prolonged silence, she huffed. "I think I've memorized the waltz."

Edmund trimmed their twirling steps to a slower tempo before he brought their warm, slightly sweating bodies to a halt in the center of the room.

She quickly parted from him. "I think I'll retire to my room and unpack the rest of my belongings."

He and Quincy had retrieved the remainder of her

furnishings from St. Giles that morning, and had placed the articles in James's former bedchamber.

The lass skirted off, flustered, hips swinging in a very pleasant manner. He watched her with keen interest as she departed from the room.

She wasn't very unlike him, he thought, for they both had to conceal their secret lives in order to fit into high society.

Chapter 9

It was breathtaking.

Amy's eyes glazed over the wondrous assortment of brilliant flowers, shrubs, tart fruit trees, and vegetable gardens: thirty-three acres of carefully cultivated land, leased from the Duke of Devonshire. Tents exhibited the finest fruits imported from around the world, hothouses protected the most delicate blooms that had traveled from various foreign climates.

It was the Horticultural Society's first-ever fete. The duke had even opened his own private gardens to the inquisitive public, who numbered in the thousands. Refreshment stands suffered under the demand for sweet juices as a series of army bands entertained the strolling guests.

It was dusk, the gardens brimming with candles in little glass orbs hanging from trees. Amy had walked the grounds all day, yet she wasn't fatigued. She was amazed. She wanted to take in every lovely spectacle. She wasn't accustomed to such natural splendor. She was accustomed to soiled streets and noisy thoroughfares and putrid stenches. The estate, so vivid, captured her imagination in such a profound manner, she'd neglected the real reason she was there: to practice the art of being a proper lady.

He rubbed against her . . . unintentionally, she hoped. She glanced over her shoulder and spotted his towering figure at her backside. One look at the handsome scoundrel and the gardens seemed dull in comparison. Her heartbeat quickened. She looked away again before Edmund sensed her unladylike stare.

"Look, James," said Sophia, an exotic-looking woman in her late twenties. She was dressed in a lily white frock with long sleeves. She had no jewelry or fancy headgear. Her dark brown hair was twisted into a charming swirl, a loose curl brushing her shoulder as she paused and examined a pristine white blossom with a burning red center. "Do you remember this orchid?"

The party was exploring a particular glass hothouse showcasing unique species of flora from the West Indies, where Sophia and her husband had first met.

James fingered the fragile petals with sensitivity, a faint smile touching his stern lips. "Aye, I remember. There was one just like it in the garden at the plantation house."

Amy stilled at the scoundrel's approach. His musk filled her lungs, making her woozy. The spicy scent mingled with the floral fragrances to create an intoxicating mixture for the senses.

"It's odd, isn't it?"

She shivered at the whispered words pressed warmly into her ear.

"Seeing James like that?"

He sounded just as flummoxed as she was about the captain's easy manner.

"Happy, you mean?"

"Pleasant," he said.

She smiled wryly.

"Look here, Amy."

Sophia gestured with her hand, bidding her toward a magnificent tree with lavender-colored blossoms. The flagstone walkway was peppered with falling purple petals as pretty as fresh snow.

"The blossom of the *lignum vitae* is Jamaica's national flower," she said, caressing a low-hanging branch with tenderness.

The woman was a botanist at heart, according to Edmund, and Amy was keen to listen to her tales about faraway lands and foreign wonders, but a part of Amy was also guarded, for she distrusted the peculiar woman. She had married James, after all. There had to be something amiss about her character.

"I see my dress fits you well, Amy."

Amy strolled alongside her chaperone as the gentlemen partnered behind them.

"Yes, it fits me very comfortably," she said, smoothing the eggshell white skirt. "Thank you."

The wardrobe Quincy had arranged for her had yet

to be delivered. She had been measured for the new attire, but it would take time for the clothing to be prepared.

Sophia slipped her hand through Amy's arm. She detected the soft scent of bay rum shampoo in the older woman's dark brown coiffure. It was an agreeable scent.

"How are you feeling, Amy?"

"A little overwhelmed," she admitted unenthusiastically.

Sophia smiled. "I was, too, when I first arrived in England from the Caribbean."

"You've adapted well. I mean, you're a respectable member of society."

She scoffed, startling Amy.

"Respectable? I'm wed to the city's most infamous rogue."

Amy paled at the ghastly remark, glancing at the other spectators who traversed the exhibit grounds, but most were too engrossed by the unique specimens to take notice of their party.

"Well, he's not such a pariah anymore," she said with a smoky chortle. "He saved me from a band of dastardly pirates, you know."

Amy's eyes widened. "He did?"

"Oh yes." She smiled coyly. "I was kidnapped by the dreaded pirate Black Hawk. It was in all the papers."

"I remember now." Amy was a bit giddy. "There was a daring rescue at sea. It was much gossiped about."

She nodded. "James saved me from a wretched fate and destroyed the notorious brigand's ship, sending him and his scalawag crew to a watery grave."

Amy heard the aforementioned hero snort at their backsides. She ignored the uncouth gesture, greatly intrigued by Sophia's swashbuckling tale, for she wasn't one to embark on an adventure herself; she was far too sensible to do that. She enjoyed hearing about scandalous exploits, though. And the strange couple's pairing seemed so much more sensible to her now. Sophia had accepted her savior's hand in marriage. It happened all the time, Amy was sure.

"And Edmund was a part of the brave crew," said Sophia. "Did you know?"

Amy glanced over her shoulder. "You've hunted pirates?"

Edmund shrugged.

Not surprising, that.

"The *ton* was very gracious toward the valiant Captain James Hawkins and his crew after my rescue . . . though not everyone likes my husband, even now."

"But you do?"

Amy blushed. She sensed the heat creeping into her cheeks, and bristled at the unsavory thought that the captain had heard her boorish remark. If he had, he politely refrained from commenting about it. Sophia, on the other hand, laughed. She didn't seem slighted at Amy's unintentional rudeness.

"I like him sometimes." There was a wicked gleam in her deep brown eyes. "But most of the time, I just want to make him miserable."

Amy sensed her chaperone was the sort of woman who, when piqued, was vindictive. She had no desire to make any further social blunders and arouse the woman's wrath. She was also more understanding about James's reason for naming the pet serpent after his wife.

The couples departed the hothouse and entered the crisp spring air. It was early May, the nights still fresh. They ambled the lush grounds at leisure, taking in the aromas, the quaint tunes, and the pruned gardens.

Amy wrapped the white fringed shawl more tightly around her shoulders as she traversed the well-manicured turf with Edmund.

"When will I be settled in my new position, do you think?"

"There's still more to teach you about being a lady."

"Your brother Quincy thinks I'm charming."

"He thinks every female is charming . . . besides, he wasn't here to hear your scandalous remark."

Amy blushed.

He smiled. "I'm sure wives beat their husbands over the head with rolling pins in the rookeries, but here in society, wives don't admit to disliking their husbands—even if they do. "

As her cheeks pinkened even more, she said tartly, "What *is* the plan to see me settled as a lady's maid or companion?"

He nudged her, steered her along a torch-lit path between a colonnade of oak trees. "You're very impatient."

She peeked over her shoulder and spotted James and Sophia engaged in deep conversation, trailing after them.

"Are you afraid of my brother and sister-in-law?" he said in a low voice.

"No," she insisted . . . though there was something dark about Sophia's nature that reminded Amy of Madame Rafaramanjaka. And what about James? He seemed unperturbed by his wife's wish to make him miserable.

"The couple are serving as chaperones, is all."

"Aha." He chuckled. "You're guarding your virtue." He murmured, "That's very wise, Amy."

She sensed the heat in her belly; it spread from her core and touched her fingertips and toes. He nettled her senses, making her more sentient of her surroundings: the crackling torchlight, the twinkling candlelight in the glass orbs. She was walking through a faerie-filled wood, it seemed . . . with a handsome scoundrel.

"I'm not impatient," she insisted, keeping the conversation more respectable.

"You always need to be in control of the situation." He brushed her elbow. "I remember."

She shivered, the touch light yet so full of bubbling energy. "Well, I can't run away at sea, looking for adventure," she snapped. "I have to be in control of the situation; I have to confront my troubles."

He was quiet.

Amy's cheeks warmed again. What the devil was the matter with her? She hadn't meant to be so churlish, but he had smothered her natural tendencies to mistrust with his easy manner and smooth words. If she wasn't vigilant, he'd tease and twist her senses until he had manipulated her movements like a marionette master.

"Is that what you think I'm doing?" he said softly. "Running away? Seeking adventure?"

"Isn't it?"

He kicked a pebble. "I'm looking for something at sea, but it's not adventure—not anymore—though there *is* plenty of it."

Am image entered her head: taut, naked skin with white lines. "The scars?"

He rubbed his belly. As his fingers ruffled his garment, the intimate gesture warmed her innards.

She flushed and bowed her head. "How did you get the scars?"

He shrugged. "I don't know; there've been so many skirmishes."

"Hunting pirates. Fighting slavers." She peeked at him askance. "Are you sure you're not looking for adventure at sea?"

He seemed thoughtful, his expression somber. "I remember the first time I boarded a slaver. I had trained and prepared for my duties, but . . . sometimes the unexpected happens, Amy."

She studied his earnest profile, detected his muscles

as they stiffened. She wondered about the unexpected happenings at sea, but she refrained from commenting about them. He wasn't prepared to share the ordeal with her, she suspected. He wasn't a gossip like his younger brother.

"Don't fret, Amy." As he gathered his features, he offered her a small smile. "Once you're better prepared, I'll ask my sister to make inquiries in society about matrons or young ladies in need of a companion. I'm sure she will find you an acceptable post."

"She's very kind to do so, I'm sure." At his silence, she frowned. "You haven't told her about me, have you?"

He shrugged.

"Why?"

"She's much to look after at home: a rogue for a husband, a disobedient daughter."

"If she's overwhelmed with domestic duties, what makes you think she'll assist me: a stranger?"

"Because I'll ask her for help," he said with confidence.

Amy looked away, an unfamiliar smarting in her breast. She had no one in her life who'd offer her aid with such assurance, and she keenly felt the aloneness.

"Thank you," she said quietly.

"Rose!"

A child danced in the dirt path far ahead of Amy and Edmund, her small figure aglow in the torchlight like an angel.

"Come away from there, Rose! You'll soil your new dress!"

The little girl was ushered away by the scolding matron. The scene triggered a flash of color, sound, and feeling in Amy's breast. She stilled.

"Come away from there, Amy!"

A soft skirt brushed her cheek. A warm, gloved hand circled her fingers.

"It's bedtime, Amy. Oh, look at your shoes." She tsked. "I'll have to change you now. Papa and I will be late for the party."

Amy pouted. "I'm sorry, Mama."

The tall figure sighed, petticoats swooshing. "I'm afraid I'll have to punish you, young lady."

Amy pinched her lips and squinted her eyes in anticipation of a sound reprimand . . . but the figure scooped her up into her arms and showered her with kisses instead.

"I shall torment you with kisses!"

Amy squealed with laughter.

"What's the matter, Amy?"

Edmund's strong voice penetrated her wistful memories, half shadows after so many years. She sniffed, confounded by the show of emotion that had unexpectedly overwhelmed her.

She took in a deep breath and shooed the hazy visions away. "It's nothing, really. I just remembered my mother. She once scolded me like that, too."

"You remember your mother?"

He seemed pensive, as if he had no memory of his own mother, and Amy's heart cramped at the thought that they shared a common, tragic past.

"Not really," she admitted sadly as she resumed her steps. "I mean, I have flashes of her: her voice, her scent, her touch. But I don't remember her face. I don't really remember her."

"I was two years old when my mother passed away. How old were you when your parents died?"

She shrugged. "About six, I think."

"How did they perish?"

The masked devils on horseback filled Amy's head. She remembered the stomping hooves and sinister shouts and rough handling as she was dragged away from her comfortable haven, her home, in the dead of night. The images still twisted in her heart, snatched her breath away.

She stilled, disoriented. She examined her unusually quiet surroundings, another distressing thought taking root in her mind.

"Where are James and Sophia?"

The woods were deserted, the dirt trail illuminated with a few torches. There was still the distant hum of voices, but the physical isolation was far too disconcerting for Amy.

She grabbed one side of her long white skirt, prepared to dash through the greenery, when Edmund captured her wrist in his robust hand.

"Don't worry, Amy."

The low light caressed his rugged features, making him even more attractive—and making her heart beat even harder.

"I'll protect you," he whispered.

She wasn't so convinced of his gallantry. How had he maneuvered her into such a private nook? And without her being aware of it?

"We should look for your brother and sister-in-law," she said in a rushed voice, jerking her wrist. "How will we get home without their carriage? What if I'm spotted alone with you, and I'm ruined?"

"Shhh." He pushed her against a tree, effectively curtailing her outburst. "Nobody knows who you are, Amy. You won't be ruined."

As he placed his hands on her hips, drawing her eyes to his lips with his lazy smile, Amy suspected she was doomed.

"You should learn to have more fun," he whispered, "to be spontaneous."

The feathery strokes across her waist bewitched her thoughts, and she stared at him with bated breath, her pulses tapping in quick succession.

"There's more to life than rules and being in control," he murmured in a smoky drawl.

Aye, she suspected there was, but it was a miserable existence, teeming with debauchery and sin and ruin. She had to keep to her planned heading or she might lose her way and never find peace.

The scoundrel's warm embrace was tempting, though, teasing her mercilessly, dangerously off course.

The man's warm, sturdy touch; his scent, smoky sandalwood; his soulful blue eyes . . . and damn kissable lips whetted her senses, her yearnings.

"Stop trying to fight Fate, Amy."

He beckoned her inside his soul. He charmed her—and she let him, the stiffness in her bones ebbing away as he pressed his sinewy muscles against her midriff, making her sigh.

"Enjoy life . . . and where it takes you."

She bristled at the sultry words; they shattered the daze she was in. As her wits returned, she curled her fingers into a firm fist, aimed for his chin—and punched.

He had anticipated her violent outburst, though. He blocked her wrist, bringing the assault to an untimely end.

"Can you do that, Amy?"

She gasped as he cupped her cheeks in both his large palms, bringing his lips even closer to her parted mouth.

"Can you let spontaneity into your soul?"

Every heartbeat pinched her breastbone, her every muscle was tight and thrumming.

"No," she whispered.

"That's a shame." He nuzzled her lips with his mouth. "A surprise can be wonderful . . . if you let it be, Amy."

Her toes curled in her leather walking boots. An unfamiliar sound, akin to a moan, welled in her throat, as a pair of seductive lips bussed her mouth. It was a soft caress, a light, ethereal touch, but it singed her blood with its heat and tenderness. Tendrils of pleasure wrapped her limbs in a tight embrace, the feeling ever so . . . wonderful.

"Was that so bad, Amy?"

She had closed her eyes at the fleeting kiss. She opened them again, lashes fluttering, as she gazed at him through a sheen of hazy light and briny moisture. Her heart ballooned, pumped with vigor like a steam engine. Her lungs expanded as she searched for more air.

"No," she admitted hoarsely. "That wasn't so bad."

He offered her a small smile; the gesture transformed the entire scope of his otherwise moody features, warming her belly.

As his rough hands slipped away from her flushed cheeks, she shuddered in disappointment, a darkness filling her, an unexpected loneliness.

She was accustomed to a solitary existence; she didn't mind her own company, but the brief, intimate kiss she had shared with Edmund had opened a door for her: a door into life, where everyone else played and laughed and made love. He had shut that door as soon as he had parted from her, plunking her back into the cold, friendless world she had lived in for so long.

"Amy?" He frowned and reached for her again. "What's—?"

"Edmund!"

The sharp reprimanded startled Amy, who quickly adjusted her shawl. She glanced at the towering, disapproving figure of Captain James Hawkins. He was making his way through the misty darkness, his cross-looking wife at his side.

"What do you think you're doing?" demanded James.

Amy flushed. The captain had directed the brusque inquiry toward his brother, however, she had sensed the accusation just as keenly.

Had the couple witnessed their improper kiss? The sanctuary of the dark woods looked ever so appealing to Amy in that uncomfortable moment.

Edmund's carriage dramatically changed. She noted the man's lazy stance was gone. He maintained a more rigid posture as he glared at his older brother.

"I haven't done anything wrong," he said lowly, ominously.

"You disappeared with Miss Peel."

"We were separated," he countered. "It's dark."

James glowered. "You should have been paying better attention to your surroundings."

"*You* should have been paying better attention to yours." He taunted the barbarian with a raised brow. "You are the chaperone."

Amy took in a swift breath, for she suspected the hot-tempered brothers might come to scandalous blows right there in the shrubbery.

"There's no harm done." Sophia stepped—wedged herself—between the two strong bodies, deftly bringing the antagonism to an end. "It's easy to get lost in such a wonderland. We shall *all* be more vigilant as we make our way back to the carriage. Come, Miss Peel." She smiled and took her charge by the arm. "You've been on your feet all day. Let's get you home."

The journey to St. James was largely passed in silence. Sophia commented on various topics regarding their sojourn, but the rest of the party remained quiet.

Amy, seated beside Sophia, glanced apprehensively at the brothers, who were stationed across from her. The men were staring out the windows in opposite directions, and it was a great relief when the vehicle rolled to a steady halt in front of the prestigious address.

The gentlemen exited the carriage first before assisting the ladies as a strong wind bustled through the quiet thoroughfare.

Edmund quickly turned toward his sister-in-law. "Good evening, Sophia." He bowed. "Thank you for the pleasant excursion."

The sassy woman lifted a dark brow. "Oh? Are we not invited inside?"

"It's late," Edmund said stiffly. "I think a storm is coming, too."

James swaggered toward the door. "Well, I'd like a nightcap."

Sophia smiled impishly and followed her husband, leaving a disgruntled Edmund staring after them.

Amy watched as the couple entered the town house, then glanced at Edmund. He was still gazing at the headstrong pair, his features taut. She wasn't thrilled about joining the Hawkinses for a nightcap, either. There was still the matter of the mortifying kiss . . . but perhaps Sophia and James hadn't witnessed the private moment. After all, the duo hadn't mentioned a word about it during the carriage ride home.

"Shall we follow them inside?" whispered Amy.

Edmund looked at her in surprise. "Yes, of course. After you, Amy."

Inside the town house, James was already waiting for them. He had propped a shoulder against the wall and was regarding them both with a stern expression.

"I'd like a private word with you, Eddie."

Amy wanted to groan. She suppressed the impulse. The couple *had* observed the scandalous kiss. Why else would the captain want a "private" word with his brother?

It would do her no good to whine about the matter. She had other, fretful thoughts to consider, like what was going to become of her now? Would James insist Edmund boot her from the house for her unladylike behavior? The brothers had to protect their sister, the Duchess of Wembury, from any whispers of impropriety. And Amy's late-night smooch with Edmund smacked of impropriety.

Edmund shrugged. "Fine."

"Shall we talk in the study?" suggested James.

"You know the way."

James looked at his wife. "We'll join you and Miss Peel in the sitting room for a nightcap."

Sophia nodded. "We'll see you both soon."

The men departed together, Amy gazing after their solid figures, her heart sinking into her belly. She would *never* be ruled by spontaneity again! she vowed. She also vowed to bloody Edmund's lip at the first opportunity; the scoundrel deserved it.

"Well, I'm parched," said Sophia.

Amy's throat was constricted as well, but for a very different reason. She silently trailed after Sophia. Amy wasn't even sure why the woman insisted on the pretense of a nightcap. Perhaps she enjoyed tormenting Amy, as the queen had done in the past? Sophia wanted to make her husband "miserable," after all.

But Amy didn't have too much time to think about the distressing situation, for the butler soon rushed into the great hall and arrested the brothers. He furtively conversed with the pair, and Amy watched as their expressions slowly darkened.

"Where is he?" demanded James.

"In the study, sir."

The brothers thundered toward the room.

Amy's pulse quickened. "What's wrong?"

Sophia frowned. "I'm not sure."

The other woman started for the study, too.

Amy remained standing in the great hall. Should she follow her chaperone? She wasn't part of the family. It wasn't right for her to meddle in their personal affairs . . . however, the sensational commotion was too tempting to resist, and she swiped the side of her flowing skirt, bustling toward the noise.

She stopped outside the door and peeked over Sophia's shoulder. Inside the study, she spied a sickly-looking Quincy prostrated across the patterned carpet, William kneeling at his side.

Amy's heart ballooned. She swiftly covered her mouth with her palm. The poor scamp! Was he dead? Good God, what had happened?

"Blimey!" James dropped beside Quincy and grabbed him by the shirt, shaking him violently. "When will you stop!"

"I'm sorry, James," he moaned weakly.

Amy sighed. The scamp was still alive!

Edmund looked at her with a forlorn expression before he shut the door, excluding her and Sophia from the dreadful scene.

The butler respectfully took himself off, but Amy remained in the passageway; she wondered aloud:

"What's the matter with Quincy?"

Sophia walked away from the door. There was a stiffness in her spine that suggested she, too, wanted to be inside the room, that she wanted to offer assistance.

"He's fighting demons."

Amy fell in step beside her. "What sorts of demons?"

"I don't know," she returned quietly.

"Should we send for a doctor?"

"A doctor cannot heal him. Come. Let's wait in the sitting room for news."

Chapter 10

❧❧

Edmund pressed his back against the door and folded his arms across his chest, trying to keep the churning darkness in his breast from bursting through his bones. He observed the glistening sweat on Quincy's pale brow, his constricted pupils. The pup looked like a wraith, an echo of his former self. The ghastly image of him gripped and squeezed Edmund's heart in a way he had never experienced, not even when he was a pirate aboard the *Bonny Meg* in the heat of battle.

James grabbed Quincy's arm in a rough manner. "Get up."

Dumped into a chair, Quincy slowly raised his head and gazed at Edmund with a sorrowful expression. The regret in his eyes was veiled, though, a hazy mist there, too. He looked as if he was trapped in a waking dream, mindful of his surroundings yet unsure if they were real.

James moved across the room and rent the cravat at

his throat. "Why haven't you put a stop to his obsession, Will?"

William bristled. "What would you have me do? Lock him away in Bedlam?"

"Can't you lock him in his room?"

William rounded the desk and placed his knuckles on the table's surface. "He isn't a babe, James. I can't follow him around all day. I have other duties, don't you know? And why didn't *you* put a stop to his obsession while you were still living here?"

"I didn't know it *was* an obsession then."

It had started out as harmless, fashionable fun, thought Edmund, but it'd soon escalated into a more serious condition, alarming all the brothers with its crippling effects upon the pup.

"Well, I'm not a physician," from William. "I can't cure his ills."

James snorted. "I'll break his legs then."

William said in an even manner, "And what purpose will that serve?"

"It'll prevent him from visiting the opium dens."

"I'd rather you not break my legs," chimed Quincy in a drowsy fashion, his shoulders slumped.

James said darkly, "Then stop chasing the dragon."

Quincy quieted.

James humphed and paused beside the fireplace. He spread his arms apart and gripped the mantelpiece. Lowering his weight on the marble fitting, he dropped his head. "I'll move back into the town house."

William scoffed. "I'm sure your wife will appreciate that."

"Sophia won't mind under the circumstances," he returned with confidence. "I know the woman."

"And the scandal that'll result from you moving back in here?" William settled into the leather seat at the head of the writing desk. "What will society think to learn that Captain James Hawkins returned to his bachelor lodgings after only six months of marriage?"

"To hell with the scandal!" James faced his brother, his features flushed. "Do you think I give a bloody damn about what the people of Town think of me?"

"No, but I think you give a bloody damn about what they think of your wife." William eyed him in a sharp manner. "Do you want them to gossip about Sophia? Whisper tales that she cannot keep her husband content?"

James fisted his palms and looked around the room as if he was trapped in an iron brig. "One of us has to look after him."

"I can look after him," said Edmund.

The rain slowly pattered against the window, the thunder grumbled as James and William stared at him, confounded. It was as if the pair hadn't noticed him standing in the room.

William frowned. "You?"

"Yes, me," he said, ignoring the affront.

"No." James was curt. "You're not responsible."

Edmund snapped, "And Quincy's flourished under your care?"

"Are you going to claim superior judgment?" James stepped toward him with a look of warning in his eyes. "How dare you after your reckless behavior in the garden tonight?"

William sighed and rubbed his brow. "What did *he* do?"

"He made love to his ward."

A sluggish Quincy chuckled. "Lucky Eddie."

"I didn't make love to her." Edmund glowered at James. "It was one kiss."

James pointed a finger at him. "I'm not going to let you disgrace this family and ruin Belle."

The heat in Edmund's belly swelled until it singed his ears. "I would never do such a thing."

"You lied to me." The man's nostrils flared and his eyes darkened even more. "You told me you wanted to turn the wench into a lady, that she had saved your life and you owed her the favor. I believed you, fool that I am."

Edmund gritted, "It's the truth."

"Don't sham me again!" He removed his coat. "You've brought your bloody mistress to live under your roof, admit it."

"It's my roof, is it?"

The growing friction between the brothers compelled William to vacate his chair. He approached the scowling men with raised hands. "Let's all keep our heads, shall we?"

James took in a ragged breath and backed away,

though his eyes still glowed with resentment. "Put her up in another house or apartment."

"She's not my mistress!"

"Too bad," Quincy quipped.

William offered him a hard look. "We're not finished with you yet."

"I figured that." He shrugged. "But it's good to know I'm not the only wastrel in the family."

"I'm not a wastrel," Edmund contested. "I really do owe Amy my life, and I intend to see her properly settled."

James circled the room like a penned bull, snarling, but he soon stilled. "Fine. If you want to see the wench settled, then you won't resist if Sophia and I take her with us to Mayfair."

"What?" he rasped.

"Sophia and I discussed it in the garden tonight," he said, eyes alight. "If you want to see Amy a lady, she should live with us, so Sophia and I can serve as proper chaperones."

"*You* want to make Amy a lady?"

"*I* don't give a bloody damn about the wench." He rolled up his sleeves. "But if she saved your life, then I'll see the debt paid."

"No."

It raised Edmund's hackles, the very thought of passing Amy off to his kin. It was his duty to look after her. It was his responsibility to find her a new means of livelihood. He had uprooted her from her home and occupation as a dancer, and he wasn't going to hand her over to his autocratic brother, to give in to the suggestion that he wasn't sensible enough to take care of the lass himself.

"It's my responsibility to look after her," he said stiffly.

"It's too dangerous for her to be here." James folded his arms across his chest. "If anyone discovers she's staying here, she'll be ruined."

Edmund moved away from the door in brisk strides, as if his feet treaded across hot coals. "No one will find out Amy is staying here. No one comes to the house, not *our* house."

The brothers were an oddity. With their sister a respected duchess, the *ton* offered the mariners a small measure of courtesy. Polite without being friendly. Inclusive without being intimate. Invitations to balls and parties and dinners made their way to the town house, and the brothers attended most of the gatherings in order to protect their sister's good name. If they refused the posh invites, their uncouth behavior would reflect poorly upon her . . . but it was all a delicate, insincere dance. The *haute monde* wasn't interested in befriending the Hawkins brothers. The *haute monde* was interested in drawing the brothers out of their gilded cage, gawking at them, gossiping about them behind their backs.

"And the servants?" said James.

"Who? The butler?" Edmund scoffed. "He's too loyal to breathe a word about Amy to the rest of the staff. Cook stays in the kitchen. The maids come twice a week to clean, and I can keep Amy away from the house while they're here."

"You see." James set his eyes on Edmund. "You *are* keeping your mistress in the house. Otherwise you wouldn't resist my prudent proposal."

To hell with the man's so-called prudent proposal! The overbearing captain took control of every situation. There was no hope for compromise in his tyrannical world. If Edmund voiced a singular opinion, he was charged with disloyalty or irresponsibility or some other rot.

In the past, Edmund had simply let James rule over his life with an iron fist. Why resist him? Edmund had had no passion worth fighting for . . . but now he had Amy. She was depending on him. She was looking to him for a chance at a better life, and he'd brawl with James first before he'd let the despot take her away.

"James is right," said William.

"Of course he's right," Edmund retorted. "He's always right, isn't he? And you always take his side."

William stared at him with a measure of ire that Edmund didn't often see coming from his unflappable, levelheaded brother. That William possessed a fiery streak was an intriguing idea yet a highly unlikely one. The man wasn't the sort to stir up trouble or make contradictions. He had always supported James as the lieutenant, and thus second in command, of the *Bonny Meg.* And now that he was his own master, he still looked to James for guidance. He had only ever gone against

"Black Hawk's" wishes once: when he had joined the Royal Navy as a privateer.

Edmund remembered the stormy row, the tempestuous atmosphere when the brothers had announced their wish to sail under the Union Jack. The contention had almost rent apart their brotherhood, for James loathed the Royal Navy for pressing their father into service many years ago. He had eventually resigned himself to their choice of occupation. He had even attended the ship's christening ceremony before their maiden voyage. For a short time, the man had relinquished control. But now he'd reclaimed his authority. And he was holding on to it with a vicious grip.

"We're going to set sail in a fortnight." William placed his hands on his hips. "What will you do with Amy then? Or do you intend to walk away from your naval duties?"

Edmund stepped beside the window and peered through the drapery, the glass, gazing into the murky street as the rain showered with greater vim. "I'll see her settled before we leave."

"You're going to make her a lady in two weeks?"

The disbelief in James's derisive voice made Edmund's muscles taut, set his spine erect. He balled his fists, breathing sharply through his nose. If either man pushed him one bit more . . .

However, Edmund wasn't worried about transforming Amy into a lady within a fortnight. The woman was already prim and proper in so many ways, the effect of her tutelage under Madame Rafaramanjaka. He would see the lass placed in a proper position soon.

"I've already lost Quincy." William gestured toward the lethargic pup. "Will I lose you, too?"

"You've not lost me, Will," Quincy protested weakly, his breathing slow and shallow.

William offered him a look of sympathy. "I can't take you with me aboard the *Nemesis* in your condition."

"I'll take Quincy home with me," said James. "I'll take them both home."

"No!" Edmund slammed his fist into the wall, pain shooting through his arm. "I can look after Quincy. And damn it, I'm protecting Amy!"

James eyed him with that familiar, piercing look. "From whom?"

From a mad queen. From a gang of assailants who want to capture her alter ego, Zarsitti. The truth sounded too fanciful, though, so he remained silent about the matter.

"It's not important." Edmund headed for the door. "But I've promised to guard Amy, and I'll see to my word."

"I can finish teaching her to be a proper lady," offered Quincy.

"First *you* need to learn to be a proper gentleman." James stalked across the room and grabbed Quincy by the shirt. "Get up."

"What are you going to do with him?" demanded William, alarmed.

"Take him to bed so he can sleep it off." He looked at his brother. "Did you think I was going to bludgeon him?"

"I'll take him to bed," offered Edmund.

He moved away from the door and took his brother's arm, but James refused to let go of Quincy's rumpled garment.

Edmund glared at the former pirate captain and tugged at Quincy's sleeve. "I'll take him to his room, James."

The men struggled over a drowsy Quincy for a moment before William stepped between them and placed his hand on James's chest.

"Let him go, James."

James glared at William with an immovable expression before he reluctantly released the crumpled fabric of Quincy's shirt.

Edmund placed his ill-looking brother's arm around his shoulder and steered him toward the door. They departed from the room, the tense atmosphere, leaving the older brothers bickering in the study once more.

"I've made a mess of things, haven't I?" said Quincy, wheezing.

Edmund guided him through the passageway, his features grim. "You've made a mess of yourself."

"But you and James are quarreling."

"We've been quarreling for a long time, Quincy. It has nothing to do with you."

"Then why are you so angry with him?"

As Edmund mounted the steps with his brother, he frowned. "Because James is a bloody despot."

Quincy staggered. "I don't remember it bothering you so much in the past."

"Well, it bothers me now," he said stiffly.

Chapter 11

A my stood beside the tall window, listening to the heavy rain fall. The water pellets beat against the sturdy pane like fists banging on the glass, trying to break into the house. Thunder rumbled, shaking the window, the vibrations chiming in her head.

The violent sounds captured Amy's imagination. She parted the fine linen drapery and peered through the wet, streaky glass into the shadowy street. There she observed the masked figures on horseback. The devils raided the lane, instigating panic. Screams filled her head.

She closed her eyes and shuddered, banished the haunting reflections. A moment later, she parted her lashes and looked through the window once more into the dead, stormy thoroughfare. She battled her own demons, she thought. She empathized with Quincy's plight.

The sound of swooshing petticoats played with Amy's ears. She half listened to the fretful struts of her chaperone as the woman circled the sitting room. Soon the door opened and Captain James Hawkins entered the space, looking bedraggled. He had removed his cravat and black coat, rolled up his sleeves, and the very *un*gentlemanly appearance of him was disconcerting.

Sophia demanded, "How's Quincy?"

"He'll live."

She sighed. The relief was short-lived, though. "And you?" She was thoughtful. "Are you all right, James?"

The captain slammed his fist into the nearest piece of furniture: a polished wall clock with a lovely eggshell-enameled face. Amy winced at the sound of splintering wood. The unfortunate timepiece absorbed the man's savage blow; its hands stopped ticking.

Amy skulked beside the thick brown curtains flanking the window, unwilling to attract the captain's notice . . . however, he soon lighted upon her, his features darkening even more.

"Pack your bags, Miss Peel."

Amy's blood chilled. The ruthless words thwacked her in the belly with such vicious strength, she was breathless.

She had anticipated the eviction. James had disliked her from their first meeting. She had prepared herself for the man's scorn . . . however, she had not prepared herself for Edmund's compliance.

James wanted her ousted from the house; she had sensed that, but she had also believed Edmund more defiant. He had submitted to his brother's demand, though. He had obeyed the barbarian's will.

She was destitute.

Again.

"I want you at the front door in twenty minutes," he said roughly.

"Twenty minutes!" she cried, pulse rampant as blood pumped in her head. "What about my furnishings? I can't possibly get everything out of the house in twenty minutes!"

And what would she do with her belongings? Where would she go? Her old lodgings in St. Giles were likely occupied by a new tenant. She might be able to return to the Pleasure Palace, to Madame Rafaramanjaka . . . but Amy doubted the queen would welcome her back with cheerfulness. And she would *not* beg the wretched woman!

"I'll fetch the rest of your belongings some other day," he snapped.

Amy was rooted to the spot, her fingers twitching, grasping at air. She would survive off her savings for a short time, but then what would she do for money?

A cold darkness stifled her spirit. She'd anticipated a dramatic shift in her circumstances: she'd expected to become a lady's maid or companion—not a tramp.

Amy muzzled the hot tears that welled in her eyes.

"Fine," she gritted. "I'll leave, but before I do, I'd like to say one thing to you, Captain Hawkins."

Slowly he lifted a brow, his eyes hard, unmerciful. He possessed the same eyes as his brother, Edmund. The same shape. The same shade of blue. And yet the men possessed such different souls.

She pointed at him, finger trembling. "You are the greatest cur I have ever met!"

Amy sniffed and started for the door with shaky steps. The denouncement had eased the smarting in her breast. She had had the pluck to tell the brute what she really thought of him. She was proud of herself for that.

Sophia quickly skirted across the room and captured Amy's hand, stroking her clammy palm with tenderness.

"I'm afraid we've offered Miss Peel the wrong impression." She smiled with chagrin. "We're not tossing you into the street, my dear."

Amy stared at the woman, bemused.

"Wh-what?" she dithered.

There was a looming shadow at Amy's backside: a cold, ominous figure. The man's voice rumbled like the thunder outside: "I see my wife's failed to mention the cur's plan to you."

Amy dropped her head and swallowed a groan. The room was suddenly stuffy and she searched for air, feeling faint.

"Don't bark at me, James." Sophia bristled. "I was worried about Quincy, and it'd slipped from my thoughts. You needn't have behaved like such a barbarian toward the girl."

The captain glowered at his wife, folded his robust arms across his strapping chest, but otherwise refrained from making one more comment.

Sophia humphed. With less heat in her brilliant

brown eyes, she looked at Amy again and offered her another, slightly wicked, smile. "We'd like you to come and live with us in Mayfair."

Amy's ears tingled with warmth. The dreadful prospects that had smothered her with despair a moment ago slowly lifted from her soul, making it easier for her to breathe . . . but she had just accused the captain of being a cur. How was she going to live with him?

She glanced at the brooding barbarian, and suspected he *dis*liked the arrangement of her residing with him and his wife entirely, but was being browbeaten into caring for her.

"Why?" said Amy in a weak voice.

Sophia squeezed her hand. "It's best if you stay with us, so I can look after you."

Amy was befuddled. It was a sound idea, that she stay with Sophia; it was safer for her reputation. But how could Edmund just toss her aside like that? And without even asking her if she'd consent to the change in address? Whatever happened to his vow of protection?

Amy gathered her wits and headed for the door. "Excuse me, please. I need to speak with Edmund."

"Wait," said Sophia.

But Amy departed from the room. In quick strides, she searched the lower level, but the elusive scoundrel wasn't on the ground floor. As she made her way toward the second level, she heard an unpleasant retching sound coming from his bedchamber.

Her footfalls swift, she skirted toward the door and knocked on the wood.

There was no response.

She munched on her bottom lip. It was rude to enter the man's private quarters without an invitation, however, the noises stemming from inside the room were too distressing for her to follow good manners.

Quickly she opened the bedchamber door.

"What's wrong?" she demanded.

She witnessed Quincy, not Edmund, vomiting into a chamber pot. The stench was foul and she wrinkled her nose in affront before she crossed the wool runner and tossed aside the wispy drapery, pushing apart the panes of glass.

The rain pummeled the lintel. A fierce wind howled and burst through the window, swirling inside the room, chasing away the rank odor, the wretched sounds coming from Quincy as he coughed and heaved into the bowl.

She shut the glass, trapping the fresh air inside the space. The lamplight that had danced in a dizzying fashion hushed. The flickering shadows in the room stilled once more.

Edmund was seated beside his brother. He guided Quincy's head toward the dish, keeping the feeble scamp from tumbling out of the bed.

She hastily moved across the room, where the washstand was located, and immersed a white towel in the ceramic basin. After wringing the water from the moist linen, she approached the bed.

The distress in the scoundrel's eyes alarmed her, for she had never detected that level of concern in his expression, not even when he had lost his memory and was homeless and alone in the world.

She handed him the towel. "Is Quincy all right?"

"He'll be fine."

"Why is he in your room?"

"We didn't make it to his."

Amy nodded and moved off.

"No." Quincy wiped his mouth and rolled back onto the bed with a loud sigh. "I want her to be nurse-maid."

Edmund frowned. "Why?"

"I have a feeling her touch is gentler than yours."

He snorted and rubbed his chin. "You'd be wrong."

Amy twisted her lips as he walked away from the bed. She retrieved the moist towel from his firm grip before she settled onto the feather tick.

She sensed the man's thoughtful gaze on her backside as he crossed the room and settled into a comfortable chair. A shiver touched her spine. She ignored the sensation and placed the cool compress over the young man's sweating brow.

His features sallow, she stroked Quincy's gaunt cheek with the back of her hand, stimulating the blood flow, bringing the color back into his pale face.

The scamp smiled, his pupils sluggish. "Thank you."

"You're welcome." She pressed the blanket over his chest, rumpled during the bout with nausea. "But now I have to make you feel uncomfortable . . . I have to box your brother's ears."

Quincy, so weak, still chortled at that. "I won't be uncomfortable, I assure you."

She bobbed her head. "Good."

She turned her sharp regard on Edmund. He was watching her intently from the chair, heat in his handsome eyes. He had rested his square chin between his thumb and forefinger, spread his long legs apart in a lazy manner.

She sensed the concentration, the focus in his brow. She was accustomed to leers and other unscrupulous stares. The patrons at the Pleasure Palace had always observed her, studied her, coveted her, but the scoundrel's hard gaze rattled her poise.

He looked past her outfit, her features. He looked right into her soul, it seemed, and she wasn't prepared to share herself with anyone. It disarmed her to think he could make his way inside her heart without much effort, that one piercing look was all it took to connect with her on an intimate level.

Amy gathered her composure and said tartly, "I'm not a piece of furniture, you know? You can't shuffle me about Town without inquiring after my wishes."

"I heartily agree," quipped Quincy.

"Quiet, pup," from Edmund. He then looked at her with fierce regard. "What are you talking about, Amy?"

She huffed. "I'm talking about you sending me off to Mayfair to live with your brother and sister-in-law."

Slowly Edmund dropped his hand from his face, and rasped, "What?"

Quincy hooted with laughter, choked on the laughter and phlegm in his breast, then rolled over and went to sleep.

Amy patted the young man's back to help clear the congestion before she demanded: "Why did you assume I'd be agreeable to the new arrangement?"

I don't even like your brother and sister-in-law.

Feelings aside, though, the ghastly confrontation she'd just had with the couple made the move to Mayfair impossible. She had denounced the captain as a cur!

Edmund bounded from the chair. "That insolent devil! I didn't give him leave to take you away, Amy."

"Well, I'm expected downstairs with my baggage in twenty minutes."

He started for the door with purposeful strides.

At the man's hardened movements, she anticipated his intentions and quickly rushed toward the door, blocking the exit with her figure.

"You will *not* fight him, Edmund."

"Move, Amy."

Heart thumping, she cried, "You will *not* come to blows with your brother over me!"

"I don't intend to fight with James over you."

"Oh." She eased her muscles, feeling somewhat foolish, yet she still maintained her position at the door. "Then what do you intend to do?"

"I told James you're *not* leaving the house." The man's eyes burned. "He had no right to go against my wishes in secret."

The possessiveness in his voice was strangely warming, for she had no one in her life to look after her interests or well-being. However, she sensed there was a deeper conflict transpiring between the brothers—all the brothers—and she was relieved to know she wasn't the source of their rift.

"Don't fight with your brother," she beseeched.

"Why?"

"Because he's your brother!"

Amy had lived alone for most of her life, but over the past sennight, she had witnessed the discord and camaraderie that made up a traditional family—and she liked it. The underlining comfort, the knowledge that one was never alone in the world, pressed upon her in the most profound way, reminding her that she was apart from everyone else.

She took in a shaky breath at the lonely thought. She soon dismissed the longing, the pang. There was still a peeved-looking scoundrel towering over her, and she had to convince him it wasn't right to quarrel with kinfolk.

"I understand you're angry, Edmund, but I don't intend to live with your brother and his wife, so there's no harm done. And so long as I can stay . . ."

He lifted a black brow. "Here?"

"That's right."

"With me?"

He queried her softly—too softly—making her pulse patter.

She returned swiftly, "And the rest of your brothers."

"They're in the way."

The skin at her brow puckered as she frowned. "I need Quincy's help, his tutelage to become a lady."

"I will assist you." As the smoldering expression in his handsome eyes burned away, a sadness entered the pools. He glanced over his shoulder at his slumbering brother. "I don't think Quincy can help you anymore."

Amy followed his gaze to the bed and the restless figure curled under the covers. She whispered, "What's the matter with him?"

"It's the opium." He sighed. "It numbs his senses and offers him a feeling of euphoria, but over time, he needs more and more of it just to feel anything a'tall."

"How did he survive aboard the *Nemesis* without it?"

"It was difficult at first, but over the weeks, he came off the opiate. He was fine for a while . . . now he's home and he's dependent on it again."

She nodded. "Killing demons."

He looked at her thoughtfully. "That's right."

Quincy tossed between the linens and murmured in his sleep: "I'm sorry. I'm sorry I killed her. Forgive me."

A spasm gripped Amy's heart, clenched it tight. She said, breathless, "Who did he kill?"

"No one." Edmund was curt, angry even. "He's dreaming, is all. Ignore him and his blathering." With more tenderness in his voice, he suggested, "Why don't you get some rest, Amy? I'll go and talk with James."

She glared at him.

"No fighting, I promise."

She sighed and moved away from the door. "I think I'll stay here with Quincy until you return."

"All right." He bobbed his head. "I'll be back soon."

Edmund departed from the bedchamber. She listened to his heavy footfalls until they drifted away before she returned, a bit wary, to the bedside.

She settled onto the feather tick again and mopped the sweat glistening from the man's pale brow, listened to his incoherent ramblings, wondering who "she" was who tormented him.

Edmund entered the sitting room. He observed his brother in the low light standing beside the window, watching the tempest, meditating.

As he regarded his kin, his muscles firmed. He balled his fists . . . then flexed his fingers. He had promised Amy he wouldn't fight with James—however much he deserved a sound thrashing.

Edmund closed the sitting room door.

"How's Quincy?" said the captain, still peering through the window.

"Amy's looking after him."

The muscles in his jaw stiffened. "You've taken a shining to the wench, admit it."

"Why do you dislike her, James?" He leaned against the door and folded his arms across his chest. "Because I didn't ask your permission before I brought her here?"

"I dislike her because *I'm* going to have to look after the wench once you're bored with her."

Edmund bristled. Irresponsible. That was his lot in life, his epithet. He wasn't saddled with important duties or trusted with confidence because he was . . . Edmund. The middle brother. The inscrutable brother. The incompatible member of the family—the one James wasn't able to control.

"Then let me put your mind at rest, James. *I* will look after Amy."

The pirate lord maintained his vigil beside the tall glass as lightning sparked and filled the room. "I suppose you've come to tell me she won't be living with us in Mayfair? Well, you needn't waste your breath. I suspected as much as soon as she'd called me a cur."

Edmund's lips twitched with mirth; the sentiment slowly seeped into his blood and warmed his heart.

"No, I've not come to tell you that, James." He looked across the room. "Where's Sophia?"

"It's a savage storm. We'll have to stay the night." He looked away from the window and pegged him with his steely eyes. "Sophia's off making arrangements for our quarters . . . since you've given away mine to the wench."

Edmund hardened again, his good temperament snuffed out. It wasn't the temporary lodging situation that raised his hackles, but the cutting tone in his brother's voice, that snide undertone that belied every austere word.

"Good," he said tightly. "I don't want your wife to hear this."

James pinned him with a sharp stare, his features grave. He had offered Edmund The Look since childhood. It was the sort of look that elicited command and respect. Edmund shrugged off the bond that chained him to the past, though. He wasn't moved by the tyrant's glower anymore.

"What is it you don't want my wife to hear?"

Edmund rolled up his sleeves as he crossed the room. "The sound of your nose cracking under my fist."

It wasn't really what he'd wanted to say to the man; it wasn't his original intent, but he had changed his mind about being civil.

The pirate lord smirked. "Have at it, Eddie."

With a shout, Edmund rammed his shoulder into his brother's chest, pushing him into the window. The glass cracked as James grunted before he wrapped his arm around Edmund's throat and tackled him to the ground.

It was a whirl of heat and energy as the brothers butted fists, slamming into the furniture. A side table teetered and the intricate model schooner of the *Bonny*

Meg toppled off the surface; it crashed onto the floor, the fragile joints splintering.

"I hate you, James!"

He jabbed his elbow into the captain's ribs, pummeled him with his fists. The wood furnishings suffered under their savage blows, rent apart and knocked into the walls.

"What the devil's going on?" cried Sophia as she entered the sitting room. "Stop! Stop it at once!" As the men still wrestled on the floor, she departed from the room in hastened strides. "William!"

In a few minutes, the space was a wasteland, filled with rubbish.

As the fire in his bones cooled, Edmund released his brother. He rested on the floor, heaving, gathering his frenzied thoughts.

He was dazed. He had never clashed with his older brother, not with his fists. He struggled against the impulse to apologize; he was *not* in the wrong. If James had demonstrated even a small measure of goodwill toward him, he would not have engaged in the brawl.

Edmund fingered his bruised and bloodied lips, wiped the thick, oozing liquid away with the back of his hand. "I want you to stay out of my life."

It was the original sentiment he had wanted to express to the man: a firm declaration that James's interference wasn't welcome anymore.

The pirate captain remained stoic, seated on the floor beside the window, rubbing his injured midriff.

There was swelling under his eyes and blood seeped from the scabs at his knuckles.

"Do you think you can manage on your own?" he said, breathless.

"I don't know." He shrugged. "I'll find out, I guess."

A muscle in the man's cheek twitched. "And the next time you get into a scrape and lose your memory?"

"Then I'll stay lost."

James's features hardened. He glowered, in truth. But Edmund was resolute. He would rather wander the world without memory than live under his brother's iron fist.

"You're not my father, James."

James had usurped the post; he had appointed himself their guardian. He had raised them since boyhood, and he *still* squeezed them by the scruffs of their necks, steering their steps.

Enough.

The pirate lord's bruised lips thinned. "No, I'm not your father."

The overhead kerfuffle seeped its way into the battered sitting room.

The brothers eyed the tremors in the ceiling, then eyed each other before both scrambled to their feet and took off running toward the second level.

Edmund was the first one out the door and he bounded up the stairs, heading for his private quarters, where he suspected the stomps and cries had stemmed from.

As he approached the bedchamber door with James

at his heels, the sounds escalated in volume and his heart pumped with greater verve, his booted steps energized.

"No, Quincy! Don't do it!"

Edmund heard Amy's frantic cries. He grabbed the iron latch and pushed against the door . . .

The shadows flickered in haste as the lamplight danced with gusto. The rainstorm had penetrated the room through the parted window. The curtains snaked around the two bodies perched precariously beside the opened glass.

Amy was drenched with water, fighting the wild tempest—and the irrational figure struggling in her embrace. She had twisted her arms around his waist in a desperate effort to keep him secured . . . but she was losing the battle with the much heavier Quincy.

"We're sinking!" cried Quincy. "We have to abandon ship!"

Amy shouted over her shoulder, "He's going to jump!"

Edmund and James charged through the tumultuous room, clasped Quincy by the arms, and yanked him roughly away from the storm-battered window.

Amy quickly shut and locked the slick panes. The shadows stilled, the lamplight steadied. Quincy thrashed, hollered, and they wrestled him to the floor, holding him tightly.

William entered the room, his arms akimbo. "What the hell happened to the sitting room?" As his eyes fixed firmly on the heap of intertwined limbs, he demanded, "What the devil's going on in here?"

"It's Quincy," gritted Edmund. "He's hallucinating."

The men struggled with their delirious kinsman.

"Blimey," snarled James. "He's as strong as a bull."

William quickly offered assistance, and together the three brothers hoisted him off the floor and tossed him back onto the bed.

James ordered, "Fetch the doctor!"

William departed in haste as Sophia appeared in the doorway. She gasped and rushed inside the room. She clutched Quincy's twitching ankles. "What's happened in *here*?"

Edmund wondered about that, too. What had happened to Quincy? How had he deteriorated to such an abysmal frame of mind? And would Edmund lose him to that seductive darkness?

"Hold still!" barked James.

Quincy gasped for breath. He thrust his breastbone out, taking in a deep swell of air before he sighed and collapsed.

Edmund maintained a sturdy hold on his brother's arm, too wary to let go and risk another violent outburst, but he soon relaxed his sore fingers, for Quincy seemed unconscious; he was murmuring incoherently in his sleep as he was wont to do since boyhood.

"I think it's over," whispered Edmund.

James stared at the troubled pup with a deep frown. "No, it's not over."

Perhaps not in the future, Edmund mused, but for the short term the ordeal had come to a surcease. He slipped off the bed, his muscles cramped after the series of scuffles. Sophia crawled across the coverlet, taking his place. She had a towel in her hand and set about dabbing the sweat and rainwater from Quincy's fevered flesh.

As James and Sophia attended Quincy's needs, Edmund glanced across the room, slightly disoriented, and located Amy still standing beside the window, wet and shivering. Fingers curled into fists, she seemed anxious, alert.

He crossed the room and gathered her into his arms. "Are you all right, Amy?"

She had combated with Quincy. She had invested every ounce of strength she possessed into keeping him from jumping through the opened window. Was she hurt? he wondered.

The lass trembled in his embrace and he hugged her tighter. As he smothered her in his arms, she, in turn, smothered the darkness in his head. She warmed him, even with her chilled bones and blood. The woman's heartbeat, so near his own, was enough to silence the nagging suspicions he concealed in his heart about Quincy's welfare and recovery, about his own estranged relationship with James. With Amy's strong body in his arms, everything seemed . . . hopeful.

"Let me see your hands, Amy."

"I'm fine," she said at last. "Truly."

He bussed the crown of her wet head, stroked her stringy locks. He should let her go, he thought, encourage her to return to her room and change, rest, yet his arms remained clinched at her shoulders, her backside.

And she didn't protest. She didn't squirm in his embrace or insist he take his hands off her. She was quiet. Still. The tremors subsided. The stress in her muscles eased, for he sensed her stiff fingers spread apart . . . and embrace him in return.

Edmund sighed. He took comfort in the woman's touch, like balm. The storm still beat and drummed against the glass, but it couldn't get inside the room anymore.

Chapter 12

Amy was alone in the dining parlor with an assortment of biscuits, scones, and jams spread out across the table's surface. She was famished, and the breakfast fare smelled ever so inviting, yet she contented herself with a cup of tea and mulled over the previous evening's happenings in her mind.

Her bones still ached from the energy she'd exerted keeping the delirious Quincy from leaping through the opened window, but she was fit enough from her training as a dancer to weather the aches tolerably well. It was her thoughts that stirred the greatest distress in her belly: the memory of the scamp's muscles slipping between her stiff fingers. If Edmund and James had not appeared in the room at that crucial moment . . .

Amy shuddered. She wrapped the shawl more tightly around her shoulders. She was still chilled from the thorough soaking she'd received during last night's storm. It was as if she wasn't able to warm her blood, she was so icy inside. Even the hot, minty tea wasn't a comfort.

She closed her eyes and imagined Edmund's arms holding her tight. The shiver that touched her spine wasn't from the cold. It stemmed from a warm place in her heart that rippled throughout her limbs. Tucked firmly in Edmund's embrace, without a breath of space between them, was the most intimate she had ever been with a man . . . and she wondered if perhaps the chill she was feeling was the result of the loss of that intimacy.

The door opened and Captain James Hawkins entered the narrow room, filling the small space with his stout presence. She noted the bruises around his eyes; the discoloration didn't negate his hard stare, though.

Amy quickly looked at the teacup nestled between her hands. She sensed the man's piercing regard on her. Was he still furious with her for calling him a cur? She suspected that he was.

The distinct clip-clop of heavy footfalls resounded in the dining parlor. The chair's legs scraped across the well-polished floor. He assumed a seat and reached for a biscuit, his meaty hand permeating her line of vision.

She twisted her lips, sifting through her thoughts, searching for something worthwhile to say to the man, but one indecorous question was all that pressed on her mind: *Where did you get the bruises?*

She didn't ask him that, though; she didn't dare.

At length, she reasoned it might be a better idea if she excused herself from the table and allowed him to eat his morning meal in solitude. She certainly didn't mind being apart from him.

Amy set the earthenware on the surface, prepared to depart.

"Thank you, Miss Peel."

She stiffened. What was he thanking her for? For preparing to leave the room so he could enjoy his food without her troubling presence?

She frowned at the assumption, so rude. However, she had learned her lesson from the previous evening's disastrous confrontation with the man. She would not voice her conjectures aloud again.

"I beg your pardon?" she said.

"Thank you for saving Quincy's life."

The low timbre in his voice disarmed her. It was pleasant. There was no animosity or underlying sarcasm in the tone of his voice. She would have detected it otherwise, for she was accustomed to Madame Rafaramanjaka's "sweet" smile and vicious taunts. The captain seemed genuinely grateful. She wasn't sure how to respond to the civility.

"You're welcome," she returned quietly.

He resumed his meal and she reconsidered her earlier decision to depart from the room, reaching for a tasty-looking biscuit herself.

Sophia soon entered the dining parlor.

"Good morning, Miss Peel."

Amy returned the convivial greeting. She watched as Sophia circled the table without wishing her husband the same felicitation. Amy wondered if perhaps the couple had quarreled, but she soon dismissed the thought from her mind as she observed the private gesture that passed between them.

Sophia slipped her fingers beneath the man's queue and stroked the back of his neck before she assumed a seat. It was a simple, fleeting expression of solidarity, and it altered the surly captain's entire visage. He seemed more at ease, comforted. The stiffness in his muscles loosened and his features relaxed . . . though a sensual fire burned bright in his eyes.

Amy was breathless. The silent communication intimated the couple's deep bond, and she sensed a pang in her breast at the thought that she was alone in the world, that there was no one in her life to chase away the demons in her head with a loving touch.

"Excuse me, please."

Amy set aside the half-eaten biscuit and quickly skirted from the room, mounted the steps at the end of the passageway, and headed for Edmund's room. She failed to knock on the wood barrier. She pushed opened the bedroom door . . . and sighed.

Edmund's long, muscular figure was slouched in a wing chair, his feet propped on the edge of the bed as he watched Quincy dream.

Slowly Edmund turned his head, his expression thoughtful, and observed her with a smoldering stare that warmed her belly and eased the pinching pressure on her airway.

"Is something the matter?" he murmured, his voice scratchy with sleep.

"No." She closed the door. "I've come to see how Quincy's faring, is all."

"He's doing well . . . thanks to you."

The look he offered her smothered her like a woolly blanket, chased off the chill in her bones. She approached him, observed his puffy lips, his bruised cheek, and her good mood quickly soured, for his brother sported a similar set of injuries.

"I know what you're thinking, Amy."

Had the scoundrel broken his vow? Had he engaged in fisticuffs with his brother? She refrained from making the accusation, though, as both men had wrestled with Quincy last night. Perhaps they had been injured in the scuffle.

She pointed at his wounds. "Are those from the tussle with Quincy?"

"No." He eyed her intently. "They're from James."

"He hit you?"

"I hit him first."

Amy rounded the chair, tight-lipped. Keeping her footfalls light, so she didn't spoil the scamp's sleep, she crossed the room and settled beside the window.

He sighed at her backside. "He deserved the thrashing, Amy."

"He's your brother."

The furniture's joints creaked as he lifted from the chair. He joined her beside the window, frowning. "He's an iron leg shackle—and last night I broke free of him."

"I see," she said stiffly. "Will you dishonor every promise you make if it suits you?"

He dropped his brows, his eyes shadowed. "I'll see you settled in a proper post, Amy."

She turned her head away. "Unless I'm a burden to you—another leg shackle—and you break free of me, too."

"You don't keep my head below water so I can't breathe." He tipped her chin with his forefinger, forcing her to meet his torrid gaze. "I don't want to be free of you."

She shivered at his smoky words, the firm touch of his finger. She turned her head away again, the sensitive underside of her chin skimming his hand, as she eyed the slumbering scamp, his features pale and twisted into a grimace.

"Is he in pain?"

"I don't think so." He dropped his hand away from her face. "I think he's dreaming."

The poor devil. It must be a frightful dream, she thought.

She looked through the window into the misty morning light. "I had a bad dream last night, too."

"Oh?"

Amy pinched the shawl more firmly at her bust, but it was not the coolness in the air making her uneasy. It was the scoundrel's expression: part dreamy, part incisive. He folded his thick arms across his chest, leaned a shoulder against the wall, and crossed his ankles.

She looked at his bare feet. She had dropped her eyes

to avoid his scrutiny, but now she wondered if perhaps she had made a mistake, for she imagined slipping her toes over his sturdy feet in playful banter.

The unladylike reflection startled her and she quickly lifted her gaze. "I dreamed about my parents."

He was watching her with keen interest. "And it was a bad dream?"

"I remembered the last time I saw them." She peered through the glass at the distant structures. "They were preparing for a party at a friend's house. My mother kissed me good night. My father tweaked my nose and told me to be good. I never saw either of them again."

"How did they die?"

She shrugged. "I don't know."

"What do you mean?"

Amy munched on her bottom lip. She looked away from the window and confronted him. "I lied to you, Edmund."

He frowned. "Amy?"

"I didn't want to tell you the truth."

"Why?"

The welter of feeling that welled in her breast was so profound, she needed a moment to gather her breath and retrieve her strangled voice. "I don't like to think about that night."

The man's voice softened. "Tell me, Amy."

At his encouraging words, she swallowed a deep mouthful of air and confessed: "My parents didn't perish when I was six years old." The truth seemed so heavy and she struggled with every word. "I haven't seen them in about thirteen years, so perhaps they're dead now, but they didn't pass away on the night of the party."

He brushed his fingers through his scruffy locks, combing the curls. "So how did you find yourself in the streets?"

"I was taken away," she whispered weakly.

"What do you mean?"

Amy's head hurt with the memories: the horses' hooves, the burning torchlight, the dark, masked figures. There was chaos in her thoughts, and it ached to sort through the disjointed images. "I was kidnapped."

He crunched the muscles at his brow. "Why?"

"I don't know. I was taken from my bed one night." She struggled with the maelstrom of emotions that stirred in her belly, making her ill. "I was carried away on horseback. The kidnappers took me into the rookeries." The first foul smells and unsightly figures from the slums bubbled to the forefront of her thoughts. "I sensed I was in trouble." She bunched her fingers into fists. "I evaded them; I jumped from the horse. I knew they would hurt me . . . kill me." She shuddered. "The villains told me my parents had hired them to take me away; that they didn't care for me anymore."

"And you believed them?"

"I was a child. I believed them at first." She shrugged. "I was a spoiled brat and their claim seemed truthful."

"You will do as you're told, Amy."

"No, Papa!"

"You will do as you're told or I will see to it that the goblins take you away and never bring you home."

"But as I matured," she said quietly, "I understood their deceit and I doubted their claim."

"Have you looked for your parents?"

"No," she returned firmly, tamping down the tears that brimmed in her eyes. "I didn't know where to begin the search. And it's been so many years; I'm sure they've forgotten about me now."

Edmund eyed her intently. "Parents don't forget about their children."

"Perhaps not, but I don't know their whereabouts. I don't remember my home; I'm not even sure I know my real name."

"Don't you want to know the reason for your kidnapping? Don't you want to know if your parents are still alive?"

Yes!

But . . . "Hope is dangerous," she said softly. "I don't want to chase after ghosts."

After another thoughtful pause, he murmured, "You look pale, Amy. Did you have breakfast?"

She sniffed, feeling silly for allowing her emotions to overtake her good sense. "Yes, I had tea and biscuits with your brother James."

He lifted a black brow. "And how did the cur treat you?"

She groaned. "You know?"

"I'm afraid so."

"I really *am* trying to be a lady, you know."

He offered her a small smile. "I admire your spirit, Amy."

She blushed at the compliment. She curled her hair behind her ear, feeling fidgety, as a profound want entered her breast and commanded her heart. She desired so much to connect with Edmund in that moment, yet she wasn't sure how to go about it.

"James treated me well," she said at length. "I think he's forgiven me for calling him a cur. He thanked me for assisting with Quincy."

"He did?"

She nodded. "Madame Rafaramanjaka would never have pardoned such insolence. She would have thrashed me, then fired me from the club."

"I don't think the queen would have fired you—ever."

"What?"

"You're too good a dancer," he said quietly.

She shuddered at the heat in his words. "But you offered me protection because you said I was destitute."

"No, you assumed you were destitute. I didn't contest the matter. I wanted you to quit the Pleasure Palace. It's dangerous for you to work there. It's too dangerous for you to be Zarsitti anymore."

She stared at him, dumbfounded. "Madame Rafaramanjaka threatened me. She said she would fire me if I ever disobeyed her."

"She threatened you to keep you in line, to control you."

Amy looked through the window and mulled over the epiphany. Was it true? Would the wretched queen have employed her services even if there had been a scandal? She wasn't so sure about that. But the matter was moot. She had an opportunity to better her circumstances with Edmund's help, and she intended to take advantage of the fortuity.

The man's eyes darkened. "I understand what it's like to be controlled."

She glanced at his brooding features. "I think you've misjudged your brother, Edmund."

He lowered his head. The morning light caressed his strong and handsome profile, making her heart flutter.

"I don't think so; I think I've pegged him right." He paused, then: "You and I are not so very different, Amy. There's always someone in our lives trying to keep us from rising too high." He looked back at her with intense purpose. "But we don't need anyone. We can go it alone, don't you think?"

Alone? That didn't sound so appealing. However, the thought of going it together sounded strangely . . . wonderful.

The smarting in Amy's breast was profound. She thought of only one balm that would soothe the deep-rooted ache.

She stepped into the light cascading through the window and the soft drapery. On spiked toes, she bussed Edmund's mouth, the tissue plump, swollen. She sucked at the tender flesh, so warm, the touch and taste of him making her giddy.

He stiffened, the kiss hard, and she hesitated, but soon the surprise in his bones passed away and his taut muscles softened . . . the kiss softened, too.

She sighed as he parted his lips and took her mouth in a more passionate gesture. She wanted him to guide her through the unfamiliar movements, to take possession of her body. And he did. The man's strapping arms circled her midriff and squeezed her ribs. His mouth moved over her lips with greater pressure, an urgent, almost hungry appeal for more, and she gave him more. She matched his hard thrusts, kissing him with zeal. She raked her fingers over his shoulders and wrapped her arms around his neck in a tight hold.

In his embrace, the world seemed at right. But it was unwise to find succor with him, a scoundrel; she knew that in the rational part of her mind . . . yet he teased her senses with such sensual pleasure she needed to let him inside her being, if only to restore the joy that had died there so many years ago.

I want you.

He growled low in his throat. *She* was moaning softly, too, so unladylike. But she wanted the scoundrel in a very *un*ladylike way. She cleaved to him, burrowed her fingernails into his stout neck. She demanded more from him than tenderness. She demanded passion. She wanted to *feel*. She wanted to keep the hot blood flowing through her veins, for it washed away the years of torment.

"I think I'm going to be sick."

Amy staggered, her footfalls fumbled. Had Edmund

pushed her away? No. He looked as winded as she was. She had pushed him away. And with reason. She glanced at the bed, where the ignominious remark had stemmed from, and witnessed Quincy as he rolled over the feather tick's edge and retched into the chamber pot.

She closed her eyes and sighed, trembling, weak. It wasn't the sight of them kissing that had sickened him, but the opium. She was still flustered, though, as Edmund dutifully treaded across the room to attend his brother's needs.

Quincy yowled as he rested again. "I hate being sick."

Edmund poured him a glass of water. "Here," he said hoarsely. "Drink this."

Quincy complied. With his brother's support, he downed the tonic.

"Ouch." Quincy massaged his arms, his midriff. "What the devil happened to me?"

"We wrestled you to the ground last night." He set the empty glass aside. "You tried to jump from the window."

Quincy looked confused. "I did?"

"You were hallucinating." Edmund glanced at her hotly. "If it hadn't been for Amy, you would've leaped to your death. You might even have taken her with you to your doom if she hadn't the strength and where-withal to keep you secured until James and I had entered the room."

The scamp paled. He looked at Amy with a welter of pain. "Did I hurt you?"

"No," she was quick to assure him. "I'm fine."

But Quincy still seemed gloomy, distraught. She, too, trembled, her nerves still frazzled. She reckoned it might be a good idea if she tiptoed from the room and composed herself, allowed the brothers some privacy, as well.

She headed for the door, casting Edmund one last, furtive look, but he had sensed her ogling and had matched her expression with a fiery one of his own.

I want you, too, Amy.

She rushed from the room, stifled. In the cool passageway, she stilled and placed her hand on the wall for support. She touched her mouth, the flesh swelling with blood.

She had kissed Edmund.

She had kissed him!

And she'd aroused the scoundrel. The sentiment had pulsed through his taut muscles, in his sensual stare, his raspy voice . . .

She quickly skirted off. She had embroiled herself in a tight fix. How was she going to disentangle herself from it now?

"Bullocks."

Chapter 13

You don't belong here, mate."

Edmund bristled. As he fisted his palms, he glanced at the looming figure that had sneaked up on him. He had failed to detect the other man's stealthy approach, his thoughts engaged elsewhere, and in a wicked den like the Red Dragon that was a dangerous misstep.

"I don't belong here, do I?"

Edmund relaxed his taut muscles and kicked the empty chair across from him, inviting the Bow Street Runner to join him at the table.

John Dunbar accepted the invitation and settled his long bones into the seat, removing his cap, allowing his mussed, sandy brown hair loose.

"You look more and more like a bloody nob, Eddie."

"The devil I do," he groused.

"It's the hair." John fingered his own unruly crop of curls, smoothing the locks. "The fashionable cut gives you away."

Edmund humphed. He might look like a gentle-man, but he didn't feel like one. He possessed the same tainted blood as the thugs and wenches who filled the flash house with their hoarse guffaws and salacious antics.

John squinted in the dim room. "Have you quarreled with one of these roughs?"

"I've quarreled with *a* rough, but don't worry about it." He thumbed the glass of gin. "Would you like a drink, John?"

"No." He set his cap on the table and placed his patched elbows on the soiled surface. "Is there a reason we always meet in the seediest pub in London?"

He shrugged. "I like it here."

"You're determined to get me killed, aren't you?" he queried askance. "I suspect it's retribution for almost arresting you last year."

Edmund snorted at the absurd idea. He had no ill will toward his friend. A year ago, Edmund was involved in a dockside brawl that had aroused the River Police. The *Bonny Meg* had waited in queue in the Thames, the quays too small to accommodate the pressing ship traffic. With the ship a prime target for robbery, thieves had attempted to unload the schooner's cargo, and a scuffle had erupted between the ruffians and the *Bonny Meg*'s crew.

The Bow Street Runners had arrived to assist the River Police in keeping the fray from turning into a riot and spilling into the city. John had attempted to appre-hend Edmund during the struggle, but in the tussle, pistols had fired. It was Edmund who had pushed John out of the way of a bullet, and it was that episode that had united the pair as comrades . . . though Edmund had yet to admit he hadn't *intended* to save John from the bullet; he'd merely tackled the Runner to the ground in hopes of disabling him and avoiding arrest.

Still, their pairing proved a curious one. Not for John, who wasn't privy to Edmund's past as a pirate, but for Edmund, who was reminded of their juxtapositions every time they gathered in public. In truth, he enjoyed keeping John as an acquaintance, for he admired and respected the man, but there was another, less wholesome, reason he maintained the amity—he knew it would turn his brothers' hair white if they ever learned he was chums with a Bow Street Runner.

The twenty-seven-year-old investigator smiled, his brown eyes brimming with jest. "Have you ever thought about joining the Bow Street Magistrates' Office?"

"No," Edmund returned brusquely . . . but the twisted humor in the matter perked his interest. A former pirate serving the law? It was an amusing idea. He also wouldn't have to confront the darker side of being a privateer in the Royal Navy's African Squadron.

The caustic smile that had touched his swollen lips quickly faded away as he remembered the deep-rooted groans and the haunting iron scuffs as hundreds of manacles clashed together. The sounds wouldn't wail in his ears at night anymore, he thought.

"The profession might suit you, Eddie, since you already combat the slave trade. And you fit into the underworld so well; you know the haunt of every villain." He scratched his chin in deliberation. "I think you must have been a member of the underworld at some point in the past."

"Do you?" he drawled.

John shrugged. "Well, I know you'd get the criminals confessing their sins, that's for sure."

"Why do you think that?"

"You have a sour look about you, Eddie. A 'give me what I want or I'll draw your cork' sort of look. Add to it the fact that *you* were a member of the crew that destroyed the infamous pirate Black Hawk, and it makes for an intimidating front. You have a sound sense of justice, too."

Edmund refrained from smirking.

"I can put in a good word for you at the magistrates' office, if you'd like."

"Thank you for the offer, John, but I'm not interested in the post." He had not invited his comrade to the flash house for idle chitchat. He had a more pressing matter to impart. "I need a favor."

"I don't know." John sighed and rubbed his brow, etched with fatigue. "I'm in the midst of an investigation. I haven't the time for favors."

"What are you investigating?"

"The dowager Lady Stevenson's jewels are missing." He yawned. "We suspect one of the servants, a footman, the culprit. He was apprehended by the other staff members, skulking from the country house after the jewels had disappeared. He must have tossed or hidden the jewels, though, for they weren't on his person when he was detained, and he won't utter a word about their location."

"Of course he won't confess to their location. He'll hang."

"Aye." John stroked his head. "It means *I*'ve got to comb the house and the grounds in search of the blasted baubles. I suspect the footman intended to evade capture and later return for the prize. I'm sure the jewels are still somewhere on the property."

"Have you checked the well?"

John snorted. "I sincerely doubt the vandal drowned the priceless ornaments."

"I would." He shrugged. "Gold doesn't rust. Besides, no one would think to look in the well . . . right?"

John stared at him thoughtfully. "All right, I'll inspect the well on the property. And if I find the jewels, I guess I owe you that favor. What is it about anyway?"

As soon as Edmund envisioned the spirited lass, his blood warmed. He rubbed his lips together at the memory of her sweet mouth pressed hard over his, seeking kisses.

She wanted him.

He was tempted to let her have him, too, but he set aside his desires, determined to put the matter of her abduction to rest. Was there a family out there, looking for her? He'd be remiss in his duty as her guardian if he didn't make some inquiries into the unpleasant affair.

"I need you to look through the files at the magistrates' office, going back about thirteen years, perhaps more."

"What am I searching for?" said John.

"A report about a missing girl. Her name is Amy. The surname might be Peel. And she possesses a birthmark."

"Do you know how many 'missing' children there are in the city? The last survey places the figure well into the tens of thousands! Most parents don't even report the child's disappearance, they're too thankful to be rid of the spare mouth."

"I understand, but I'd still like you to search for the potential record."

John sighed. "Why the interest in the girl?"

"I can't tell you that." He stood and prepared to depart from the flash house. "Don't reveal our conversation to anyone. Let me know what you find."

"*If* your tip about the well proves fruitful."

"It will."

Amy entered the dining parlor—and paused. She admired the elegant table settings and inhaled the rich scent of freshly cooked fare. Candlelight flickered across the green-and-gold striped papered walls. In the narrow room with a high ceiling, the flames skipped over the dark woodwork, giving the polished furnishings a warm and lustrous glow.

Slowly she lifted her gaze and narrowed her eyes on the scoundrel standing behind one of the high-back chairs, carved in the classical baroque style. He offered her a sensual smile.

"Good evening, Miss Peel."

A tremor skipped along her backbone. "What's going on, Edmund?"

"I thought we'd continue our lessons." He pulled out the chair for her; its legs scraped softly across the floor. "With dinner etiquette."

She remained standing beside the door, transfixed on a single thought. "Alone?"

"James and Sophia have departed for Mayfair, William's away on business, and Quincy's still resting." He gestured toward the chair. "That leaves you and me, Miss Peel."

Amy stared at the offered seat and balled her fingers into fists. What must he think of her after their morning kiss? That she was a brazen harlot? Was that why he'd arranged for such an intimate dinner? To seduce her?

She wanted to be a lady's maid or companion. She hadn't behaved like one, though. She had forsaken her good sense and polite manners for a scandalous kiss. And now he was treating her like a strumpet.

"Edmund—"

As she was still rooted to the spot beside the door, he crossed the room and cupped her elbow, escorting her to the round table. She assumed the seat with a sigh.

"We don't use first names at the table," he said, and occupied the seat opposite her. "It boasts a level of intimacy one might not share with the other dinner companions."

She glanced around the room. "But it's just the two of us at dinner."

He removed the napkin from its gold ring, flapped the crisp linen, unraveling it, then set it across his lap. "And are we intimately acquainted, Miss Peel?"

"Ed—"

He raised a brow.

"Mr. Hawkins," she said tightly as she followed his mannerisms, covering her skirt with the napkin. "I must talk with you about—"

"You've placed the ring on the wrong side of your plate."

She looked at the table. "What?"

"The ring sits to the left of your plate."

She moved the article. "It matters where I set the napkin ring?"

"It matters if you'd like to be invited back to dinner. Don't underestimate the smallest detail, Miss Peel."

The weighty warning sobered her, and she quickly firmed her lips, studying the man's movements, mimicking his posture.

As the soup was already presented in the bowls, Edmund picked up a spoon and tasted the steaming first course.

Amy followed his movements. "Shouldn't you wait for the lady to begin?"

"It's old-fashioned and crude to wait for the other guests. One dines as soon as one is served."

"Oh."

Amy brought the spoon to her lips and sighed at the

refreshing scent, rather hungry herself. She tasted the soup; scrumptious.

Edmund set down the cutlery. "You've just ruined yourself, Miss Peel."

Aghast, Amy placed the spoon into the bowl. "How?"

"I heard the little noise you made."

Heat filled her cheeks. "I beg your pardon?"

"You slurped your soup. You must *never* make a sound while eating soup."

"I see," she said stiffly.

She picked up the spoon again, drinking the repast with an unsteady hand, but she managed not to make another indelicate noise.

"The soup was delicious. Can I have—?"

"No." He cleared the table of soup dishes and retrieved two plates with roasted ham and potatoes from the serving cart. "One doesn't ask for seconds." He set the plates over the gold chargers. "It holds up the next course for the other guests."

Amy wiped her mouth.

Slowly Edmund lowered himself back into his seat, staring at her.

"What?" she demanded.

He lifted his napkin. "Tap your lips." He gestured. "Like this."

Her heart fluttered as he caressed his mouth in demonstration, his lips sensuous, inviting. Her mouth slightly ajar, she quickly clamped her lips together, chastising herself for her folly. The etiquette lesson was stirring very *im*proper feelings in her blood, and setting aside her desire to learn and practice proper dinner manners, she realized she still had to set the scoundrel straight about their earlier kiss.

He poured her a glass of wine. "A miss might drink up to three glasses of wine during dinner; however, a married woman might have up to six."

"Six?" She cut into the ham. "I'd lose my faculties after one."

He arched a black brow again.

"I mean, I have to talk with you—"

"Never speak with food in your mouth."

She quickly swallowed and parted her lips to speak—

"And don't talk about yourself at the dinner table; it's rude."

She glared at him. "All right," she said tightly. "What did you do today, Mr. Hawkins?"

"I visited with a friend."

"That's nice. Well, I—"

"Keep your elbows off the table." He gestured. "Wrists only."

"How about if I slit your wrists?" she muttered under her breath. At his questioning look, she swallowed the threat. "Well?"

"Yes?"

"Aren't you going to ask me about my day?"

"I already know what you did today." There was heat in his eyes, his voice. "And it isn't necessary to reciprocate with the same question."

Amy shivered at the man's knowing expression, the approval in his gaze. He wasn't the least bit put off by her scandalous behavior, scoundrel that he was.

"Tell me, Miss Peel. What do you remember about your childhood?"

She stiffened at the unexpected query. "Very little."

"Are you sure?"

"Why are you asking me about the past?" she snapped.

"I'm curious to know more about you."

Amy took in a deep breath. It was one thing to collect trinkets that reminded her of better days, but it was another thing entirely to dredge up the past, to talk about wistful memories.

She folded her napkin and set it aside. "I've lost my appetite, Mr. Hawkins." She headed for the door. "Good evening."

"Amy, wait."

But she disregarded his entreaty and bustled toward her private room. Once inside the large bedroom, she sighed and examined her surroundings. A small fire burned in the hearth, casting the furnishings in a glistening aura. The bulk of the pieces belonged to her; she had arranged them in such a way that the configuration reminded her of . . . a time long ago.

She approached the tall vanity, skipped her fingers over the scattered toiletries: hairbrushes, hand mirrors, perfume bottles—remnants from the past. She found little comfort in the familiar articles, now.

A knock at the door.

She ignored the bounder.

The rapping persisted.

She huffed. She inspected her countenance in the mirror and smoothed her scowling features before she walked across the room and opened the door.

Her heart trembled.

"Are you all right, Amy?"

He peered at her from the misty darkness, his expression inscrutable, his eyes veiled with shadows. He queried her in a low voice; the sounds teased her senses, like fingers thrumming her spine.

She gripped the wood frame. "I'm about to retire."

"Can I come inside?"

He pressed his palm against the door frame, brushing her fingers. She pulled her hand away. Jerked it, really.

He shifted his weight, leaned closer to her. "I need to talk with you."

She detected the scent of wine on his breath.

"Now?" she snapped.

"It's important.

She firmly pressed her lips together, but stepped aside, muscles taut, allowing him entrance.

The man's long figure sauntered inside the room. He stirred the air as he passed, making her shiver. She closed the door after him and waited.

He scanned the bedchamber and remarked in a thick voice, "I see you've made yourself at home."

"Was I not supposed to?"

He turned around and offered her a small smile. "No, I want you to feel at home."

She humphed at the friendly gesture, still perturbed.

He soon settled on the bed, the feather tick sinking. The ropes stretched, supporting his weight. In the firelight, one side of his body glowed, the other remained in shadow.

She was sentient of his slightest movement. He rested his figure on the spot where she slumbered, and if he shifted a thigh, she sensed the hard muscles rubbing her leg; she imagined it.

He looked across the room and set his gaze on a particular piece of furniture. "I've often wondered what sorts of treasures you keep locked away in that chest."

"You have your secrets and I have mine."

He chuckled. "And what secrets would you like to know about me?"

It sounded like a dangerous invitation; like he might bundle her up in a potato sack and drown her in a pond if she learned too many intimate details.

She eyed him with intent. "What happened when you boarded a slaver for the first time?"

He looked at his hands as a heavy silence entered the room. "I can't tell you."

She walked across the wool runner and sat on the wood chest. "I guess you can't see my treasures then."

He glanced at her with wry humor, but the flirtatious light soon faded from his eyes, and he sighed.

"It was dark belowdecks," he said slowly, "the air ports too small and too few to offer light or a fresh breeze. I had to crawl. The ceiling was low, too low to stand. I followed the sounds: the cries, the iron manacles striking. The smell was foul, putrid. I found the slaves, chained together tightly without space to move. Naked. Filthy. A woman nursed a dead babe at her breast. I . . . I set about my duty and unlocked their shackles."

He looked into the firelight as if seeking escape from the memory.

"How many were belowdecks?" she whispered, aghast.

"Two hundred and fifty."

A staggering figure.

Amy had suffered over the years, too. She had endured hunger and isolation and hopelessness, but she suspected the depth of misery Edmund had encountered aboard the slaver alien even to her.

"Is that why Quincy takes to the opiate? To forget about the ordeal at sea?"

"No."

"Did he kill someone aboard the slaver? A woman?"

"No!" he said sharply, eyes fierce. "He's not a murderer."

"He thinks he is."

He quieted at that. After a short pause, he confessed, "It's our mother. Quincy believes he killed the woman."

She gasped. "What?"

Edmund rubbed his head, scratching his scalp. "She died in childbirth to the pup. The damn fool thinks it's his fault."

"I understand." Amy sighed. "He feels guilty about her death."

"He's got no reason to feel guilty about it; he didn't do anything wrong."

"He thinks he did, though."

"Aye," he grumbled. "That's the trouble. And I can't convince him otherwise, I'm afraid."

She looked at her hands, rubbed them together. "I suppose it's only fair that you learn some of my secrets now."

She carefully removed the iron key from around her neck, knelt beside the chest, her skirts pooling, and unlocked it.

He hunkered beside her as she pushed up the cumbersome top and revealed the assortment of curios: a gentleman's top hat, a crinoline, silk fans.

"Why so many gloves?"

At the low timbre in his voice, she shivered. "They remind me of my mother." She opened one of the twelve boxes. "She used to wear gloves just like these. I purchased one pair, then another, searching for the right match."

He fingered the soft white leather. "And do you think, if you surround yourself with these knickknacks, you will recapture the past?"

She closed the glove box, pinching his fingers between the cardboard; he was tardy in pulling them away.

"I want to remember the past."

"Why do you want to remember painful memories?"

"I don't want to remember the bad memories," she said stiffly. "There were good ones, too."

"Your mother kissing you good night?" He fixed his sharp eyes on her. "Your father tweaking your nose?"

"That's right."

She swallowed the knot of tears forming in her throat. "What is this about?" She closed the chest and locked it. "Why did you come here, Edmund?"

"I think it a good idea we look for your parents."

She scrambled off the floor and treaded toward the firelight, hugging her upper arms. She stared at the snapping flames, seeking warmth. "Why?"

"If your parents are alive, don't you want to see them again?"

She watched as his shadow moved across the ground, approaching her. She burrowed her fingernails into her arms. "It's a waste of time; it's been too long."

As she gazed into the firelight, fuzzy images stormed her mind: a garden filled with fragrant blossoms, a rambunctious puppy, a bright nursery room. The memories welled in her head with such vividness, she almost sensed . . .

A set of thick arms circled her midriff. "I didn't mean to upset you, Amy.

"Really?" She struggled in his tight embrace, breathless, as the comfort of past dreams and the uncertainly of her future prospects clashed together in her heart. "Then what did you mean to do? Offer me false hope?"

"Amy?"

She pushed away from him; she staggered. "I have *one* chance to better myself as a lady's maid or companion, and you want me to dream about lost parents and faerie-tale endings." She brushed her hair away, the tresses trapped between her trembling lips. "Well, I won't be distracted from my goal."

"I don't want to distract you."

"Liar!"

The man's sensual lips firmed. "What did you call me?"

"My parents are gone." She swatted at the wretched tears that welled in her eyes, burned her sight. "I'm not going to waste my time and effort hunting ghosts. Get out, Edmund."

"Amy," he drawled, "what the devil's come over you?"

"There's nothing the matter with me. I won't be pushed about, is all. I won't let you torment me!"

She had suffered under Madame Rafaramanjaka's cruel dictatorship. She had endured the leers and abuse from the patrons at the Pleasure Palace. She had evaded the kidnappers. She had survived—alone—for most of her life. And she wasn't going to let the disdainful, arrogant scoundrel taunt her with worthless dreams about long-lost parents for his amusement and selfish curiosity.

"Torment you?" He glared at her. "Are you daft?"

"I said get out!"

He bristled. After a moment, he growled, "I know you've been without friends for so long you suspect a saving hand, but I am not your enemy. I am your friend. And you damn well *don't* treat a friend with such disrespect. Why don't you learn *that* lesson before you tout yourself a lady."

He stormed from the room, leaving Amy biting back her tears.

Chapter 14

At breakfast the next morning, Edmund gathered a portion of every serving: biscuits with jam, smoked ham and cheese. He devoured the steamy fare without prejudice. As his belly filled, so, too, did the troublesome thoughts in his head. He had hoped to bury the haunting reflections with a hearty meal, but the shouts from last night's row with Amy still resounded in his mind.

Did the lass really think him such a beast, he would *torment* her?

He frowned at the disturbing thought. He might be a scoundrel, but he wasn't a bloody sadist. What was Amy thinking, accusing him of such loathsome conduct? Hadn't he protected her, sheltered her for more than a sennight? Hadn't he vowed to find her a respectable livelihood? And yet she still deemed him a reprobate. Why? Had she always harbored such a low opinion of him?

The idea seized Edmund's imagination and he stiffened at the wretched prospect. If she considered him such a swine, why had she kissed him? What the devil was the matter with the girl?

Quincy entered the dining parlor, his features drooping, morose. He dropped into one of the sturdy chairs and sighed, massaging his temples.

"You look like shit," remarked Edmund.

Quincy ignored the surly comment, pegged him with a beseeching expression. "You have to talk with Will, Eddie."

"About what?"

"About letting me sail aboard the *Nemesis*. James is threatening to house me at Mayfair while you're both away at sea."

Edmund snorted. "I'm half inclined to let him. It'd be a fitting punishment for being so daft."

"I *can't* live with him, Eddie."

Edmund commiserated with his younger brother's plight. Quincy's misplaced grief and regret transcended their mother's death. He had watched their father mourn for the beloved woman over the years, and while no one had blamed the pup for her death, *he* had blamed himself. The foolish man believed he'd devastated all their lives with his birth, James's most of all, for the demise of their mother had pushed James into the role of caregiver. A role, Quincy suspected, James had loathed. Edmund, however, wasn't so sure James had despised the position; he had yet to relinquish it.

"No, I suppose you can't live with James. It'd drive you even deeper into the opium dens."

Edmund eyed his brother with scrutiny as a series of words from a mysterious stranger echoed in his head: *Have you come looking for salvation?*

"What do you find in the smoke, Quincy? Salvation?"

He lifted his eyes, his expression black. "Don't preach to me, Eddie. I hear enough sermons from James."

"Bite your tongue. I'm not James." He frowned. "But you're not going to find forgiveness for sins you didn't commit in the opium dens."

Quincy rubbed his brow, gnashed his teeth before he entreated, "Are you going to talk with Will?"

Edmund stuffed a biscuit into his mouth.

"I'll talk," he mumbled. "But I doubt he'll listen to me."

"Well, he won't listen to me." Quincy scratched his head, restless. "I've already quarreled with him."

William entered the room next. He glanced at his brothers with a critical glare before he assumed a chair and gathered the food onto his plate.

Quincy quickly excused himself and departed from the dining parlor, offering the brothers privacy.

"What?" snapped Edmund. "Now?"

There was still a fortnight before they had to set sail and resume their naval duties, but Quincy, it seemed, was too impatient to wait that long and learn his fate . . . or perhaps he was anxious to get more opium.

"What's going on?" from William.

Edmund sighed. He stroked his lips and chin, grooming himself for the confrontation. "We should take Quincy with us aboard the *Nemesis*."

The captain paused. "I've already talked with him about the matter."

And with James, surely, he thought.

Edmund persisted, "You can't leave Quincy with James."

"I can't leave him alone, either."

"You know what I mean, Will. Being with James will only make his nightmares worse. You know he feels guilty about Mother's death. He thinks he's ruined all our lives, and James's iron hand will only compound the guilt."

William observed him as if he was an oddity, a bloody ape capable of reason. "So what would you have me do?"

"Take him with us."

William wiped his mouth with the linen napkin. "You know I can't do that in his condition."

"He'll come off the opiate at sea, like last time. He always feels better at sea."

"And then he'll return to it when he comes home."

"We'll deal with that trouble when we return to London."

"*We* will?"

Edmund set his teeth together, raked his molars. He gritted, "Giving him to James won't make things better, and you know it."

The captain sighed. "I've lost my appetite."

"I'll take care of him aboard ship, Will."

"You're a seaman, not a nursemaid," he said sternly. "You have other duties to attend aboard ship."

"I'll do both."

"And when do you intend to sleep?"

"Damn it, Will!" He pounded the table with his fist, making the dishes dance. "You know it's the right thing to do. Why do you always listen to James?"

The man's lips firmed. "The decision is mine. *I* believe it's the right thing to do, to leave Quincy behind in London. And have you considered I might be right? That keeping him on land might sober him, encourage him to stop smoking the opiate?"

Edmund countered in a stiff voice, "And leaving him here to fight his demons alone might drive him deeper into the elusive smoke."

"Perhaps." William was thoughtful. "But there's nothing more I can do for him."

Edmund looked away from his brother as the blood in his veins burned. He wasn't so ready to give up on Quincy.

The butler stepped inside the room. "A letter, sir."

The servant handed the folded missive to Edmund. He recognized the penmanship in the address. The note was from John.

With swift movements, Edmund rent the red wax seal and scanned the epistle. As he read the words, his hot blood cooled, turned to ice.

"What's the matter?" said William.

Edmund's visage was stoic, like stone. He quit the dining parlor without answering his brother's query, and headed for the stairs. He scaled the carpeted steps in methodical strides, two at a time. Strapped for words, he moved through the passageway and paused beside the set of double doors depicting a jungle motif.

He gathered his errant thoughts and rapped at the door.

After a few moments of quiet, he knocked again.

"Amy?"

But she still refused to respond. He sighed and pushed open one of the doors without a proper invitation. He found the chamber empty.

"Where are you, Amy?" He inspected the adjoining dressing room. "I have important news."

However, the lass wasn't inside the room.

He frowned.

Where the devil was she?

Edmund next explored the sitting room, then the dining parlor again. He located William, who had regained his appetite and was eating his meal, but there was no proof that Amy had been inside the room, the other chairs and plates still untouched.

"*What* the devil is wrong?" demanded William.

Edmund departed once more without remarking about the situation, though his heart thumped with greater verve. He searched the rest of the house, including the kitchen and even the attic loft.

Amy was missing.

No, she wasn't missing, he thought grimly. She had deserted the house, run off after their unfriendly quarrel.

The daft girl!

Edmund scrunched the letter in his hand and shoved

it into his pocket before he vacated the town house and strutted through the streets of the St. James district, heading for Covent Garden.

It was there, amid the bustling traffic, he spotted the unruly minx, toting a leather bag, standing across the street from the Pleasure Palace in an idle manner.

He watched her for a brief time, observed her lonely figure as pedestrians scampered past her. She seemed fine. No bruises. No scuff marks on her skin. She was wearing a full green skirt with a fine white shirt tucked beneath a deep blue, form-fitted waistcoat with shiny brass buttons. The woman's long blond hair was un-secured, the wavy tresses falling the full length of her backside. She sported a woolly red cap; it highlighted her rosy lips.

Edmund warmed at the delightful, eclectic sight of her appearance. She had dressed in a hurry, he sus-pected. She wasn't hustling now, though. She seemed in low spirits; it gouged his soul to see her in such a manner. He relinquished his vantage point, crossing the busy thoroughfare.

He joined her on the other side of the lane, ap-proached her quietly. She noted his movements quickly, for her eyes darted in his direction, but she didn't scut-tle away. She remained rooted to the spot, lost amid the noisy streetgoers.

She looked at him glumly. "I thought it'd be easier to return to my old life."

Edmund regarded her thoughtfully, disarmed by the steady stream of emotions that teemed through his head.

He had failed to reflect upon the hollow, vast emptiness that had overwhelmed him at her disappearance. It wasn't until he'd reunited with her that his bones ached from the pressure of his girded muscles.

He eased the stiffness in his joints with a comfortable sigh. "You don't really want to go back to your old life, that's why you can't set foot inside the Pleasure Palace."

She pondered that, it seemed. He noted the lines across her brow.

"No," she said with passion in her voice. "That's not the reason. I just won't give the mad queen the satisfaction of hearing me beg."

Pride. He chuckled at that. She really was . . . He smoothed his lips and lowered his eyes.

Amy sighed. "I'm not really sure where I should go now."

"How about home?"

She looked at her brown leather walking boots. "What home?" She made a wry face. "I think I've overstayed my welcome at the town house, especially after what I said to you last night."

"No, not my home." He was hard again, his muscles taut. "Listen, Amy, I didn't mean to upset you when I mentioned your parents. I just wanted to prepare you."

An inattentive pedestrian bumped into her, and she, in turn, bumped into him, flushing. "Prepare me for what?"

He circled her arms with his fingers. She stiffened under the bold, public expression of intimacy, yet he maintained his embrace, for he suspected the lass was going to need the added support when he confessed his findings.

"I had a hunch about you . . . about your past."

Her eyes widened. He noted the shift in her breathing. It was deeper, louder.

She whispered, "What sort of hunch?"

"I received a note from a friend this morning. He's a Bow Street Runner and I had him look into old records, search through missing children reports . . . for you, Amy."

She paled. She dropped the bag at his feet.

He gripped her tighter. "I think I've located your parents; they've been looking for you these past fifteen years."

She licked her lips. "Fifteen?"

He teased her cheek, brushed the white flesh, stirring the blood, the life back into her features again. "If you're their daughter, you're one-and-twenty years old."

She snorted, still looking dazed. "I'm a lot older than I thought I'd be."

Her bravado was a distraction; it masked a welter of emotion that welled in her eyes. She wobbled even, and he steered her toward the nearest building's façade, dragging her bag with him.

He pressed her against the shop's stone wall, giving her more support. "I think you should meet them. I don't want to raise your hopes; I know you don't want to chase after ghosts from the past, but I've looked into the matter, and I believe it's important you meet the couple. I'll send word to them about you, set up a reunion."

"No!" She jumped. "You can't tell them I'm still alive." She grabbed his coat. "You can't let them know."

He fingered her wrists, so tight. As he stroked her thumping pulses, he murmured, "Let them know what?"

"Who I am," she returned weakly.

"You might be their daughter."

She chewed on her bottom lip, then: "I'm Zarsitti."

He pulled her rigid fingers away from his coat and hushed her with a few tender strokes across the brow. "You were Zarsitti. No one knows your true identity."

"The queen knows." The lass's voice quivered. "She's vindictive. She can tell them my past. And once my parents learn the truth, they'll regret my coming home. They'll wish I'd stayed lost . . . my parents."

She wavered as the possible truth fully impacted her thoughts.

Edmund circled her waist in support, dismissing the noisy snorts of disapproval from the bustling citygoers.

"Madame Rafaramanjaka won't betray your past, I assure you. She'll never get an audience with the couple who might be your parents," he said firmly. "Not *this* couple."

Amy blinked. "Why? Who are they?"

*   *   *

The party traveled along Brook Street, making their way toward Grosvenor Square. Servants fussed with the knockers and cleaned the front steps with brooms in preparation for the arrival of their wealthy masters and mistresses, who were making their way into Town for the start of the Season.

Edmund was seated beside Amy in the coach, James and Sophia positioned on the opposite squabs. The journey into the heart of Mayfair was a silent one in deference to Amy's comfort. The lass still looked bemused at the possible turn in her fortune. It was quiet inside the vehicle for another reason, too: the brothers were still at odds.

Edmund regarded Amy's profile; sleek, prim. He remembered her haughty manners in the rookeries, her distaste for the lower classes, her desire to better herself, and as he studied her aristocratic contours, he wondered how he'd overlooked her likely heritage . . . or perhaps he'd not wanted to see the blue-blooded indicators; perhaps he'd willfully ignored them.

She was covered in rich, honey yellow linen taffeta. The fine fabric fit her figure in snug fashion; it was especially designed for her shape. The piece was part of the new wardrobe Quincy had ordered for her. He had instructed the seamstress to create the dress from the best material—and had forwarded the bill to Edmund.

Edmund had lost his temper upon first reading the outrageous amount, but as soon as he'd witnessed Amy in the handsome garment, his dander had cooled. Now he admired her. He memorized the sight of her pristine features and meticulous coiffure, the locks styled and pinned in the current, smart manner with small butterfly hairpins.

She was lovely.

So lovely.

And she might part from him forever today, he reflected in a dour mood.

The vehicle rolled to a steady halt before the imperial dwelling. The magnificent structure boasted architectural artistry with its robust Ionic pilasters and proud, tall windows. Hand-crafted, wrought-iron gates and a marvelous lintel with an ancient coat of arms bedecked the main entrance.

Amy stared at the towering structure.

Edmund observed her fixed features; he noted her slightly trembling lips. The desire welled inside him to ease her anxiety. He wanted to take her mouth in a soft kiss. He wanted to hear her sigh in contentment, moan in arousal. He wanted to taste her one last, miserable time.

But he tamped down the unruly feeling. If she was a lady, she wasn't to be touched. Not by him. Not ever.

"Are you ready, Amy?" said Sophia.

She licked her lips and nodded.

Edmund and James exited the stationed coach first, assisting the ladies.

As soon as Amy's foot, sheathed in a sparkling, heeled shoe, stepped onto the pavement and clicked, she winced. She pulled away from them, and Edmund pinched her wrist, keeping her from fluttering off.

She looked at him with a beseeching expression to let her go, but she belonged at the town house in Mayfair; he sensed it. She belonged with her family.

Not with him.

"Come." Edmund tugged at her hand. "We're expected."

He sensed her fingers fold into fists. She desired to strike him; the intent welled in her eyes. But he firmly yanked her wrist, disabusing her of the unladylike gesture. She would have to fight with her words and her wiles, not with her fists. She would have to learn better decorum, adapt to her new way of life. The expectations placed upon her would be great, but she would survive the rigorous vetting. He knew it in his soul. She was a fighter.

"It's time to confront your past," he whispered.

She eyed him, willful, but the defiance in her soft green eyes soon gave way to submission. She had always wanted to be a lady. If the couple within the luxurious dwelling weren't her parents, her dream would be shattered; however, the dread in her heart didn't warrant an end to the investigation. There was no sense in turning away from the door now. She might be home.

Edmund steered her toward the front steps and rapped on the imposing entranceway with the decorative brass knocker.

It wasn't long before the couples were escorted inside the main parlor, the furnishings in sensuous, pastel shades, the wall hangings and draperies in splendor.

A large woodland scene on canvas with a thick, ornate frame stood above the white marble fireplace, the polished stone gleaming in the sunlight as the focal point of the room.

Edmund was unimpressed with the lavish surroundings, accustomed to the pomp, but Amy seemed awed. Moreover, she touched the fine woodwork and upholstery, her lips forming a small "ooh."

He regarded the celebrated dancer from the city's underworld as she traversed her potential new residence. The posh abode suited her, he reckoned. She might soon settle into her new life as a proper lady . . . and forget about him.

Footfalls encroached. Hard steps and quick, lighter taps. Edmund eyed the parlor door just as the Duke and Duchess of Estabrooke entered the spacious room.

The older couple remained still for a time, silent. They looked between Amy and Sophia, and at last settled their thoughts on Amy. She had fair hair and green eyes that matched those of the duchess: a woman in her late fifties. It was she who first stepped toward Amy, her lips, her chin quivering.

Amy curtsied with aplomb; she had practiced the greeting myriad times with Quincy. Edmund still detected the fretful glimmer in her eyes, though, the uncertainty, the mistrust. He sensed her vulnerability, too. He suffered it with her.

"Your Grace," Amy said in deference to the woman who might be her mother.

"None of that." The duchess's words clipped as she

struggled with her tears. She rasped, "Come here, my dear."

Amy stepped toward the matron with obvious restraint, but the duchess was quick to do away with formality. She embraced Amy in a warm, hearty hug.

The duke eyed their reunion with a blank expression. "The physician is waiting in the salon," he said tightly.

Amy glanced at the man. "A doctor? I'm feeling fine."

"My daughter possesses a distinguishing mark."

The kiss.

The duke regarded her with an inscrutable air. "We've had many young ladies come forward, claiming to be our lost child. However, there is only one way to be sure. You, of course, will not refuse the examination."

Amy's lips firmed. "No, of course not."

"Very well, then." The duke offered a curt nod. "Off with you both."

The duchess simpered. It was clear from her mannerisms she had recognized and acknowledged Amy as her missing daughter. The duke needed more tangible proof, however.

"Come, Amy," said the duchess in a shaky voice.

The ladies headed toward the door.

Amy furtively glanced at Edmund. The intensity, the vividness in her eyes captured his breath. He was tempted to snatch her away from the duchess and carry her off. He firmed his muscles instead, keeping his hands secured at his backside.

He smiled at her.

Good-bye, Amy.

As soon as she passed through the doorway, Edmund looked at the floor, his head smarting.

"Where did you find her?" the duke questioned James, his features stony. "What has she been doing all these years?"

"I understand she was raised in a foundling asylum," the captain returned. "After that, she worked as a maid for various respectable families."

"I see."

The stiffness in the duke's voice betrayed his displeasure. He had anticipated an unseemly upbringing. He had expected a garish tale about thievery or prostitution perhaps. But the Hawkins brothers had vowed to keep her occupation at the gentlemen's club a secret. Edmund wasn't sure how much of the falsehood the duke had believed, though.

"A maid?" he said primly. "And why do you believe she's my daughter?"

James said in an even manner, "She resembles you and the duchess."

The duke remained stoic. "And you associate with maids, Captain Hawkins?"

Sophia lowered her brow and intervened with "*I* associate with maids, Your Grace. As you might know, the captain and I are recently wed." She looped her hand through her husband's arm. "I'm in the process of acquiring staff for my household here in Duke Street— we are neighbors, you and I—and I was prepared to offer the young lady a position."

"I see," he said again.

"Why was the girl kidnapped all those years ago?" wondered Sophia.

The duke bristled. "As a man of great wealth and importance, I suspected it a case of avarice, however, the kidnappers never contacted us with a ransom demand."

"As she evaded her kidnappers," from James, "the bounders had no cause to contact you for the ransom. She was lost to them."

"She was lost to us all," he returned.

Until now, thought Edmund.

A few minutes later, a servant appeared with a note card from the physician. The footman handed the paper to the austere duke, who quickly parted the folds and scanned the missive.

The man paled.

It was favorable news, Edmund estimated. Otherwise, the duke would have turned bloodred from rage at the thought that another fraud had entered his midst.

Amy was his daughter.

Edmund rejoiced for her . . . and mourned for himself. A part of him had wanted to keep her as . . .

He shrugged at the half-formulated thought.

"I must thank you, Captain Hawkins," the duke said quietly, "for bringing Amy home."

"It was an honor to serve as the young lady's chaperone, Your Grace." He looked at Edmund. "However, the accolades belong to my brother. It was he who first suspected her your daughter."

The duke turned toward Edmund, and hardened. "I see. Might I have a private word with you, Mr. Hawkins?"

The crispness in his voice raised Edmund's hackles. Slowly he nodded his assent. "Your Grace."

The duke departed from the parlor in brisk strides.

His mood dark, Edmund followed the tall, slim man through the ornate passageway, and into a masculine-looking study with large, dark furniture and thick, leather-bound tomes.

"Thank you for returning my daughter, Mr. Hawkins."

"You're welcome, Your Grace."

The duke rounded the wide writing desk, the papers, the books all neatly positioned across the surface. He lowered himself into a high-back chair and removed a quill from an ivory inkwell. "Will five thousand pounds suffice?"

Edmund listened to the scratching sound coming from the fine-tipped pen, making strokes across the mysterious paper.

He frowned. "Pardon me, Your Grace?"

"For your trouble, Mr. Hawkins."

Edmund hardened at the distasteful insinuation. There was a burning feeling at the backs of his eyes as he watched the duke make out the check in the unseemly amount.

He said tautly, "It was no trouble, Your Grace."

The man paused. He eyed Edmund coldly before he rent the paper apart and started anew. "Ten thousand then?"

"I don't want your bloody money," he growled.

Slowly the duke returned the pen into the inkwell. He placed his hands across his desk and folded his fingers, glaring at the young seaman. "Then what do you want?"

Edmund curbed his temper, and said with more restraint, "Nothing, Your Grace."

The man's eyes darkened. "My wife and I have suffered sorely these last fifteen years, searching for our daughter, hoping for her return. And you discover her in your brother's household, working as a maid. Do you expect me to believe that? Do you expect me to allow scandalous tittle-tattle to be spread about Town? Now what do you want for your silence?"

"I don't want anything from you, Your Grace. I am honored to return Amy—"

The duke glowered.

"—Lady Amy Laetitia Peele to her rightful home. I hope she will be happy."

The man narrowed his steely gray eyes on Edmund. "Have you befriended my daughter?"

"Your Grace?"

"I know who you are, Mr. Hawkins. I hope the last few years you've spent playing gentleman in society has taught you one important lesson."

The fire in Edmund's blood burned with reckless intensity. He pressed his lips together. Tight. He didn't deign to answer the remark. He'd shout an obscenity, he was sure.

The duke pressed onward: "A woman of noble blood does not associate with a seaman."

The truthful words cut Edmund's heart with painful precision.

He offered a curt bow before he vacated the study with long, heavy strides. He returned to the parlor. There, James and Sophia awaited him.

Edmund said tersely, "Let's go home."

He stalked toward the main hall as if hellhounds dogged his heels.

James followed him toward the front door, inquiring, "What was that about?"

"The duke wanted to express his thanks in private, is all," he gritted.

The three unwelcome visitors departed from the imperial dwelling and entered the waiting coach, setting off for home. All the while, Edmund mulled over a dismal certainty—he wasn't good enough for Lady Amy.

Chapter 15

"If you dance with a gentleman at a ball, then see him the next afternoon while riding in Hyde Park, are you expected to acknowledge him with a greeting?"

Amy munched on her bottom lip. "Yes."

"No. No. No." Mr. Hurst pinched his shriveled lips together, making a sour face. "A single dance does *not* imply an acquaintanceship. You ride past him. Ignore him."

Amy sighed and leaned back in her seat, her head throbbing.

"Why don't we rest?" suggested Helen, the Duchess of Estabrooke, her voice tender in the heated room.

Mr. Hurst bowed. "As you wish, Your Grace."

As he sauntered from the drawing parlor, murmuring something about "barbarity," Amy eyed his scrawny figure and imagined snapping it in half.

She looked at her mother. "I'm sorry, Mama."

The woman smiled and poured her a cup of tea. Together at the small round table, the ladies sipped their refreshments without the intrusive presence of the strict tutor.

"You're doing fine, my dear."

"Not according to Mr. Hurst," she returned petulantly.

"Mr. Hurst wants you to shine during the ball tomorrow tonight. We all do."

Amy shifted in her chair at the mention of the ball: her debut ball. After three months of endless lessons and preparations for her grand reentrance into society, the time had approached for her fashionable come-out, and her return to posh civilities had to be seamless. If not, there'd be rumors about her character, her reputation. One blunder and her tainted past might come to light and ruin her—and her parents.

"Are you all right, my dear?"

"I'm a little nervous about the ball, is all."

Amy sipped her tea—without slurping. She still remembered the scoundrel's lessons in good manners with crisp precision, while her tutor's lessons flittered away. She still remembered the seaman's reprimands, his tutelage . . . in matters beyond etiquette.

You should learn to have more fun . . . to be spontaneous.

She closed her eyes and sensed his firm fingers at her waist, cupping her hip bones in a teasing manner.

There's more to life than rules and being in control.

Such soft, kissable lips, she reflected.

Stop trying to fight Fate, Amy.

She tightened as she imagined his mouth pressed warmly over hers. The sensual memory unsettled her nerves, already taut as a result of the approaching festivities, and she dismissed the unwelcome intrusion with a brisk shake of the head. She shouldn't think about him. Not him. It was improper. She'd have to make a greater effort to heed Mr. Hurst's shrill-pitched sermons, for she needed him to buff away her rough mannerisms.

All her rough mannerisms.

"Don't be nervous, my dear," said the duchess in encouragement. "Your dress arrived this morning. We'll have a fitting soon after our instruction with Mr. Hurst. How are you progressing in your piano lessons?"

Amy grimaced.

"I see." The duchess chortled. "You disliked your music lessons even as a child."

"I remember." She had remembered more and more about her past since her return to the town house in Mayfair. "I also remember a porcelain doll named . . . Regina. I had a puppy, too."

"Sasha. A gift from a Russian diplomat. She died two years after you'd disappeared. I cried for that dog." She appeared sheepish. "I can get you another pooch, if you'd like."

"No, thank you." She looked at her mother with fondness. The duchess had welcomed her home with exuberance and love, fussed over her like she was still a babe. It'd troubled Amy at first; she'd grown accustomed to her own company, her own way of thinking. But soon she'd sensed their bond, still unbroken after so many years, and the uneasiness had faded from their relationship. "I've too much to look after already."

Helen set aside her tea. "I don't mean to upset you, my dear, but I feel I must prepare you for some unfortunate news." She looked at her hands. "I've received a note from Lord Gravenhurst."

Amy stiffened. "Oh?"

"He sends his regrets; he will not be able to attend the ball due to pressing estate matters."

"I see." Amy also set aside her tea, the fine porcelain unsteady in her hands. "How did Father take the news?"

The duchess eyed her with a half smile. "Well."

Amy snorted inwardly. Her father was furious at the report, she was sure. She wasn't the least bit put off by it, though, content to enjoy the evening without the lord's presence; however, her father likely considered it the greatest affront that her own fiancé wasn't going to be in attendance at the ball.

Amy sighed. Apparently she had been betrothed to the Marquis of Gravenhurst since she was a babe, and her father was determined to see the engagement honored. The gossip surrounding her unexpected return didn't make her the most eligible female in society, even if she was a duke's daughter. Her father believed it her only chance at a respectable match—and the only way to save their family name from vicious tittle-tattle.

"Don't fret, Mama. It'll all turn out well." She mustered a smile. "I'm sure the night will be a smashing success even without the marquis's presence."

"A few more steps, Will."

Edmund supported his brother's cumbersome weight, hooking him around the waist as they exited the hackney coach, keeping the injured captain's arm slung over his shoulder. He guided him toward the town house as the rain pounded their backsides, banged on the secured door with the tip of his boot.

James appeared, looking cantankerous.

"What are *you* doing here?" demanded Edmund.

The former brigand hoisted William, wheezing, into the house. "I received word from one of your tars about the accident."

Edmund remained rooted in the doorway, the rain pellets slipping off his shoulders and pooling at his feet. There was a bloody spy aboard the *Nemesis*? He shouldn't be surprised by his brother's skullduggery, and yet . . .

Edmund balled his fingers. He watched as James steered William's movements, commanded the staff as if he still resided at the town house and was master of the domain. In a few moments, the party had bustled up the elongated stairway.

Feeling the fire in his toes, Edmund headed for the study. He entered the dark room and slammed the door closed. He wasn't needed anymore, so he settled into a wing chair and propped his wet, dirty boots on the table, staring through the window at the raging storm, breathing sharply through his nose.

"What happened?"

Edmund detected Quincy's voice. He glanced toward the corner of the room, where his brother was seated in the shadows, observing the tempest, too.

"William was shot," he retuned brusquely.

"How did it happen?"

Edmund sighed and rubbed his tired brow, stained with rainwater and sweat. "We had a slaver in our sights." He paused, the memories welling in his head. "She put up a fight. The captain took a bullet in the chest."

Edmund quickly pressed his palms over the gash in his brother's chest. He watched the dark blood ooze between his fingers, sensed its warmth as it bathed his hands.

"We almost lost him to the fever and the infection," he said pensively.

Quincy shifted from the corner seat and approached the small table peppered with liquor bottles. He filled a glass with spirits, corking the decanter again with the glass stopper.

He handed Edmund the drink. "Here."

Edmund took the offered tonic and downed the fiery liquid in one greedy gulp. He stroked his unruly beard. "We needed your healing hand aboard the *Nemesis*."

His brother had steady fingers with a needle and thread. A sound healer, he had attended many an injured seaman during a pirate battle.

Quincy returned to the corner seat. "Then you should have taken me with you."

He sighed. "You know I tried to convince William to bring you aboard ship."

"I know."

Edmund looked over his shoulder and eyed him thoughtfully. "How are you, Quincy?"

It had been three months since he had last seen his younger brother. James had compelled Quincy to reside with him in Mayfair during their voyage at sea. And Quincy's uncharacteristic reticence told Edmund the rooming hadn't been pleasant.

Edmund thumbed the empty glass and looked back out the window. "How is she?"

The words had escaped his lips before he'd thought too much about them. The warm spirits in his belly aggravated the bile already stirring in the bowel of his soul. He pressed the glass between his fingers with greater vim.

"I haven't seen her," said Quincy, "but I've heard there's a ball in her honor tomorrow night."

"I don't suppose we received an invitation?"

"No. Belle did, though."

Edmund snorted and rolled his thumb and forefinger in the corners of his burning eyes. Of course there wasn't an invitation in the post for him. He might suspect the duke and duchess privy to his tour at sea, that they hadn't issued an invitation card because they believed him out of the country, but he doubted Their Graces followed his movements. It was much more likely they believed him in Town—and had simply chosen to snub him.

"Do you want to go and see her?" wondered Quincy. "Amy, I mean."

"I know who you mean." He scratched his beard. "It's better if I don't go and see her."

He wasn't good enough to be in her company, according to Their Graces. The couple had deliberately omitted him from the guest list, and *he* had found the girl, returned her to her rightful home. But after five years in high society, he was accustomed to the proud and arrogant ways of the *ton* . . . and perhaps the duke and duchess were justified in their unfriendly gesture. As a former pirate, he wasn't proper company for Lady Amy.

"I can get the invitation from Belle," suggested the meddlesome pup.

"No."

"You can just look at Amy from across the dance floor."

"No."

"All right, one waltz."

Edmund glared at his brother.

"I'll even come with you, Eddie."

"No!"

"Fine." He shrugged. "I'm off to see Will." He headed for the door. As he opened the wood, he paused. "It's just as well you don't go to the ball, Eddie . . . James would disapprove."

Edmund squared his jaw. He turned his head away from his troublesome brother . . . but he didn't reject the suggestion again.

Chapter 16

∽◦◦◦◦◦∽

There was a glamorous assortment of high society guests. Floral garlands festooned the many tall windows, the bright blooms bringing natural splendor into the sumptuous interior. The lavish drapery matched the yellow roses and white lilies, fresh from the hothouses. With heaps of elongated candles around the rich ballroom, the circular chamber scintillated under the dappling glow.

Amy absorbed the lush atmosphere, her senses teeming with delight. It was her first public appearance, and she was giddy with the fanfare in her honor. The flourishing spectacle had an unfortunate side effect that tapered some of her enthusiasm, though.

"I truly don't know what happened to our invitation."

The Duchess of Wembury frowned. It was really a slight wrinkling of the lips. Otherwise, she maintained her poise. She was a dramatic presence in the bustling ballroom with her striking features and elegant satin dress, shimmering in the light like liquid gold.

Amy was parched for her company; standing next to the attractive woman deflected some of the attention away from her. That was the unpleasant consequence of her exhibit, the curious stares. The inquisitive looks reminded her of her time at the Pleasure Palace, being showcased on stage, scrutinized, lusted after . . . stared at.

"The card was sitting on my desk this morning when my brother Quincy came to visit, and then *poof*, it was gone."

Amy half listened to the mystery of the missing invitation card, comforted instead by the duchess's companionship. She possessed a high rank, yet she didn't exhibit any of the fussy qualities her contemporaries so often insisted on as proper etiquette. Amy sensed her tight bone corset a little less clinching in the woman's sociable presence. In truth, she had wanted to meet the duchess for some time. She was Edmund's sister . . . and Amy felt closer to Edmund being so near his kin.

"How is Quincy?" wondered Amy, stifling her other, inappropriate reflections. "I hope he's well."

"Yes, he's fine." The woman's umber eyes narrowed. "Are you suggesting there might be something amiss with my brother?"

Amy balked. She quickly gathered her thoughts, so unruly even after months of rigorous training. She had studied and memorized countless rules about etiquette, her tutor strict. She had been primped and polished for her grand debut, yet still she possessed the improper tendency to blurt out her innermost thoughts. It was obvious from Mirabelle's befuddled expression she was ignorant about her brother's condition.

"Not a'tall." Amy rushed to conceal her blunder with "I just haven't seen him for such a long time."

"It's been three months, I understand." The duchess looked at her thoughtfully. "You've not formed an attachment to Quincy, have you?"

Amy groaned inside her head. She gathered a deep breath and righted her disorderly thoughts. "I've not formed an attachment to Quincy, Your Grace. I mean, he's very charming, but I've only feelings of friendship for him. He was my tutor for a time," she rambled. "He helped me become a lady."

"Quincy?"

Amy squirmed in her corset, feeling constricted again. "I owe him, I suppose, for his guidance. It was very much appreciated. In truth, I owe all your brothers a great debt of gratitude."

Mirabelle smiled. "Think nothing of it, my dear. You protected Edmund from harm when he'd lost his memory, and then my brothers returned you to your family. The debt is paid."

And yet Amy's thoughts so often returned to the scoundrel of St. James. He was at sea, patrolling the coast of Africa. She had heard tales of sickness and savages, fierce battles with determined rigs unwilling to give up their slave cargoes. The images of Edmund wounded . . . sinking . . . fighting for survival filled her head. She had learned to quash the dark reflections whenever they pressed upon her. She had learned to ease her troubled heartbeat with a few measured breaths.

"Are you all right, Lady Amy?"

"I was just thinking about your brothers at sea. Do you ever worry about their welfare, Your Grace?"

"All the time, I'm afraid." She sighed. "I've learned to live with the underlying anxiety." She rubbed Amy's hands. "But don't *you* fret about the Hawkins brothers. They've been through scrapes and catastrophes, and they've weathered them all. I've learned that about my brothers, too." She gestured toward the ballroom. "You should be thinking about your come-out party, Lady Amy. How do you like your new position as a woman of consequence?"

Amy's employment at the Pleasure Palace had trained her to perform in front of strangers, and while she wasn't dancing on a stage anymore, she still had to summon every ounce of her theatrical savvy to mingle with the critical *haute monde*. She wasn't one of them. Not really. She had the same blue blood, but she still had to wear an invisible veil to conceal her true thoughts and feelings, her past.

Her wretched past. It was impossible for her to escape it. Even now the spacious room was filled with myriad "strangers," and yet she recognized many of the male faces. The gentlemen now had lofty titles and accomplishments that went along with their familiar features; however, she remembered them without their polished veneers. She remembered them when they had salivated at her feet, bombarded her with requests for private rendezvous.

Amy shuddered. It hounded her almost every moment of the day, the dreaded prospect that her sinful spell as Zarsitti might be revealed. She often imagined the horrid news spreading across the city, shaming her parents.

Amy sighed. "It's overwhelming, Your Grace."

The duchess patted her arm. "Yes, it is, my dear. I was thrust into the position of duchess without much knowledge about the post or the duty. Give it some time. You'll be fine."

Amy simpered at the much-needed encouragement. "Thank you, Your Grace."

The duchess smiled in return, but her features quickly gathered in bewilderment. "What are you doing here, Eddie?"

Amy bristled.

Edmund?

Impossible. The man was at sea. And yet she sensed his familiar figure at her backside, warming her very bones with his presence. Her heart thumped with greater energy, every pulsing beat unraveling her delicate pretense.

He was home . . . On land . . . Here . . . Beside her.

"I've come to ask Lady Amy to dance," he said in a low voice.

Slowly she turned around and confronted the handsome scoundrel. The noisy din from the other guests, the animated candlelight intensified. It all seemed so much more palpable. She was sure everyone inside the ballroom was privy to her scandalous thoughts, her flickering heartbeats.

She licked her lips as she perused him, noting every detail. He was dressed in formal evening wear, the dark, finely tailored ensemble hugging him with precision, setting off his most admirable features, like his wide shoulders and his sinewy legs. She fanned herself with the silk accoutrement secured at her wrist, eyeing his smooth cheekbones, his square chin. She yearned to rub her fingers over his mouth, so sensual, so inviting.

She dashed the unfitting thoughts. He was safe, untouched by danger . . . and yet that wasn't true. He had evaded serious injury, even death at sea, but danger still manifested from his pores, tempting her, coaxing her from her prim position as a lady, bidding Zarsitti into the light.

Amy pinched her bottom lip between her teeth as he looked at her with fierce regard, the smoldering stare imploring: *Dance with me, Zarsitti.*

Mirabelle interjected, "But you're supposed to be at sea for another six months!"

He kissed his excitable sister on the flushed cheek. "We returned home early, Belle."

"Why?" she snapped.

"I'll visit with you tomorrow," he promised. "I'll tell you the story then. Why don't you dance with your husband?" He set his fine eyes on Amy again. "I'm presently engaged with Lady Amy."

He clasped her hand with confidence and guided her toward the dance floor. She released the fan, let it dangle from the cord at her wrist, as the desire to move her hips and undulate her belly welled inside her. She wanted to dance with Edmund. She wanted to dance for him.

She looked at his strong, robust hand. It was wrapped around her slim fingers. She wedged the appendages deeper between his palm, seeking a firmer, unbreakable connection. He responded to her probing pokes, gripping her more tightly before he clinched her waist in a snug embrace.

The heat from his touch, the security that radiated from his presence, lured her into a forbidden entanglement. She breathed with greater zest in his arms. It was as if he was the one missing piece from the ball preventing her from thoroughly enjoying herself, and now that he had arrived, her spirit danced.

But as soon as Amy detected the Duchess of Wembury's audible groan, the enchantment shattered, and her muscles stiffened at the prospect that she was making a spectacle of herself with Edmund.

She struggled, a cold sweat coming over her. "We can't do this, Edmund."

"Yes, we can," he said suavely as he whirled with her across the ballroom. "We've danced before."

"No, you don't understand," she said, almost frantic. "It's improper. I'm—"

"Shhh . . . I've missed you, Amy."

And with those whispered words the defiance in her soul passed away, like an ailing body taking its final breath after a hardy battle with death. And without the defiance in her soul, there was only the pleasurable feeling of being trapped between the scoundrel's arms . . . and savoring the delicious sensation.

"What are you doing here, Edmund?"

He tsked, his sensual lips snapping. "Is the music too loud? I said, I've come to dance with you, Amy."

"I'm not deaf, but you've not traveled the ocean for a waltz."

He fingered her spine like a violin player. "Perhaps I have."

"Bullocks," she mouthed.

He smiled at her tartness, his eyes teasing, and she shivered in her bones, charmed by the coy expression that so often hung from his churlish brow.

"What about your naval duty?" she charged.

"Our patrol ended early; the captain was injured."

As his lush lips thinned, her heart swelled in her breast. "Is William all right?"

"He will be," he returned with confidence.

"What happened?"

"He was shot in battle."

Amy gasped. "Shot?" She glanced at the duchess in distress. "You have to tell your sister!"

"I will. Tomorrow."

"What are you doing here, dancing?" She glowered at him. "Why aren't you at home, nursing your brother?"

He snorted. "I'm not needed at the house." The bitterness in his voice was thick. "James is there."

"Are you *still* at odds with your brother?"

"I don't want to talk about him. I've come to see you, Amy." The heat in his words charred her innards. "Are you happy?" he murmured. "Is it everything you dreamed it would be?"

"Why do you ask me that?" She sensed every pair of eyes on her, ogling her, cutting into her like a hundred pinpricks. She added peevishly, "To rest your mind?"

He frowned. "You're unhappy then?"

"I didn't say that," she snapped, "but I belong here. Happiness isn't a consideration."

"Do you dislike your parents?"

"No, of course not." She huffed. "I love my parents. I've always loved my parents."

"The balls. The dresses. The respectable company. It *is* what you've always wanted, isn't it?"

"I *didn't* say I was unhappy."

He twirled with her across the polished wood floor with aplomb. "And yet you are unhappy."

"I'm overwhelmed."

"You're not overwhelmed," he said, thumbing her spine, rubbing the knobs of bone in slow and teasing movements. "My sister might believe that rubbish, but I know you better than that, Amy. You've been dreaming and preparing for this event for most of your life."

Flustered, she stammered, "I-I'm afraid then."

"Of what?"

"Of disappointing my parents."

"Perhaps. But there's more to it than that." He eyed her with stern reproach. "Why are you lying to me?"

"Why don't you just tell me why you think I'm unhappy." She twisted her lips. "*You* know me best, don't you?"

As he guided her with ease, mixing effortlessly with the other couples, he maintained his sharp blue eyes on her, ruminating. "I think there's something missing from your life."

She sucked in a deep breath. "Like what?"

"Fun."

She exhaled slowly. "I don't have fun, remember?"

"A pity." He whispered, "You once had fun with me."

She bristled. The banter, the seductive repartee had to come to a surcease. If he persisted in the intimate manner, he'd ruin more than her reputation; he'd devastate her fragile heart with memories and promises of things that might have been . . . but would never be.

"You have to leave the ball."

Now!

He frowned. "Why?"

"Because . . . I will never be happy so long as you're in my life. You don't belong here, Edmund."

He stiffened. "I see."

A darkness entered his eyes. It squeezed at her breast, the discomfort, the shame she had caused him, but it was the only way to disentangle herself from his bewitching spell. She *had* to part from him. She was promised to another man.

"I don't want to cause you unrest, Lady Amy," he said in crisp fashion.

As the music died, he coldly escorted her back to his waiting sister. There, the duchess was conversing with her youngest brother, Quincy. Perhaps grilling him, by the looks of their heated exchange. When the scamp noticed Amy's approach, he smiled. She returned the convivial gesture; however, she felt nothing but a distaste in her soul.

She felt like a cur.

Edmund bowed. "You won't ever have to see me again, Lady Amy."

Chapter 17

$\sim\!\!\!\sim\!\!\!\infty\!\!\!\sim$

A my traveled through the rose-paneled passageway, making her way toward her private suite.
She was fagged, the merrymaking at an end. As her
bones ached, she wanted nothing more than to snug-
gle under the coverlets and dream—dream away the
night's events.

The exchange with Edmund pressed on her thoughts.
She imagined his sturdy embrace, his soulful blue eyes.
She envisioned the twinkling smile that so often lurked
beneath his sardonic expression. The sound of his deep
voice still rumbled in her breast, the resounding timbre
making her shiver.

She sighed as the warm sentiments gave way to
more disturbing reflections. The memory of her cal-
lous conduct still made her flinch. She had not desired
to hurt Edmund, but he'd captured her imagination in
an illicit manner. Musing about him—about a life with
him—was a forbidden dream.

She belonged to another man.

"Amy?"

She paused, bemused, her thoughts tumbling in discord. Retreating a few footfalls, she stepped through the study's door frame and smiled in a weak manner.

"Yes, Father."

"I'd like a word with you, Amy."

Her pulse quickened as she entered the large room. With fretful strides, she approached her father, his arms folded at his backside. He stood behind the wide and ancient desk, watching her closely as she traversed the long wool runner.

George Peele, the Duke of Estabrooke, was a tall figure with a slim build. His brusque manner and rigid countenance offered the impression that the dignified gentleman was dispassionate. He was rational and prudent, a stern patriarch, yet he possessed passion. He concealed a passionate temper.

Amy remembered the night in vivid detail. She had furtively sneaked belowstairs, knowing her mysterious fiancé had been summoned to the house. Desiring to meet the fellow she was intended to marry, she had witnessed a far more alarming exchange between the duke and her fiancé:

"It's been fifteen years, Estabrooke! Do you really expect me to honor the betrothal?"

"I expect you to honor your word. Or will you shame your family name by breaking the contract?"

"And if she had not returned? Did you think I would've waited for her forever?"

"You haven't wed another in that time, so the point is moot. You will honor the vow you made at her birth!"

"I made that vow as a boy of one-and-twenty."

"You were of legal age and your father's successor. You are duty bound to keep your promise. Do not think I've forgotten your past indiscretions, Gravenhurst. I hope you've learned from your former mistakes, that you will do what is right."

"Yes, Your Grace."

Amy chilled. The biting "Yes, Your Grace" still haunted her thoughts. The curt words had underlined her fiancé's true feelings toward her, his repressed contempt, yet theirs was a necessary union, for she'd been apart from society for fifteen years. A hasty marriage to a respectable gentleman was of the utmost importance; it'd safeguard her reputation, protect her family from gossip.

Amy peered at her father with solemnity.

"How did you enjoy yourself tonight, Amy?"

"I enjoyed myself very much," she returned, maintaining a steady inflection in her voice. "It was a lovely evening, Father."

"I'm glad to hear that." The man's gray eyes darkened. "I spotted you with that seaman on the dance floor."

Amy's heart fluttered. "Yes, he came to the ball with the Duke and Duchess of Wembury."

She had emphasized the couple's title, raising her voice, fashioning more pomp. If she reminded her parent that Edmund was related to such a prestigious family, he might frown at her less.

"I see." The duke's lips firmed. "How very bohemian of the seaman to disregard convention, to attend the ball on his brother-in-law's coattails."

She winced. "If it wasn't for Mr. Hawkins, I might still be lost to you, Father."

"Yes," he drawled. "About that, Amy."

The scoundrel's kinship with the ducal couple had clearly failed to meet her father's ostentatious standards. And as she had danced with the "bohemian," she imagined her parent's great displeasure, his ire at the improper spectacle.

She lowered her eyes, avoiding the stern patriarch's cutting stare. If he was disappointed in her for waltzing with the mariner, what would he think to know she was smitten with him?

"I have a confession to make, Amy."

"What is it, Father?" she wondered quietly.

He rounded the desk and approached her with steady steps. At length, she was compelled to meet his gaze as he settled right in front of her, his arms still secured at his backside.

"After the kidnapping, I didn't think I would ever see you again. Your mother, of course, believed you'd return to us, but, over the years, I waned in my dedication."

"I understand, Father." She twisted her fingers together. "Fifteen years is a long time to wait."

"No, Amy, you do not understand." He looked at her with intent, his eyes hard. "Parents should never give up on their children, just as the Lord Almighty never gives up on us." He brushed her chin with his thumb, stroking it in a maladroit fashion. "But now you've returned to your rightful position, and tonight we've celebrated your homecoming with our dearest friends."

A celebration? The ball had rivaled a street carnival with its fanfare. The guests had represented the finest crop of social dignitaries. It'd been an exhibit. Of her. A declaration. It'd announced her refinement, her respectability. It'd quashed any doubt she was a lady. Almost. There was one last test she had to endure: marriage to the marquis. She had to prove she'd make an upright gentleman a suitable wife. *Then* she would be welcome as one of them.

"I am very proud of you, Amy. You've matured into a beautiful, charming young lady."

Her blood pounded in her head, making her dizzy. "Thank you, Father."

He placed his hand at his backside again. "I have every confidence in you, Amy." He returned to the sturdy oak desk. "I trust that all my disappointments are now behind me, that we can move forward with our lives at last . . . the way we should have done before your kidnapping." He looked at her pointedly. "Fate cannot be denied, my dear, only delayed."

She curtsied, her leg muscles weak. "Good night, Father."

"Good night, Amy."

She quickly departed from the study, her head feeling pinched. The fatigue in her soul had been trampled by her father's stern sermon. She needed fresh air, not sleep. She needed freedom, not the cloistered confines of her private chambers.

With light, swift steps, she scurried through the long passageway and, through the terrace doors, entered the blooming garden.

The fragrant blossoms, an olfactory tonic, calmed her nettled senses. She breathed in the sweet night air, gazing at the delphiniums and lilies, the hydrangeas and irises. In the bright moonlight, the pink and white carnations formed a brilliant ring around the stone patio, the cool blocks comforting under her sore, silk-slippered toes.

She sighed, looking beyond the flowers and trees toward the dark, towering structures on the horizon. She peered longingly at the full moon, so brilliant and low in the heavens. It seemed an inviting place to be, a faraway land where dreams flourished.

She chastised herself for thinking such wistful rubbish. She had reunited with her family. She had reclaimed her rightful heritage. All her dreams had come to fruition. So why was she still gazing at the moon?

"Good evening, Lady Amy."

Amy stiffened at the rusty voice that nibbled at her backside like a hungry pest. She maintained her eyes on the celestial ball, ignoring the dark presence; however, approaching footfalls ruffled her concentration. At last she peeked at the tall, shadowy figure that had settled beside her. Fortunately she also witnessed a footman positioned in the offing, keeping an appropriate distance from the affianced couple without offering them complete privacy.

"I'm sorry I missed the celebration tonight."

He stood with his hands at his backside, an imposing figure. He might be considered handsome, with his fine features and well-tailored garments and polite mannerisms . . . if it wasn't for his icy temperament.

"I'm a cad," he said without a flicker of genuine remorse in his voice. "I should have been in attendance during such an important occasion, but I'd estate matters that needed my attention." He shifted his stony eyes to meet hers. "I trust you will forgive me."

"I forgive you, my lord," she said stiffly, mimicking his aloofness.

Samuel Hale, the Marquis of Gravenhurst, smiled at her with artificial tenderness. He was two-and-forty years of age, with sandy brown hair and gold eyes that pegged unsuspecting citizens with their coldness. She was accustomed to their often vacant expression, yet she still shuddered each time he settled them on her.

It was a heavy truth that pressed on her breastbone: *he* was to be her husband. It wasn't a binding, legal union, their betrothal. She'd like nothing better than to call it off, but it was an honorable pact made between the marquis and her father. If she cried off, it'd disgrace the duke. It'd shame her, too, for she'd be branded a jilt. A single social misstep and she'd be ruined. Besides, her father was depending on her to do the right thing . . .

I have every confidence in you, Amy. I trust that all my disappointments are now behind me, that we can move forward with our lives at last.

The duke's stern words still resounded in her head, quashing the hope she might disentangle herself from the disagreeable marquis.

Fate cannot be denied.

"Did you enjoy yourself this evening?" He lowered his voice and murmured, "Did you dance with all the beaus?"

The shiftiness in his manner unsettled her nerves, and little, icy bumps appeared across her tingling flesh.

"Not all the beaus, I'm afraid."

She'd much prefer it if he refrained from looking at her at all. With such a warm hue, it was a wonder the pools of his eyes expelled such frosty, even wicked regard.

"Should I be jealous of anyone in particular, my lady?"

"I think not." She glanced at him askance. "You need a heart to feel jealousy, my lord."

"True," he said darkly.

She shivered under his creeping stare, restless. He had a polished air, an unblemished reputation, yet she sensed a tenebrous quality lurking behind his sophisticated affectations.

The harmony in the garden, the milky glow from the moon no longer offered her solace, not with the moody marquis in her company.

"I remember an evening like this many years ago." He gazed at the late-night sky. "I was young, about your age, and the world seemed so full of promise. There was a blue moon then, too. Do you know what it means, Lady Amy? A blue moon?"

She shifted. "It's the second full moon in one month."

"That it is," he praised. "It's very rare." He took in a deep breath, as if wanting to ingest the haunting atmosphere. "It's a false moon, you know? We are standing under a false moon, you and I."

She girded her muscles. "How do you mean?"

"There is a full moon every twenty-nine and a half days, twelve in a year. But every so often, the half days accumulate and another full moon appears in the calendar year, the thirteenth full moon. It's a fraud."

Very much like their relationship, she mused. Was that the devil's point? But she wasn't willing to prolong their unpleasant exchange by making any more inquiries. In two weeks' time, she would wed the morose marquis. She would have a lifetime of unpleasant exchanges then.

"I have an interest in the sky: the stars, the moon," he murmured. "I'm fascinated by the concept that our lives are ordained, recorded in the constellations."

"Why?"

He said thickly, "A long time ago, at a country fair, a fortuneteller prophesied an ill omen. I believed it rubbish . . . until misfortune followed." He shrugged. "I'm afraid it's been an insidious obsession of mine ever since."

"Searching for more misfortune?"

"Trying to prove the heavens wrong," he returned darkly.

She shivered.

"Do you believe in astrology, Lady Amy?"

"I don't need the stars to tell me my fate."

"I see." He paused, then wondered, "Do you rely on your heart? Your wits?"

"I do."

"And what does your heart tell you about our approaching union?"

Her lips firmed. She struggled with the need to tell him what she *really* thought of him. In the spirit of camaraderie with her betrothed, though, she returned tautly, "That we will endeavor to please one another."

"Hmm . . . would you like to know what the stars foretell?" He whispered, "You might be surprised."

"I'm fagged, my lord," she snapped. "I've had a long day." And an even longer night, she mused sourly. "Good evening," her words clipped as she bustled away from him.

"Lady Amy."

She paused and hardened. "Yes, my lord?"

"Sweet dreams."

At the insidious farewell, she bustled off the terrace.

Chapter 18

⁓◦◦⁓

Edmund's horse pranced about the crowded Hyde Park trail. It was half past six in the afternoon, too early in the day for him to take himself off to the rat pits or pugilist arenas. He needed the distraction, the amusement of a pounding ride, yet the three-hundred-and-forty-acre parkland still teemed with the city's most fashionable dwellers.

He frowned. A bloody storm was approaching. Wasn't the threat of rain and wind persuasive enough to curtail the daily parade of nobility? To send the fastidious lords and ladies scampering indoors? Apparently nothing tempted the *haute monde* from their cherished rituals.

Was she here? he wondered. Strolling with the rest of the riders?

Edmund dismissed the thought and sighed as he dismounted. He steered the gelding toward a wooded niche and tethered the beast to a low-hanging branch, waiting for the other riders to vacate the park.

He glanced through the patches in the leaves, noted

the brewing gray clouds. Thunder rumbled and rolled across the heavens. He imagined galloping through the deserted oasis, the downpour washing away the restless fire that burned in his bones. He itched for the freedom, the comfort.

I will never be happy so long as you're in my life.

He hardened at the reflection. He made the woman miserable, did he? He soiled her ducal presence with his lowly upbringing?

Edmund snorted. He should have stayed away from *Lady* Amy. He should have listened to his better judgment, not heeded Quincy's rot about the ball. The duke had espoused the same belief, that Edmund didn't belong with his daughter. He accepted that now. He accepted the truth: he wasn't good enough for anything.

"Edmund?"

The lily softness in her voice caused his muscles to stiffen even more. He snatched the reins from the tree without even glancing her way. "What are you doing here?"

"I've sneaked away from my chaperone to talk with you. Edmund, wait!"

He stalked deeper into the woods. "I wouldn't want to make you unhappy with my company, Lady Amy."

She rounded him and set her hands across his chest. "Don't call me that."

He stopped. The muscles at his breast capered under her warm palms. She looked so bloody beautiful in her riding outfit with wide brown skirt and matching coat, clipped at her hips and snugly hugging her bosom. The woman's long and wavy blond locks spilled over her spine. She had a riding cap, pitched to one side of her head. And he observed the riding crop pinched between her fingers; it rested against him like a lash, and he bristled at the thought that he was her pageboy in need of a sound whipping.

"What should I call you then?" he demanded. "Zarsitti?"

Thunder groaned as the wind whooshed through the trees, stirring the leaves into a cacophony of rustling jabber, twisting her hair wildly, too.

"I feel like her almost all the time." A sadness entered her brilliant green eyes. "I hate her. She's robbed me of myself. I will never evade her, will I?"

He resisted the mawkish desire to put his arms around her. He tightened his grip on the leather reins instead. "You have my sympathy."

"Don't patronize me, Edmund." She tucked her loose locks behind her ears. "You don't know what it's like, keeping a tainted past secret, praying your former misdeeds don't come to light and shame your family, those you love most."

The rain started, a light shower. He watched the droplets strike her cheeks, watched her swipe at the pearled beads as if she was swatting at tears. It welled inside him, the resemblance between their situations, and the truth lessened the darkness in his soul.

"I understand," he said in an even manner.

He, too, had to safeguard his past to protect his sister

from disgrace, his brothers from the noose. It was a burden at times, a weighty yoke.

"How can you understand, Edmund? You live as a mariner and a gentleman, and the world treats you accordingly." She pointed at herself with the riding crop. "But I have to hide who I am—was. I have to pretend I'm worthy of the title 'Lady' Amy."

"You *are* a lady."

"No!" She shuddered. "I was a lady. Once. I'm just pretending to be one now." She looked at him with such fierceness in her eyes. "It's why I can't be with you, Edmund. I can't offer you friendship."

"Fine," he gritted.

The horse snorted as lightning flickered in the distance.

"You keep her alive." She hit her bust with her fist. "You keep Zarsitti alive. Do you understand?"

He frowned. "No."

She stepped nearer to him, setting his senses alight with her warm proximity, her intoxicating scent.

"Being with you means keeping Zarsitti breathing, her heart burning, wanting, desiring things I can never have." She munched on her bottom lip. "And if I'm ever to be happy, if I'm ever to accept my new position in life, I have to let her go."

"Fine. You never have to see me again."

A white light sparked.

The kiss was hard.

She wrapped her arms around his neck and he bristled at the bold, unexpected gesture. At first, he believed the lightning had pierced him, scorched him straight to his toes, but then the passion in her mannerisms convinced him it was the hunger in her mouth unleashing the fire in his belly. She wanted him, despite her protestations to the contrary.

Edmund released the reins, he looped the leather lead over the nearest branch and slipped his arms around Amy's midriff, squeezing her in a tight embrace.

The rain beat hard. The thick shade of summer leaves sheltered the couple from the brunt of the storm. Lightning cracked like a blistering explosion, followed by the low moan of thunder. Amy moaned, too. He sensed the vibrations in her throat. He tasted the sweet rainwater on her lips as the leaves slowly softened and sagged under the pressure of the tempest, gradually soaking through their attire.

Edmund moved his fingers across her spine and snagged them in her moist hair, tugging at her locks, pulling her away.

Amy gasped as he ended the kiss; her cap slipped and landed in the grass. She stared at him with a dreamy expression, a lustful look. He stiffened at the sight of her swollen lips, so sinfully tempting.

"You're not behaving like a lady, Amy . . . or am I kissing Zarsitti?"

"I-I'm both, I guess."

The muscles in his back firmed at her words. "You're not both."

He still gripped her midriff, keeping her flush against him. With his other hand still secured in her tresses, he was only a short distance from her lips . . . yet their positions in life separated them by leagues.

"You can't be both," he said roughly. "I know it's impossible to be two different souls. The duality will destroy you one day."

Something glistened in the deep green pools of her eyes. "That's why I need you now."

The white light flashed, spooking the tethered horse, who snorted and struggled with the secured trappings.

"You don't need me. Now or ever." He bussed her lips. "You fit in with society just fine. You *are* a lady." He twisted his fingers even more tightly in her wet hair. "It's your rightful home."

"Th-then I want you."

The rain dribbled between his stiff collar and hot flesh; it trickled down his backside and bathed his pulsing muscles.

"That is a different matter," he said gruffly.

He guided her head, pulled her back toward his mouth, and kissed her with the same gusto as the rowdy storm. She filled his veins with a thirst for existence. In her arms, there was purpose and meaning in his soul. In her arms, he was at peace.

The lass's skirt ballooned around his legs. He rolled with her in the grass, pinned her against the ground as he deepened the kiss. He didn't even remember falling to the turf with her, but the fierce noise and heavy rain that surrounded their undulating bodies washed away so many senses.

The deep, booming beats of his heart anchored him in the moment, maintained some semblance of order in his head as he guided her skirts over her legs, rubbing her soft calves draped in silk stockings, stroking the sensitive undersides of her knees.

"I want you, Edmund."

He pressed his hand between her legs and fingered her moist quim. "I know."

She bucked her hips and gasped, pinched his wet, straggly hair between her fingers as if he might flee from her.

"Do you think I could walk away from you now?"

Do you think I could ever walk away from you, Amy?

He had tried; he believed it the right thing to do. And yet . . .

She rasped between kisses, "I think the gentleman inside you might trounce the scoundrel."

He snorted. "You don't know me very well, Amy."

She laughed. Amid the hellish weather, the restless wants teeming inside them, she laughed. It cut through his bones, the unexpected joy in her voice, and he hardened for her even more.

"Have you ever done this before, Amy?"

"I've seen it a hundred times."

At the Pleasure Palace.

He unfastened his trousers in quick strokes. "That's not what I asked you."

More lightning flared throughout the treetops. He shielded Amy's body from the rain, the frantic, sidestepping horse, covered her with his length as he positioned his hips between her soft legs.

"No," she admitted, breathless.

He looked into her eyes, filled with expectation, desire. He kissed her with a deep, thrumming need. He was engrossed with the feral, rutting instinct, yet somewhere in the rational part of his thoughts, he remembered her condition and slipped inside her with a steady thrust.

She stiffened and bared her teeth. He closed his eyes and settled within her, maintained his position, giving her the time she needed to adjust to the feel of him. The savage impulse to bump his hips, give her a thorough bedding, gripped him. He beat back the wild craving.

As soon as he sensed her muscles ease, as soon as he heard her audible sigh, he opened his eyes and rocked his hips.

"You feel so good, Amy."

He groaned at the tight, slick sensation of her. The rain poured over her legs, lubricated her thighs, making his entry even smoother. He had never tasted such delicious passion. He was tangled in her hair, her arms, her legs. She ensnared him with her being. And he blessedly welcomed the feeling of being bound by her . . . to her.

Amy closed her eyes and cradled Edmund's head. He was soaked, heavy with rain. His hair was rough and teeming with beaded moisture that dripped over her flushed features as he slowly pumped inside her.

The drops splashed on her cheeks, rolled down

her throat and between her breasts, tickling her. She gasped for air, moaned. She was lost amid the whirling winds and biting rain. The scoundrel's steady yet tender thrusts teased her other senses with distracting precision. She wasn't sure about anything in the world right then but his sensual penetration.

She opened her eyes and stared into a pair of deep blue pools. The connection between them intensified. Her heart thumped with vigor, her muscles undulated at a matching tempo. She harmonized her movements with his, as in a dance . . . an erotic dance.

It welled within her, the thought that she was dancing with Edmund without her veil, that her muscles and limbs rolled and rocked in sensuous waves with the scoundrel, the stormy heavens their music.

He pressed his mouth—his sardonic mouth with an upturned quirk—over her lips, savored her. She adored his mouth . . .

"I adore your mouth."

She blushed at the sound of husky chuckling. Had she uttered the intimate reflection aloud? Amy munched on her bottom lip; however, he quickly offered her another heated kiss, appeasing her chagrin with the sound strokes of his passionate mouth.

He tasted so bloody good, too, but she was sure to keep that thought private as she hugged his sinewy biceps. The pressure at her apex was starting to build, a low and teasing ache.

She lifted her legs slightly.

He pushed deeper inside her.

He groaned at the added room. She groaned, too, the girth of him stretching her, filling her with its thick arousal. The virginal pain had whittled away with each soft stroke, replaced with a feeling of pleasure: soul-wringing pleasure.

She scraped her fingernails over his neck. "Edmund . . ."

She wasn't sure what she was asking for; the words trailed away.

"I know, Amy."

He smothered her with kisses as his hands cupped her hip bones and his penetrations deepened, quickened. She gasped with new awareness. Yes, it was what she wanted. It was . . .

The electric light flickered, a bright flash that blinded her for a second. She witnessed the colorful spots swirling in her line of vision as the thunder boomed, the crescendos overhead.

An urgency gripped her. A primitive instinct took over her senses and guided her body. She lifted her hips as he bored down on her, the contact more intimate, the friction more intense. She wanted him with such abandon, she neglected all other thoughts, all other feelings in light of the brilliant moment.

"Oh, Edmund!"

She chewed on his ear nestled near her lips with wicked delight. The strain between her legs snapped. She cried out. The muscles shuddered, pulsed with release. The scoundrel drummed her core with piercing strokes before he poured himself into her, as well. He groaned with pleasure, his dark growls snatched away by the howling winds.

Amy was breathless. She trembled in Edmund's arms, bemused. He still smothered her with his figure, protected her from the elements. Yet she was weak. She wondered if she possessed the strength to stand. She didn't care. Not really. She was more mindful of her heated tussle with the scoundrel. She wanted to remain in his arms, right there in the sheltered wood. The trees concealed their intertwined bodies. The tempest guarded their sensual shouts. The storm surrounded them: two wet butterflies fresh from cocoons. She didn't want to leave the haven. She didn't want to leave him.

Edmund stroked her brow with his fingertips, brushed away the moist lines of hair. "I didn't think I'd meet with you when I ventured into the park today."

"I thought you believed in spontaneity?" She smiled. "I thought you wanted me to have more fun?"

He snorted with laughter. "I like your idea of fun, Amy."

She chuckled and sighed as he nuzzled her cheek. "You'll have to walk home, Edmund."

He nipped her ear. "Why?"

She shuddered. "Your horse is missing."

"Bloody hell."

"I'm sorry."

"Don't say that," he said roughly. "You didn't do anything wrong."

"I distracted you."

Slowly he smiled again, the handsome scoundrel. "Aye, you did. But I didn't mind the distraction."

He kissed her once more with both passion and tenderness.

Sated, Amy thumbed his backside. "I have to go."

He sighed. "I suppose you do."

He shifted his weight. The rain was still pouring, but the lightning, the thunder had ebbed away. He circled her arms and lifted her to her feet, wobbly after the vigorous bedding.

She smoothed her rumpled skirts, soaked and stained with soil. She grimaced and rubbed her fingers over the dark blotches, smudging them even more. No, the dress was ruined.

She shrugged. "My cap?"

Edmund fastened his trousers and retrieved her riding hat, her crop. As he handed the articles to her, their fingers linked, and she shivered at the sweet touches.

"Will you be all right, Amy?"

"Hmm? Oh, I'll be fine. I'll tell Mama I fell from my horse in the storm. She'll believe me. I'm a terrible equestrienne."

He stroked her wet cheek. She peered into his smoky eyes; the raindrops lined his lashes like tiny diamonds.

"I can't go with you, Amy."

"I know." She bussed his thumb as it swept across her lips. "I understand."

She would be ruined if she was spotted in his company, emerging from the sheltered woods.

"But I'll come and see you again soon," he promised.

Amy smiled, her lips trembled. She quickly skirted away as a coldness entered her heart. The man's words seeped into her bones. She imagined the restless delight, the thrilling anticipation of their next rendezvous. But it was a hopeless dream, for she would never see Edmund again. Soon she would wed the Marquis of Gravenhurst. Soon she would surrender to her husband's icy touch.

Amy struggled with her tears as she scurried through the park. She comforted herself with the knowledge that she had tasted pure passion at least once in her life . . . but perhaps it would have been better if she had never known it. In the dark days to come, their intimacy in the park would be a bittersweet memory: a reminder of how things might have been if she hadn't been betrothed.

Chapter 19

Edmund walked the horse toward the rear of the town house and secured the beast within the private stables. He had eventually spotted the animal wandering through Hyde Park, nibbling on the wildflowers. After smoothing the gelding's coat with a brush and pitching fresh hay into the stall, he entered the main dwelling.

The storm had passed, yet Edmund's clothes were still damp with rainwater, sticking to his flesh. He didn't notice his disorderly apparel, though. He was much too engrossed with thoughts of Amy.

His body still ached for the lass. In an instant, he conjured her fingernails digging fiercely into his arms, imagined her undulating hips, listened to her sultry cries of passion.

He shuddered. He needed to see her again. He needed to be with her again. And not just one more time. All the time. Every day of his life. He had to protect the lass, too, for she might be enceinte. But how to go about it? What would it take to prove to her father he wasn't just "playing" gentleman? That he had honorable intentions toward the duke's daughter? That he wanted to marry Amy?

He mounted the steps, needing advice. As he reached the middle of the staircase, he stilled, sensing a presence. He glanced toward the towering figure on the second level, his spine straightening.

James regarded him with a staid expression before he sauntered down the steps, his footfalls strong and steady. Edmund stepped aside, allowing his brother passage. As soon as the captain had reached the lower level, he headed for the door without offering his kinsman a farewell.

At the deliberate disregard, Edmund glared after the surly brigand. Was James ignoring him now? He shrugged. If the despot desired an even greater estrangement, so be it, but one day he'd learn the truth; that he'd pushed away more than just Edmund, that he'd driven off all the subjects in his kingdom with his ruthless ways.

Edmund ascended the rest of the steps.

"The physician was here to see Will," remarked James in an offhanded manner. "The wound is healing well. There are willow leaves beside the bed."

Edmund stilled and followed the captain's movements with his eyes.

As James opened the door, he looked pointedly at his brother. "Mix the leaves in tea and make sure he drinks the tonic every four hours for the discomfort."

"You're leaving?"

He bobbed his head. "I am."

The door closed.

Edmund stared into the empty passageway for a moment, wondering what sort of calamity had appropriated the captain's attention, for James would *never* willingly set off from the town house, not with a wounded brother in residence.

Still bemused, he scratched his head. On the second level, he knocked at William's bedchamber door.

A faint "enter" welcomed him; he stepped inside the warm, dim room.

He eyed his convalescing sibling, resting under the layers of bedding. The drapery in the room masked the two windows, allowing the captain to recover in relative darkness. There was a fire in the hearth; it drew out the dampness in the air and permitted some soft illumination.

"You're wet," said William.

"I was trapped in the storm." He closed the door. "How are you feeling?"

"Smothered," he returned succinctly, his features sallow. "First Belle served as nursemaid, then James." He rasped, "Do you know what that does to a man who's been shot in the chest?"

"Takes your breath away?"

"What little I have of it."

Edmund settled into a chair at the foot of the bed and stretched out his legs, crossing them at the ankles. "I saw James a moment ago. He left the house."

"He's going home to be with his wife."

"He's leaving you?"

"In your care, aye."

The serpent stirred in the aquarium positioned on the table beside the chair.

Edmund knocked on the glass with his knuckle, a light rap. "Is Sophia all right? His wife, I mean."

William chuckled. "Aye, she's fine, but I think James realizes he doesn't need to be here all the time. I think he trusts you to take care of things."

"Why?"

It didn't sound like James, the tyrant. He needed to be in control of every situation. He needed to be in control of all their lives. And yet he had walked away?

"I told him what happened aboard the *Nemesis*, that you had served as lieutenant to the acting captain in my stead . . . that you had saved my life."

As the unsettling ordeal stirred in his mind, Edmund glanced at his hands.

He quickly pressed his palms over the gash in the captain's chest. He watched the dark blood ooze between his fingers, sensed its warmth as it bathed his hands.

Edmund rubbed his brow, his head smarting. "I didn't save you. You stepped in front of me, remember? The bullet was meant for me."

"You stopped the bleeding," he said in a low voice. "You did your part . . . and I did mine."

The gloomy reflection had smothered Edmund's otherwise buoyant spirit, and he concluded it was not the right time to beseech his brother's counsel about Amy.

"I'll let you rest, Will." He lifted from the chair. "I'll return in a few hours to serve you the willow-leaf tea."

"Eddie."

He paused beside the door. "What is it?"

"I've had to write to the Admiralty. I don't know when I'll be returning to duty."

"I understand."

William eyed him thoughtfully. "What will you do with yourself in the meantime?"

He shrugged. "I don't know."

"You could sail with James again."

Edmund placed his hands on his hips and looked at the shadows on the floor. "I was thinking about staying on land for a while."

"Because of Amy?"

He looked at his brother. "Aye."

"Is that wise?"

He frowned. "Why?"

"Quincy was here looking for you. He wanted to know if you were all right. He told me about Amy and the Marquis of Gravenhurst."

Who the devil was the Marquis of Gravenhurst?

Edmund's heart tightened. "What are you talking about, Will?"

"I'm talking about the couple's engagement."

Edmund stared at his brother, confounded. He assumed William confused, suffering from some sort of dementia . . . but he hadn't a head injury. The bullet had pierced his chest. He had a sound mind, which meant . . .

"Engagement?"

"The couple will wed in a fortnight, I understand. Quincy had just learned the news."

Edmund's head throbbed with vivid images as he remembered the heated tussle in the park, her sweet words and urgent touches. A darkness filled his head, his blood. A cold and cutting pain sliced through his muscles. He gnashed his teeth at the rising pressure in his skull. He wanted to smash something, pound it with his fists.

"Perhaps it's a good idea if you sail with James for a time," suggested William.

Edmund raked his fingers through his ruffled hair. That conniving little— He firmed his fists. Why had she come to him if she was going to marry another man? A bloody marquis?

He soon imagined her heavy with child—his child! If she was enceinte, the marquis would likely claim the babe as his heir. He'd have no reason to think it wasn't his offspring, for the couple would wed in two weeks time.

Edmund's fist went into the door. A marquis. She was going to wed a fucking lord! He sneered at his own stupidity. What lady of consequence would marry a lowly seaman? He was such an idiot!

"Are you all right, Eddie?"

He took in a deep, seething breath through his nose. Was he all right? He wasn't so sure about that. One damnable question hounded him. Why? Why had she come to him, the deceiver? Why had she rolled in the mud with him like a common harlot if she was going to marry the Marquis of Gravenhurst?

Amy gazed at her reflection in the tall mirror. As it was late, the candlelight glistened in the room, the illumination playing softly across the fluffy, pale blue wedding dress.

The garment swallowed her in a neat ensemble of pleated linen. It was the last fitting before the wedding. She stood on a small stool in her private room, listening to the seamstress, who prattled in French. Fortunately, the Duchess of Estabrooke was also in the chamber and was well versed in the foreign tongue. The two ladies conversed around the bride-to-be, and, as Madame Léger didn't speak a word of English, Amy relied on her mother's translation to communicate with the finest seamstress in Town.

"How does the garment fit, my dear?"

Helen smoothed her fingers across the wide skirt in a fond manner, raising Madame Léger's hackles as the woman's features burned red. The short, prim seamstress looked as if she wanted to blast the duchess for running her fingers over the pleats and ruffling the carefully stitched garment; however, she refrained from the outburst, pinched her lips in displeasure instead.

"It's still a little loose in the hips," returned Amy.

The duchess communicated the alterations to the seamstress, who bobbed her head in understanding and proceeded to pin the garment at the appropriate spots.

"Is something the matter, my dear? You look pale."

It was the wedding dress, thought Amy. It reminded her of her approaching nuptials. The attire seemed so heavy on her thin frame. It wasn't really too cumbersome, but as soon as she imagined her soon-to-be-husband waiting for her at the end of the church aisle, the dress weighed on her even more.

"I'm fine, Mama."

The duchess smiled. "I've missed hearing you call me Mama."

Amy looked at her mother, her heart pulsing with longing. "I remember seeing you at the orphanage in Town a few months ago. Well, I saw your gloved hand. But I remembered the sound of your voice, your laughter."

"I've been involved with such charities for years. After I had lost you, I had always hoped I might find you at such a place: a place for lost children."

The duchess wiped at her eyes.

"What's the matter, Mama?"

The older woman sniffed and retrieved a white kerchief from the nearest table. Madame Léger tsked and brandished her fingers, and although Amy wasn't sentient of her odd-sounding words, she comprehended the seamstress's meaning, that she wanted the duchess and her briny tears to keep away from the sensitive fabric.

Helen dabbed at her eyes with the kerchief. "I've only just welcomed you home and now I have to give you up again."

Amy simpered. She longed to stay with her parents for a greater time, too. She longed to postpone her marriage to the marquis indefinitely. But . . .

"But the marquis will make you a fine husband." Helen's soft green eyes smiled. "It's a good match, my dear. Your father negotiated the betrothal with such zest all those years ago. He wanted our two families to be united for many years."

"Why?"

"It's a respectable match between two wealthy, distinguished dynasties. As our only child, you were your father's greatest hope for such a prestigious alliance; it'd been his fondest wish that you wed the marquis."

Amy said quietly, "And produce a noble legacy?"

The duchess nodded. "It almost didn't come to pass. The betrothal, I mean."

Do not think I've forgotten your past indiscretions, Gravenhurst. I hope you've learned from your former mistakes, that you will do what is right.

The chilling words still hounded her. She wondered, "What happened, Mama?"

"I don't know the particulars." She shrugged. "I wasn't part of the talks that detailed the arrangement, but it all worked out in the end." She smiled again. "You look so lovely, my dear."

The seamstress twittered some words in brisk succession.

"Madame Léger wants you to remove the dress now."

Amy wriggled out of the flowing garment with the

aid of the seamstress and her mother before she donned her white frock again. After bussing her mother's cheek, she parted from the ladies, who remained inside the bedchamber, discussing the bridal dress's final, finishing details.

Amy headed for the garden. She entered the private oasis with high stone walls. There was no moonlight, but glass lanterns flickered with candlelight. She followed the soft aura through a narrow, winding trail and settled on a curved stone bench, backless, keeping her spine straight as she lifted her eyes to the dark heavens. Without the moon, that faraway land, the sky looked so bleak. The stars didn't shine through the murky clouds of soot, and Amy looked away from the unfriendly black canvas.

The blossoms and trees and shrubs offered her some companionship, their fragrances pleasing after the brisk rainstorm, their lilting movements in the breeze comforting. But soon her thoughts darkened her spirit as she reflected upon her future husband and his secrets.

What "past indiscretions" had almost prevented their union? Her father was clearly willing to overlook any impropriety to ensure her marriage and subsequent good standing in polite society; however, she wondered if such an indiscretion—made public—might prevent her union now?

It was a wicked desire to go against her father's dearest wish in such an ungrateful manner, but she wasn't so sure she could carry the yoke of her duty. She hadn't the strength to leave the marquis of her own volition and shame her parents; however, if she unearthed her fiancé's tainted past, and made it public, perhaps the scandal would force her father to break the betrothal contract?

It was worth some investigating.

"Good evening, Amy."

She started, scanning the shadows in the garden with wide eyes, searching for the source of the familiar voice.

"What are you doing here, Edmund?"

He emerged from between the fruit trees and crossed the pebbled path. The lamplight at his back cast a long shadow over Amy, and she shivered at the man's sensual presence, his robust strength. Her heart ballooned in her breast. She sensed her blood, her pulse quicken with delight.

"I promised I'd come to see you again."

He straddled the stone bench beside her, his long legs spread wide as he caged her between his thighs. The sound of his voice, so gravelly, stirred the fine hairs at the back of her neck to sensitive life.

She licked her lips. "You have to leave, Edmund."

Slowly he brushed her cheek with the pad of his thumb, his touch warm, gentle. "You didn't mind my company in Hyde Park."

She shivered under the tender gesture, the hotly spoken words. Little goose pimples sprouted over her skin, making her flesh tingle with the memory of their intimacy in the park. In vivid detail, she remembered the heat, the rain, the wild wind as he'd shielded her from the tempest with his body, pressed his sturdy weight between her thighs, offering her pleasure, closeness.

"I don't mind your company now," she whispered, a need growing inside her. "But if you're discovered here—"

He bussed her mouth with a soft, light kiss, curtailing her protest. As the kiss deepened, she matched its sound and steady pressure, offering him the same passion he offered her, feeding his desire as he fed hers.

Would it always feel so good? she wondered. Kissing him? Being caressed by his sensuous mouth? She wanted him. Always. She wanted his lips a hairbreadth away from hers at all times. She wanted to take his mouth whenever the need compelled her, welled within her.

"I need you, Amy."

A firm hand rubbed her waist, petted her breastbone. She raised her bosom, taking in a deep breath, as he rested his large palm over her breast, her thumping heart. She trembled with a fiery want, a familiar anxiety.

"I need to touch you."

He stroked the buttons of her dress in a lazy manner, making her shiver with delight at his teasing promise of pleasure. Slowly he unfastened the row of beads and parted the fabric folds. The warm breeze tickled her spine and she trembled under the scoundrel's sensual seduction, quivered with need as he strummed her boned corset and loosened the lace bindings with ease.

"I need to taste you."

She gasped at the dark hunger in his voice. "Here?"

"Right here."

He plumped a swelling breast with his strong fingers, kneaded the soft flesh, so tender. She cooed at the delightful sensations, her heart pounding, her muscles firming, but as soon as he parted his lips and took her stiff nipple into his hot mouth, she groaned, unprepared for the erotic attack on her senses.

"You and I belong with the trees and the flowers," he murmured, lapping his tongue over the puckering nub. "We belong with nature."

She moaned and burrowed her fingers tightly into his hair as he undulated his tongue over her hard nipple, drawing her further into his mouth, flicking the rigid, sensitive surface again and again.

"Do I please you?" he rasped.

"Yes."

She ached for him deep inside her belly, a knotted sensation that constricted the muscles in her body; she felt only warmth and expectation and longing.

He tugged at her corset with firmness, searching for her other breast. "Do you want me to please you like this all the days of your life?"

"Yes!"

Amy chewed on her bottom lip as he took her other breast into his mouth and sucked hard, making her so tight inside, so full of energy. She gasped, a deep craving in her soul; she cried out in need.

He rent the corset slightly, exposing the birthmark

between her breasts. He touched the mark with reverence, thrummed his thumb over her taut midriff.

"Do you want me to come to you in the garden and pleasure you every night?"

He bussed the birthmark, matched his lush lips with the smaller configuration. As her heart shuddered, she closed her eyes and sighed.

"Yes," she said weakly.

"Do you want me to come to you, Amy?" he said fiercely. "After your husband's finished with you?"

She hardened. It was like a nasty imp had dumped a bucket of icy water over her head. She sensed the goblin's mordant laughter as a chill seeped right through to her toes.

"After the marquis's dutifully rutted with you," he said stiffly, "do you want me to come and give you more fun?"

He knows about the marquis!

She opened her eyes and pushed him away, struggled with her dress. "I know you're angry with me, Edmund."

He grabbed her trembling wrists and pinned her hands behind her back. "I don't think you do, Amy."

Her breasts still exposed, she was trapped between his thick arms. He pegged her with his steely eyes, his expression darkening.

"I have to marry him, Edmund," she said, breathless. "We're betrothed. We've been betrothed since I was a babe. It would disgrace my father's good name if I refused to wed the marquis."

"Why didn't you tell me?" he demanded.

"I . . ."

"You wanted me for your lover, is that it? Your poor, lowly lover, who otherwise isn't fit to be seen in your company."

"No, Edmund, I—"

"I won't be your lover, Amy." He gritted, "If I'm not good enough to touch you as . . . then I won't touch you at all."

Her breath hitched at the implication. If he wasn't good enough to touch her as her husband . . .

Her heart cramped at the wonderful thought.

He released her and stalked away, deep into the shadows.

"Edmund wait!"

She grappled with the garment, attempted to fasten the buttons, but her fingers quivered with emotion. In the end, she was too ineffective. She grabbed the material and pressed it against her bust, concealing her breasts. She bounded along the winding path in search of him when she detected the sharp whiff of tobacco smoke.

She stilled and studied her surroundings.

"Do you need assistance, Lady Amy?"

She bristled.

She looked askance and spotted the marquis smoking beside a tree. A creeping chill spread over her limbs, her spine. Had he watched her with Edmund?

"H-how did you get into the garden undetected?" she stammered.

"You didn't ask your lover that question?"

He stepped away from the tree and approached her as if he might offer her assistance with the garment. She quickly skirted off a short distance. He paused. She shuddered at the thought that he might rub his fingers over her body. She wasn't his wife yet . . . would she ever be now? she wondered.

Amy's heart pumped with vigor. She was ruined. One word from the marquis and her betrothal was finished. She imagined the disgrace, the shame her parents would suffer as the scandal spread across Town. She imagined clobbering the marquis and dragging his carcass into the bushes to rot.

She tamped down the tears that brimmed in her eyes. "What do you want?"

The wretched lord might be persuaded to keep his ogling a secret. If she offered him something valuable, perhaps—

"I want to give you this necklace." He presented her with a dazzling ruby choker in a velvet-lined box; the gems glistened under the lamplight like hot coals from Hades. "It's a family heirloom. I'd like you to wear it on our wedding night."

She stared at the twinkling stones, the bile burning in her belly. "Our wedding night?"

The marquis still wanted to marry her? There had to be a wedding day if there was going to be a wedding night.

She shivered. The black-hearted devil! He had sneaked into the garden, lurked behind the trees, waiting for her, so he might offer her the necklace, an intimate gesture. It wasn't proper for him to meet her in the sitting room and talk about such private matters . . . like their first night together.

She firmed her lips. He wanted to torment her. She suspected it pleased him to see the distaste, the resistance in her eyes. He loathed her. Why? And why was he willing to proceed with the wedding after witnessing her lovemaking? Family honor? He had vowed to wed her, and he would keep his word, even if she'd dallied with another man?

"Did you think your transgression with Mr. Hawkins a sin?" He looked at her with stony eyes, the tobacco smoke swirling around his head. "I'm not such a puritan, my lady."

She clutched the fabric even tighter at her bust, her heart knocking against her breastbone with vim.

"Tell me," he drawled, "do you like his touch? Does it give you pleasure?"

She shuddered at the whispered words, hissing like wet wood in the firelight.

"In the breeze, your moans sound like sweet music." He lowered his gaze to her bosom, leering at her. "How does it feel to have him in your arms, at your breasts?"

The warmth of Edmund's touch soon dissipated, her skin feeling cool and clammy under the marquis's seedy glare.

"It feels glorious, I suspect. I envy him the comfort he finds at your bosom and warm, beating heart."

Amy spread her shaky fingers apart, tamping down the nausea in her belly.

"I don't care if you keep Mr. Hawkins as your lover," he said slowly, looking back into her eyes through a haze of cigar smoke. "It won't prevent our wedding."

She squeezed the velvet box with the ruby choker between her stiff fingers. It welled within her, the desire to cry off and escape the lecherous fiend, but she smothered the unruly impulse. She had her parents' feelings, their reputations to consider, as well. She needed to make a good match, to squelch the rumors regarding her past, and the only eligible gentleman prepared for the task was the marquis; he'd already committed to the duty.

He pulled away from her. "Don't despair, Lady Amy. I would never stand in the way of true love, I assure you."

And with that cryptic declaration, he blended with the garden shadows once more.

True love? What did *he* know about true love, the creeping devil?

Amy shuddered at the words. She dismissed them, in truth. She hadn't the wherewithal to sift through her complicated feelings for Edmund. And what about the marquis's deviant promise that he'd permit an affair between her and the scoundrel?

The situation was too distasteful. She needed to prevent the wedding. She needed to foil the betrothal.

Chapter 20

Amy skulked through the shrubbery. She parted the foliage and peered at the churchyard a short distance away. The sturdy gravestones dotted the level terrain like silent sentries, guarding the dead.

She shivered at the morbid atmosphere, searched the landscape for a sign of the sordid marquis. She had followed the man in the hopes of learning more about him and his unseemly interludes, but she wasn't likely to uncover anything scandalous in the quiet parish. She sighed, shifting from her crouching position, her legs cramped. She'd tracked him thus far; she thought. She'd wait a few minutes more before declaring the day a failure and skirting off.

Amy spied the deserted hallowed grounds with growing impatience. She had watched the marquis pass through the church gates. She had slunk after him shortly thereafter, but she was having trouble locating the man now.

She moved stealthily through the bushes. After

searching the entire churchyard with her eyes, she realized the marquis wasn't there and huffed.

Where had the man disappeared?

At length, she heard soft murmuring. She stooped
as she approached the wooded enclave, and peered
through the leaves at the patch of land set aside from
the churchyard. She counted a few headstones there—
and the marquis.

He hunkered beside a monument, speaking softly.
As he stroked the cold, gray stone his voice deepened,
darkened. An almost wretched blathering passed between his lips as if the man was in distress and needed
attention.

Amy chewed on her bottom lip, wishing him an apoplexy, but she quickly quashed the wicked thought, for
the marquis hadn't ruined her after witnessing her tryst
with Edmund, and for that he deserved some consideration, she supposed. She glanced at the church steeple,
shadowed by the late-afternoon sun. Was the parson
inside the holy dwelling today? If not, she'd have to
dash toward the nearest village to fetch assistance.

She looked back at the hunched figure. The marquis
had quieted. He scraped his fingernails along his scalp
and grasped his sandy brown hair.

He was weeping

Amy was disarmed. She stared, transfixed, at the
haunting spectacle. The man was such a cold beast.
How did he keep such heavy feelings concealed?
Where did he keep them? But the grief that poured
from his soul convinced her the black-hearted devil

had a heart pressed somewhere deep within his being. It was a wounded heart, and she empathized with the mysterious man for a moment.

After a thorough atonement with the body in the grave, he righted himself. Quietly he vacated the grounds and returned to the church courtyard where his coach was stationed.

As soon as Amy heard the wheels crackling over the pebbled road, she emerged from her hiding spot and slowly approached the tombstone. It was a simple, rounded marker with two doves engraved on the façade.

She squatted, touched the rough surface, weathered with age. She brushed her fingers across the birds, symbols of peace. She next pressed her fingertips into the crevices that marked the name, the letters vaguely familiar to her. She was learning to read. She traced her fingers over an R and a U. Next she fingered a D . . . but she wasn't able to spell out the rest of the name.

The dates she deciphered as 1791–1811. The deceased was twenty years of age. Not a lost child, then. The marquis had never wed, so it wasn't his spouse interred in the earth. The occupant was too young to be an aged parent. A sibling, perhaps? No, the marquis was an only child, like her. Who then?

Amy made the sign of the cross and lifted off her haunches. She approached the small church. She stepped inside the ancient structure and was greeted with the pungent aroma of burning tallow candles. The rows of pews seated about forty parishioners, she estimated. She caressed the wood seats, skipped her fingers over them as she stepped down the aisle.

A chill gripped her bones as she imagined her wedding march, the sinister groom waiting for her at the end of a similar aisle, his eyes cold, biting, filled with rancor . . . despair.

"Good day," she called out. "Is there someone here?"

A young curate, with a mop of curly brown hair, appeared from a small office behind the pulpit. "Good day, miss. How can I be of service?"

Amy smiled. She was dressed in a simple white dress, respectable, but otherwise plain, her long hair plaited and secured with a ribbon. She wanted to protect her ducal heritage. It wasn't right for her to be traipsing through the countryside without an escort, and she didn't want word to reach the marquis that she was snooping into his private affairs.

"I need some information," she said. "There's a grave marker with a pair of doves just beyond the church grounds. I'd like to know more about the deceased."

The Church of England maintained records of births and deaths and marriages, so the information shouldn't be too hard to ascertain, she thought.

The curate frowned. "That's unconsecrated land, miss."

"Unconsecrated?"

"The land isn't blessed; it isn't sacred." He smoothed his clerical vestments. "It's where we bury the suicides or the unbaptized, the nonconformists."

Her pulses leaped. "I see."

"Why do you want such information?"

He sounded ominous. Amy suspected the pious curate was affronted by her unbecoming questioning, and she refrained from making any more inquiries.

"I've made a mistake, is all." She bobbed a curtsy. "Good day."

Quickly she scurried away from the holy house—and the curate's sanctimonious stare. She wandered the churchyard for a brief time, trolled the grounds as she assessed the news that the corpse was laid in unconsecrated ground.

Who was buried there?

She would have to find some other way to learn the name on the headstone, the identity of the deceased—and why the bones were so important to the marquis.

Amy headed for her own stationed vehicle; it was a short distance away and concealed. As she traveled the pebbled road, she detected the faint shuffling of feet and glanced over her shoulder.

Two figures ambled down the road at a distance.

She eyed the bodies, those of two men. Farmers, perhaps. Or tradesmen. She looked away again . . . but a niggling suspicion hounded her thoughts and she examined the figures once more.

"Oh, bullocks!"

Amy took off running.

"You eat like a pig."

Edmund glowered at his brother, standing in the door frame. "Sod off, Quincy."

The pup entered the room and rounded the dining

table before he settled into a chair, scratching his chin. "What's wrong, Eddie?"

He took a bite from the roasted lamb, mumbled, "Nothing."

"If you're stuffing your belly, something's wrong. Care to tell me about it?"

Edmund chewed his food in silence.

"It's Amy, isn't it?"

He gnashed his teeth.

"And her pending marriage to the marquis?"

He slammed his fist into the table, rattled the dishes. "I'm about to flatten your nose, pup."

"That won't really make you feel better."

"It might," he growled.

Quincy raised an amused brow. After a short silence, he pressed on with "Are you going to fight for the lass?"

"No."

"Why?"

"She's betrothed to Gravenhurst." The blood in his skull pounding, he gritted, "What am I supposed to do about it? Duel with the marquis? He's not dishonored her good name."

Quincy snorted. "No one duels anymore, Eddie."

"What did you mean, then?"

He shrugged. "Break the engagement."

"Why?"

"You care for her, admit it."

Edmund stiffened at the provocative suggestion, girded his muscles against the rising pressure in his chest, the unfilled longing. "I can't."

"Why?"

I have to marry him, Edmund. It would disgrace my father's good name if I refused to wed the marquis.

"Shut up, Quincy."

He folded his arms across his chest and sighed. "You don't feel you deserve her, do you?"

Edmund mustered a surly expression. "You don't understand."

"I understand better than you think. I've lived in their shadows, too. Breaking away from the past isn't easy, I know. But *you* have a chance to make a new start for yourself with Amy, and if *you* don't take it, it's your own damn fault."

Edmund humphed and stared at his plate, feeling less hungry. He sucked the meat's juices off his fingers just as the butler appeared in the door frame and announced in his classical, brusque manner, "Lady Amy."

Edmund bristled. Slowly he lifted his gaze, set it upon the piquant lass as she stepped into the room, draped in fine white linen, her fair hair plaited in a charming fashion. She was so damn lovely. In her presence, he was sentient of his every defect—and his every desire to be a better man. It was a stupid, wistful desire.

"Hullo, Amy," from Quincy.

Edmund firmed his jaw, feeling less hospitable. "What are you doing here, Amy?"

She was pale. She possessed light features, but her skin seemed even more pallid, iridescent in the sparkling sunlight.

He demanded roughly, "What's happened?"

"I'm being followed," she said, breathless.

The brothers exchanged knowing glances.

Quincy bounded to his feet. "I'll take a look outside."

"Be careful," she beseeched.

Quincy smiled at her before he and the butler departed from the dining room in brisk strides.

Edmund wiped his mouth, his fingers in the napkin; he lifted to his feet. With steady footfalls, he approached the trembling woman, resisting the impulse to draw her into his arms, comfort her.

"Did you recognize the men, Amy?"

"Yes, they're the same two assailants from the Pleasure Palace." She dropped her reticule on the table. "They must have discovered my identity as Zarsitti. They'll ruin me, Edmund!"

"Is that what you're worried about?" he said darkly.

"What else is there?"

"Kidnapping? Death?"

She snorted. "They want money, I'm sure of it. A bribe. I'm not Zarsitti anymore; they can't collect the hundred-pound bounty on my head, but they can blackmail *me* into giving them the lost amount."

She circled the table in a fretful gait. He spied her anxious mannerisms, heard her harried breaths. She was working herself into a frenzy. If he embraced her, he'd smother her fussy movements . . . but he'd ignite an unquenchable fire in his belly, too.

He said sharply, "Why don't you just pay them off and be done with it?"

"And *where* am I going to get a hundred pounds?"

"From your father."

"I can't go to my father." She knotted her fingers. "I can't confess my past!"

"I'll give you the bloody money."

She stilled, looked at him with wide green eyes. "You'd do that? Even after . . . ?"

"Last night?" he said roughly.

She flushed. "Do you hate me?"

He breathed slowly through his nose. "You lied to me, Amy."

"I never lied to you."

"Aye, you did." He closed the door and folded his arms across his chest. "You had no business coming to me in the park, giving yourself to me when you were promised to another man."

He choked on the last word, a wretched truth.

Amy munched on her bottom lip. "I wanted to come to you in the park. I wanted to be with you, Edmund."

The quiet confession disarmed him, upset his moody disposition. He quelled the rampant need to touch her, taste her. She looked at him with such hopeless longing, he very nearly crossed the room and took her in his arms for a savage kiss.

I want you too, Amy.

He smothered the unfit impulse. She was a duke's daughter. He was a pirate's son. If desire burned between them, the damnable heat was moot.

"I'll fetch the blunt."

"Wait!" She circled the room again, brandished her

hands. "The assailants haven't approached me with any demands. What am I supposed to do with the money?"

The sound of her swooshing petticoats rattled his sensitive senses even more. "What do you want from me, then? Do you want me to kill the blackguards?"

She paused and gasped. "I'm not asking you to commit murder . . . not yet."

He looked at her with a wry expression. "Then why did you come here?"

"I need your help. You have a friend, a Bow Street Runner. Can he look into the matter for me? Arrest the men?"

"You'd prefer a stranger's help to mine?" he said tightly.

"*You* trust your friend, so I trust him, too."

The stiffness in his muscles loosened, and he warmed at the thought that the woman believed in him, trusted him.

She said quietly, "Will you help me?"

He gazed into her eyes, so imploring. He might never stand beside her in society as her social equal, but he would always stand behind her as a friend. "Yes."

She sighed. "Thank you."

"What about your fiancé?"

She hardened. "What about him?"

"Why didn't you ask him for assistance?"

She grabbed a chair, crushed the wood between her fingers. "I'm not very fond of the marquis."

"Trouble, Amy?"

"Yes," she bit out. "I have to marry him, the lout."

He stared at her, confounded. It was the ambition of every chit in society to snag a titled husband, even if he was a lout, and her betrothal to the marquis assured her position within the *ton*.

"What's going on, Amy?"

She stroked her fingers across the chair's ornate headpiece. "I have to marry the marquis . . . but I don't want to be with him."

Gravenhurst was a bloody peer of the realm, though. He offered her respectability and security and every other social advantage that she had longed for since being in the rookeries. Was she really displeased with such an advantageous match?

"Why?" he demanded.

"I don't like him," she said in a flat voice. "We don't suit."

"Are you sure, Amy?"

"Yes, I'm sure," she snapped, still rubbing her fingers across the chair's headpiece in a mindless fashion. "I don't want to be with the marquis."

Who do you want to be with, then?

He'd almost asked her the daft question. In truth, it didn't matter whom she set her cap on, for *he* would never be one of her suitors. He was a former pirate. He wasn't good enough for the woman.

"Cry off," he suggested.

"I can't." She balled her fingers around the chair. "It's complicated, Edmund. I've been away from society for so long, folks view me with suspicion. A respectable match will assure my standing in good society, but if I cry off, I'll disgrace my parents, especially my father, who made the betrothal contract. I'll be branded a jilt, too."

"I understand," he said gruffly, her words sinking into his skin like sharpened teeth. He looked at her thoughtfully. "I'm sorry you're unhappy, lass."

She quieted and shrugged. "I might not be for very long."

"Do you intend to poison your fiancé?"

"No."

"I won't breathe a word of it, I promise."

She huffed. "I'm *not* going to poison him."

"Pity."

She glared at him. After a short pause, she said, hesitant, "I have another idea."

That she was scheming to be rid of the marquis livened his heart, warmed his blood, and while some other coxcomb might woo her one day, he'd enjoy the subterfuge for a time—even if it offered him false hope. "What is it?"

"If the marquis's reputation is publicly tarnished, my father will break the betrothal contract; he'll insist I *not* marry the lord, and no one will think ill of me for obliging him. After all, I can't be expected to wed an unrespectable gentleman."

He snorted at her mettle. She'd acquired the manipulative traits of every other gentlewoman in society, so her marriage to the marquis seemed a pointless front to Edmund; she *was* a proper lady.

"And how do you intend to tarnish his reputation?"

"I can make a past indiscretion public. Anonymously, of course. Once the tale's printed in the scandal sheets, I'm free."

"Oh?"

"I know it sounds hypocritical. I lived as Zarsitti for three years; I've my own past indiscretions to hide, but I *can't* wed him. Besides, he's a man. A marquis! He'll endure the gossip without discomfort."

"I'm not judging you, Amy."

"You judged me last night," she countered with spirit, her green eyes bright. "You thought me a selfish harlot, admit it."

He rubbed the back of his neck, the muscles taut. "I was angry with you."

She humphed. "Well, I'm not, you know."

He looked at her bottom lip, pouting. "I know." After a short pause: "Well, what's the indiscretion?"

She lowered her voice. "I'm not sure. I followed him today."

"Where?"

"A small churchyard on the outskirts of Town. It's also where I first spotted the attackers. There's a grave there with a pair of doves etched into the marker and the letters RUD."

There was a growing warmth in his belly. "You're learning to read?"

"I am, but I've still more to learn." She pushed a lock of loose hair behind her ear. "The deceased is twenty years of age and he or she is buried in unconsecrated ground."

"Really?"

She nodded. "The grave means a lot to the marquis."

"And you hope to unearth some salacious gossip about it?"

"I don't *want* to hurt him," she contended, her cheeks a deep rose. "But I don't see any other way out."

He stroked the back of his head, disorderly thoughts stomping through his skull. "Fine. Let me take care of it."

She looked at him with wide eyes. "The grave?"

"The grave. The bandits. Everything."

"Edmund—"

Quincy entered the dining room; he opened the door without rapping on the wood, breathless, as if he'd sprinted through the streets.

"Anything?" from Edmund.

"It's clear." Quincy then glanced at Amy. "You're safe."

She sighed. "For now."

And always.

Edmund turned toward his brother. "Take her home, Quincy."

The pup nodded.

Amy gathered her reticule, her eyes alert, probing. "What are you going to do, Edmund?"

"First, I'm going to muzzle the hounds chasing after you."

Chapter 21

The low candlelight, the soft furnishings ensnared the senses. It was easy to dream at the Pleasure Palace. It was easy to imagine a shapely figure, outfitted in sensuous silks, dancing across the platform, gyrating its hip bones, undulating its waist in rhythm to the haunting drumbeats.

"Mr. Hawkins."

Edmund shifted his gaze away from the stage area. He eyed Madame Rafaramanjaka as she slowly approached him, swinging her voluptuous hips in a lush ensemble of fine green glacé silk.

"How charming to see you again," she said in a throaty voice as she joined him at the corner table: the same corner table where he'd first set eyes on Zarsitti. "You wished to speak with me?"

"Good evening, Madame Rafaramanjaka."

She folded her smooth hands, wove her fingers together, and rested them on the table's polished surface. "And to what do I owe the honor of your visit?"

"I'd like you to call off your hounds."

She lifted a dark, slender brow. "I beg your pardon?"

In an idle manner, he skimmed his eyes across the thinly populated gentlemen's club. "It's quiet here tonight." He looked at the shrewd queen again, her features aglow. "Isn't Zarsitti scheduled to perform?"

"Zarsitti doesn't perform here anymore," she returned tightly. "She's been kidnapped by a Turkish sheik. I'm working on retrieving her from the harem."

"Hmm . . . without the dancer, you're operating just another whorehouse—and not a very popular one at that."

The woman's lips soured. "What do you want, Mr. Hawkins?"

"You must be very angry with Lady Amy for deserting you."

"Who?"

"I'm sure you read the papers . . . Your Highness."

She narrowed her black eyes on him. "You're the bitch's lover, aren't you?" She firmed her fists. "I hope she slowly roasts in hell. She abandoned me, the ungrateful harlot."

"She's the daughter of a duke."

"She's a slut! And she left me without a show. I'm still training her replacement. It'll take the new girl many more months to learn all the seductive dances."

"I'm sure it will," he drawled. "I'm also sure you'd like nothing better than to see Lady Amy suffer for it."

"That's right," she said succinctly.

He glowered at her. "Well, that's why I'm here. Call off your hounds."

"Is the whore in trouble?" She smiled. "How marvelous."

"If you hurt her," he said with a darkened expression, "I'll see you hang."

The woman's eyes flashed. A dark fire burned in the murky pools. "I'd like nothing better than to see the tart dead, but I'm not willing to hang for the pleasure." She lifted from her seat and leaned over the table. "I've sent no hounds after her. I don't hate the slut enough to burn alongside her, Mr. Hawkins."

Slowly the dethroned queen sauntered away.

Edmund stared after her curvy figure, frowning. The deceitful woman refused to admit her involvement with the attackers. The arrogant, narcissistic queen might cherish her neck, but she possessed a wicked, vengeful spirit, too. She'd orchestrated the threat against Amy, he was sure. But how was he going to prove it?

Edmund departed the Pleasure Palace in brisk strides and headed through the Covent Garden district. He passed through Bow Street, making his way toward Anne Street, where he entered an apartment structure. On the third floor, he located the proper loft door and pounded on it with his fist.

In a few moments, the barrier opened, and Edmund swaggered inside the room, disgruntled.

"I need a favor, John."

The investigator yawned and closed the door. "Didn't I already do you a favor?"

As Edmund folded his arms across his chest, he leaned against the wall. "What do you do when you know someone's guilty of a crime but you don't have enough evidence to prove it?"

"What's going on, Eddie?" He scratched his head, somnolent. "Are you in trouble?"

Amy was in trouble, at the mercy of bandits, but it was their "employer" who really posed a threat, for if the attackers were apprehended, there was nothing preventing the queen from hiring more cutthroats to torment the lass.

"Just tell me, John."

John rubbed his eyes. "Look for more evidence, I guess."

Edmund frowned. "I'm not in the mood for jests."

"Nor am I. What time is it, anyway?"

"I don't know." Edmund stalked across the room, restless. "Well?"

"Why don't you just beat a confession out of your suspect?"

"I can't."

"Why?"

"It's a woman."

The investigator lifted a curious brow. "Are you going to tell me what this is about, Eddie?"

"No."

John stroked his chin, then sighed. "Well, what's your suspect's motive?"

"Revenge," he returned succinctly. "And why were *you* so sure the footman from the dowager Lady Stevenson's estate had nabbed the family jewels? You didn't even have the baubles in your custody at the time."

"There were too many coincidences." He shrugged. "It was logical to assume the footman had discarded the jewels to protect himself."

That was Edmund's trouble, too. It was too great a coincidence, the circumstances between Amy's attackers and the Pleasure Palace: a coincidence he wasn't able to ignore. But coincidence wasn't akin to proof.

"What about another suspect?" suggested John. "Can the clues point to a different villain?"

Edmund pinched his brows in contemplation. Another suspect? He mulled over the prospect that the attackers were working independently of a master, but he quickly dismissed the idea, for it implied the bumbling cutthroats were savvy enough to orchestrate an abduction on their own.

Could one of the guards at the Pleasure Palace be involved? But what would be the man's motive? Greed? Did he think to sell Amy to a real Turkish sheik? Edmund doubted the athletic yet dim-witted sentries capable of formulating such a complicated plan. And there was still the matter of Amy's anonymity. She had always veiled her features and painted her eyes to protect her true identity. The attackers knew her as the lowly dancer from the city's rookeries. How had they discovered she was Lady Amy, the Duke of Estabrooke's daughter?

Someone *had* to have informed the attackers about

her true heritage . . . and every bit of evidence pointed to the queen.

"No," said Edmund with confidence. "I'm certain it's her."

John scratched his belly. "Follow her, then. If she's engaged in criminal activity, catch her in the act."

Madame Rafaramanjaka was too shrewd to be prowling the streets at night, hunting Amy, hence she'd hired the attackers to hound the lass. She'd not associate with the brutes again, he was sure. He had to find some other way to implicate the cruel woman.

"That won't work, either."

John chuckled in a hoarse voice. "Why don't you do what I do when I'm flummoxed . . . sleep on it?"

Edmund sighed, disgruntled. "Not yet, I'm afraid. I've still a cemetery to visit."

The shouts from the rowers mixed with the babbling ladies and trilling birds, the mesh of vivacious voices such a contrast to the quiet sunset.

The riverside terrace at Mortlake was brimming with an evening tea party. Amy observed the enchanting parkland from her seat at the table. She twirled her parasol between her fingers as she admired the glowing sun, sinking behind the arched bridge. The water shimmered like liquid fire, the ripples like small flames. Boats glided across the surface, dark silhouettes against the brilliant backdrop.

"Is everything all right, my dear?"

"Yes, Mama," said Amy. "It's a beautiful summer night, isn't it? I think I'll take a turn through the grounds."

The duchess smiled. "Don't soil your dress."

Amy chuckled. She was one-and-twenty years of age and yet her mother persisted in treating her like a child. She didn't mind, though. She had to make up for fifteen years of missed coddling.

Amy excused herself from the gaggle of matrons. She strolled the terrace in harmony with the cool breeze that floated off the river, stirring her pristine white hemline. She descended a series of stone steps, leading toward the well-hewed turf. As she passed between the noble trees, she searched the terrain for the marquis. He was at the tea party, too, trolling the grounds. She soon spotted his solitary figure.

Amy paused. She observed the morose man as he stared at the sunset in silent contemplation. She had learned his secret at last. It was a sad tale; he hadn't a tainted past worthy of the scandal sheets. And his "indiscretion" was a matter of opinion. It'd disturbed her father, an elitist, but it had saddened Amy.

As she spied the lonely lord, she reflected upon her own bitter, turbulent past. A more compassionate tactic might suit her aims better. If she appealed to his heart, she might get *him* to end their engagement, instead.

She gathered her composure and slowly approached the brooding figure.

He turned his head slightly. "Do you grow tired of the gossip, Lady Amy?" He looked back at the sunset.

"I'm afraid that doesn't bode well for your future as a marchioness."

She stilled beside him. "And what qualities should the future Marchioness of Gravenhurst possess, my lord?"

"She should be of good stock, prideful, manipulative . . . a gossip."

"I'm afraid I won't make you a very fine wife, then."

He glanced at her sidelong. In the burning twilight, his gold eyes sparkled red. "I think you have your father's blood."

She looked away from him, suppressed a creeping chill. What did her father have to do with her being a good wife?

Confounded, she pressed on with "I can't even read."

"I'm aware of your defects," he said tersely. He folded his hands behind his back. "But your faults won't prevent our wedding."

"And what will?" she wondered, trembling.

He returned quietly, firmly, "Nothing."

Her heart shuddered. "We are not suited, my lord."

"I'm not concerned with our suitability, Lady Amy."

"But you didn't even *want* to marry me a few months ago; I heard you tell my father so in the study."

He shrugged. "I've changed my mind. I've decided to honor my duty. And I suggest you do the same." He peeked at her askance, his eyes seedy. "I'll not take too kindly to being jilted, Lady Amy. In truth, I'll be *very* displeased."

She frowned at the veiled threat, her skin warming, yet she resisted quarreling with the unpleasant man. He was a wounded soul, she reminded herself. He had suffered, *still* suffered. She might reach his heart yet.

"You must see that's impossible, my lord." She looked at the distant terrace, at her beloved mother. "I'd disgrace my family."

"Even if it means losing your lover?"

She stiffened at the murmured words and blushed at the memory of the marquis's inappropriate regard that night in the garden. He had peeped at her and Edmund, ogled their most intimate encounter. It roiled her blood, the recollection.

"I don't have a lover," she returned in a stiff voice.

He chortled; the vibrato rattled like chains. "There's no need to be missish, my lady. I've already told you, I won't stand in the way of true love . . . you do love Mr. Hawkins, don't you?"

Amy's heart cramped. She firmed her muscles, pinched her lips to keep the marquis *out* of her soul. He was rummaging through her innermost reflections, and she bristled at the thought that he'd pried into her most private ruminations.

"I've been away for fifteen years," she said tightly. "Do you want me to cause my parents even more pain?"

"I care nothing for your parents' feelings!"

The savageness in his voice disarmed her, and she blinked. "There is compassion in you, I know it."

"Do not fool yourself," he said brusquely as he stepped in front of her, glaring. "You will be very disappointed."

"You have a heart, Gravenhurst," she insisted, and clutched the parasol with greater vim. "Call off the betrothal and spare us both a lifetime of misery."

"I am already miserable." He eyed her with fierce, piercing regard. "My life will not change for having you as my wife . . . and I've not a heart for you to milk, Lady Amy."

"Yes, you do." She maintained her poise even as he blustered and her heartbeats increased. "You've concealed it well, but I know you have it . . . I've seen it."

"What do you think you have seen?" he drawled in a low voice.

Amy licked her lips. "I saw you at the cemetery . . . a-at Ruby's grave."

He quickly rotated his heavy form and presented her with his towering backside. She spied his knotted fingers at his rear, the appendages white. The man's wide shoulders ballooned as he swallowed deep mouthfuls of air.

Amy sagely waited for him to gather his composure. She had received word from Edmund about the grave at the outskirts of Town. She had misread the letters in her ignorance, and the "RUD" was, in truth, the start of "RUBY": a Miss Ruby Duncan.

"I know you loved her," she said softly. "I know she ended her own life and you're grieved by her loss, so have mercy—"

Amy shrieked and dropped the parasol as two fists came at her. He slammed his knuckles into the rough bark behind her head, blood spurting from the wounds; she sensed the light spray on her cheeks.

"If you utter one more foul word, I'll rake my knuckles over your teeth."

She trembled, pinned between his snarling features and the tree. She wanted to scream. She glanced at the terrace and the coterie of females engaged in gossip. If she screamed, it'd cause a scandal. She pinched her quivering lips before she attracted their attentions, her heart in her throat, constricting her airway.

"Never," he growled. "Never again."

He pegged her with a black expression. Tears welled in her eyes. She struggled with her gibbering thoughts, her harried breath. She ached with a stiffness in her bones as she girded her muscles in anticipation of the madman's savage blows.

"Never say her name in my presence, you cursed, wretched spawn!"

Amy swallowed her tears, choked on them. She flinched as he pressed his bloody thumb across her cheek, smearing the warm fluid.

"Is this the heart you were speaking of, Lady Amy?" There was a darkness in his eyes, black as cinder. He burrowed his thumb into her cheek, grinding the bone, making her wince. "Is this the compassion, the mercy you believed rested inside me?"

He shuddered as he said the words. He resisted thrashing her right there in the park; she observed it in his twisted visage. He grimaced with the pulsing need to maim her, and he grappled with his wits to keep his feral instincts under control.

"Well, take a good look at me, for I will soon be your husband," he hissed. "I will *not* cry off. *This* is whom you will have to endure for a lifetime of misery. Accept it." He stepped away from her, haggard, his eyes flashing. "Begone from my sight! I don't want to see you again until our wedding day."

Amy clamped her sweating palm over her mouth, curtailing her cries as she stumbled and dashed into the woods.

She looked over her shoulder to make sure the mad marquis wasn't in pursuit before she slowed her frenzied steps and sobbed.

She wiped the blood from her cheeks with the kerchief she had tucked up her sleeve; her tears sluiced the red stains.

"Never," she vowed as she scrubbed her face with zeal, washing away the lord's vile touch. "Never will I wed the Marquis of Gravenhurst."

Chapter 22

The distant clock tower chimed the hour of midnight. Edmund remained at the garden's edge, observing the town house, the occupants asleep, the rooms dark—but for one burning light.

He had spotted the figure in the window an hour ago. He wasn't able to see inside the bedroom, for it was too highly elevated, but he maintained a watchful eye on the shimmering lamplight—and the restive shadow prowling behind the wispy drapes.

At length, the illumination expired.

"Sweet dreams, Amy."

He guarded the house, concealed by the tall stone wall, the shrubbery and fruit trees. He had yet to determine how he was going to apprehend the queen. In the meantime, he was prepared for an all-night vigil. If the attackers approached the quiet dwelling, it'd be a swift doom for the pair.

A few minutes later, Edmund spotted a lone figure. It skulked from the structure through the arched terrace doors, lugging a carrying bag.

Amy.

It was her unique frame; he recognized it even in the darkness. He moved toward her with quiet footfalls and whispered, "Where are you going, lass?"

She yelped and started, peered into the blackness. "Who's there?"

He emerged from the shadows.

"What are you doing here, Edmund?"

"Protecting you." He took her by the wrist and dragged her off the flagstone walkway, steered her beneath a shelter of trees. "What are *you* doing?"

She dropped the bag at his feet. He sensed the chamomile wash in her hair; the soft scent kissed her flesh and welled in his lungs like a spell, charming him. She was so warm. He sensed the heat from her pores. She was breathing at a slightly rapid rate, too.

"Well?" he said in a low voice.

"I'm going to Gretna Green."

He stiffened. "You're eloping with the marquis?"

A coldness entered his heart. She had changed her mind about marrying the man. It was the right thing for her to do, for the marquis was her social equal *and* he was her father's choice for a mate. She would be more content with the marquis in the long term . . . and yet Edmund gnashed his teeth at the thought of it.

"Don't be daft," she chastised. "I'm eloping with *you*."

He blinked. "What?"

"It's a good thing you're here." She picked up her bag. "It saves me the trouble of making my way into

St. James. If we leave tonight, we can be in Scotland by Sunday. I'm at the age of consent, so I don't need my father's permission to wed."

"Amy." He rubbed the back of his head. "Stop."

A welter of thoughts in his brain, he paused for a few seconds, sorting through the dissenting voices . . . and the cheering ones that crowded in his head. The lass had changed, he reflected. A few months ago, she would never have suggested anything so spontaneous—or reckless—and yet here she was, in the garden at midnight, demanding that he marry her.

"What's the matter?" She set down the luggage again, frowning. "You want to marry me, don't you? You said so right here in the garden, I remember."

"I did?"

"Aye, you did." She folded her arms over her breasts. He sensed the soft swishing sound of her skirts as she tapped her foot in rapid strokes. "You said you would only touch me as my husband."

He hardened at her provocative words—and the sweet promises the words suggested. He struggled with his reflections. "I don't remember saying that, Amy."

"It was something similar, I'm sure."

A need filled him, a wretched longing. He wanted to take her away. Far away. Into the Highlands. Before he surrendered to the irresponsible impulse, he distracted her from the passionate entreaty with "What happened with the marquis?"

She spat. "The black-hearted devil!"

He brushed her cheek, so soft, so warm, pulsing with blood. "Tell me, Amy."

"I implored him to end the engagement."

He sensed the frailty in her voice, and his every muscle cramped in response to it. Without a word, he opened his arms. She stepped into his embrace, wrapped her hands around his midriff, squeezing, filling him with her heat. He hugged her tight in return, smothered her until his stiff joints sighed in comfort.

"I appealed to his heart, but he doesn't have one," she mumbled into his shirt. "He's an infernal beast!"

Edmund buried his lips in her sweet-smelling hair and bussed the crown of her head, weaving his fingers through her thick tresses, breathing in the essence of her. He stroked her rigid spine, too, strummed the knobs of bone in an even manner.

"He didn't cry off, like you'd hoped?"

She rolled her face in his chest, shaking her head. "And I won't wed him!"

He sighed. "You don't have to wed him, Amy."

She looked up at him. In the dark shadows, she was a part of him, for the night concealed her noble attire, her aristocratic profile. In the dimness, she was an outcast in the garden, like him. And for a moment, he believed . . .

"My parents will get over the shock, Edmund."

He rubbed the base of her skull, cradled her neck in his palm. He pressed his thumb against the pulse at her throat and memorized the rhythmic beats. The life teeming inside her stirred something within him, moved his heart to thump at a matching tempo.

"Yes," he murmured, "your parents will get over the shock of your broken engagement."

"No." She fisted his coat between her fingers. "I mean, they'll get over *our* wedding. I still need to marry, Edmund. I need to wed a respectable gentleman, so there won't be any whispers about me in society."

A cold, rugged pain twisted in his gut. He grabbed her fingers and loosed her tight hold before she severed his veins with her wistful promises.

"I can't marry you, Amy."

She blinked. "What the devil do you mean, you won't marry me?"

He raked his fingernails along his scalp. "I said I *can't* marry you."

She was quiet. Still. He listened to the sound of her breathing as it steadily increased in sound and speed.

"I'm sorry, Amy. I once thought I could make you happy, but it isn't true. I'm *not* a respectable gentleman, and your family will *never* approve of our marriage. If we wed, your parents will disown you, and you've lived apart from them for fifteen years. You can't lose them again, not because of me."

She stared at him, unmoving. After a few silent moments, she turned away from him, rubbing her temples in circular movements.

He reached for her, stretched his fingers toward her arm, but a stringent voice in his head censured him, and he pulled his hand away, firmed it into a fist.

"One day, you'll grow to hate me, Amy. As you come to miss your parents' company, you'll see me as the cause of the estrangement."

Slowly she confronted him again. "You have good relations, Edmund. Ducal in-laws. My father will come to accept you in time. Mother even sooner, I'm sure. And the *ton* will forget about my broken engagement to the marquis. Once I'm properly wed, that is."

He returned stiffly, "Your father will *never* accept me."

"Why?" she demanded.

"I'm a pirate."

She offered no expression of outrage or even disbelief. As the quiet seconds lengthened, he thought about commenting on the situation, but she soon flicked her forefinger and stabbed him in the chest with it.

"If you don't want to marry me anymore, then say so, but don't invent such outlandish, childish tales."

He circled her wrist with his fingers, sensed her pounding pulse. "I'm telling you the truth."

"You're a pirate?" she said with sarcasm. "And I'm really Zarsitti, a Turkish princess."

Edmund cupped her defiant chin. "I was a pirate for many years."

She snorted.

"We were all pirates."

"We?"

"My brothers and I." He thumbed her chin. "After Belle married the duke, we retired from piracy."

"I don't believe you."

He pressed his thumb against her plump lips, silencing her. "It's true. I served under my brother James . . . Black Hawk."

She parted her lips, gasping. "James is the infamous pirate Black Hawk?" After a few thoughtful moments, she said, "I can believe that." She pulled her chin away from his fingers. "But Black Hawk is dead. James killed him at sea when the marauder kidnapped Sophia."

"It was staged to put an end to our past, to protect Belle from the threat of our identities being revealed."

"So you *are* a thief?"

"That's right," he said succinctly. "I might be a gentleman now, but that doesn't negate who I once was at sea. Do you see now why I can't be with you, Amy?"

"No."

"I'm a cutthroat," he reiterated.

She tsked. "I'm not going to tell my father about your past."

"You don't have to tell him . . . he already knows the truth."

"What?"

The bile in his belly burned at the memory of his last heated encounter with the Duke of Estabrooke. "He isn't privy to the details, to my years at sea as a pirate, but your father *knows* I'm a wastrel; he senses it. He will never approve of our marrying. I'm not good enough for you, Amy. I'll never be good enough for you."

She caressed his hips in eager strokes. "That isn't true, Edmund."

"Damn it, Amy!" He fisted her wrists again, for she tempted him with her sensual touches . . . tormented him. "It can't be between us! Don't fool yourself into thinking we have a future together. You *don't* belong with me."

She kissed him.

It was a hard, passionate gesture; it snatched his wits away. He cried into her hot, needful mouth with longing, and, in an instant, he smothered her in his embrace, keeping her locked between his arms as if he might cease to breathe if he let her go.

"No," he said hoarsely.

"I want to be with you, Edmund."

He gritted his teeth at the wretched pain that churned in his belly, for he knew the words hollow, however sweet and tempting.

She silenced his protests with another sultry buss; it seized his breath, his resistance. He was hungry for her, for every wistful fancy that she'd promised him. A darker sentiment prevailed, though. A miserable truth: He wasn't fit to be her husband.

"I can't, Amy." He cupped her cheeks in a firm hold. "Damn you, woman. Stop!"

"You can't do this to me," she said, breathless.

He gnashed his teeth. "Do this to *you*? Do you think I don't cut my own heart out, turning you away?"

"Then *don't* turn me away." Biting back the tears that had formed in her shaky voice, she pleaded, "Come with me to Gretna Green."

"No," he returned tersely. "I have to protect you."

"From what?"

"From myself!"

"Arrgh!"

She stepped away from him. He watched her fretful movements as she trolled the grounds in a circle, wringing her fingers, her each disorderly step mirroring the havoc in his soul.

"I can't marry the marquis!"

"You'll find a more respectable husband in time," he said in a broken voice. "You don't have to wed the marquis."

"He's promised to make it *very* unpleasant for me if I cry off. And I'm to be married in one week! Where will I find another husband in that time?"

He returned darkly, "I'm just preferable to the lout, then?"

"He's mad, Edmund!"

"What?"

"Gravenhurst is *mad*." She paused and stared at him, her lips quivering. "He's vowed to make me miserable. At the party at Mortlake, he offered me a glimpse of our future together. It's dreadful." She shuddered. "I can't endure it."

"Did he hurt you?"

The dark sentiment passed between his dry lips in a throaty rasp; his blood burned, pounded in his head.

"He frightened me," she returned in a low voice.

He softened as he spotted the tears in her eyes, sensed her anguish. "What about your parents, Amy?"

"I know, I'm a failure." She sniffed. "I've not the strength to do my duty, to wed the marquis."

He hardened at the familiar sentiment; it festered in his head, too. "I *mean*, are you prepared to go against their wishes?"

She wiped at her eyes with her sleeve; he hadn't a kerchief to offer her, he thought sourly.

"Yes." She rubbed her nose in her sleeve, too. "I know they'll be upset at first, but if we wed, it'll lessen the scandal. I'll be married to a respectable gentleman; there won't be anything the marquis can do about it, either."

His ears burned. "Are you sure, Amy?"

"Yes!"

He stiffened with indecision, hounded by the primitive instinct to follow his wants and desires, to marry the lass and protect her from harm, even if she merely preferred him to the mad marquis. And yet he was troubled by the thought that *he'd* make her unhappy, that *he'd* harm her with an unsuitable match.

As the contention within him intensified, he sifted through his muddled reflections, grasping at reason. Had she quarreled with the marquis over the engagement? Was that why he'd frightened her? Could she reconcile with the man? Be happy?

The prospect gripped him, for if there was hope for a reconciliation, he shouldn't whisk her away to Scotland for his own selfish motives; she belonged with a better man than he.

He rubbed his brow. She was frightened, though. She had survived the rookeries. She had served the vicious queen for three years. If such hardships hadn't frightened her enough to escape them, then her ordeal with the marquis *had* to have truly alarmed her . . . and he'd never leave her to such a dismal fate. If she asked him for everything in his possession, he'd give it to her.

Breaking away from the past isn't easy, I know. But you *have a chance to make a new start for yourself with Amy, and if* you *don't take it, it's your own damn fault.*

Edmund closed his eyes; he let the scoundrel in him win.

"I'll wait for you in front of the house, Amy."

She gasped. "Oh, Edmund!"

She ravished him with another hearty kiss, wrested the groaning desire chained in his belly, and at the warm and pulsing thought that she'd be with him forever, he relished in the hot blood that drummed through his veins.

"Do you want . . . to be . . . in Gretha Green . . . by Sunday?"

"You're right," she whispered as she ended the shower of kisses. "I'll sneak through the garden with you. I don't want anyone to see me in the house."

"You can't scale the wall in your skirt."

"I can try."

"Amy."

She huffed. "Oh, all right."

She picked up her bag again. She was teeming with

energy. He sensed every breathless, bouncing movement. It nourished him as well, stilled his reservations.

"Go, Amy."

She dashed across the terrace, through the parted doors. As soon as she'd entered the dark passageway, he scaled the stone wall and skulked through the shadows, making his way toward the entrance of the town house, where he waited for her.

He spied the deserted street, the light fog rolling across the road. He rubbed his fingers together even though the late-summer night wasn't very cool. With his eyes on the door, he listened to the blood throbbing in his head. His older brother's stern reprimands resounded in his skull, too. Bellowed, really.

Irresponsible!

But he silenced the outcry, convinced himself he was making a wise decision, he was protecting Amy . . . and yet the niggling doubt remained, vociferous. It gnawed at his spirit, slowly turning cold. He was making a mistake. He was going to disgrace the lass with their marriage. A respectable gentleman? Him?

I hope the last few years you've spent playing gentleman in society has taught you one important lesson. A woman of noble blood does not associate with a seaman.

The duke's biting warning filled his head, cramped his other spirited reflections. As he fingered his hair, feeling the pressure building in his skull . . . a blackness came over him, snuffing his thoughts.

Chapter 23

"Dearly beloved, we are gathered together here in the sight of God, and in the face of this congregation, to join together this Man and this Woman in holy Matrimony . . ."

Amy stood at the foot of the altar in St. Paul's Cathedral, staring at the old bishop with wide eyes. He was so aged, his bony fingers trembled as he read the verses from the Book of Common Prayer. She spied his shaking mannerisms; he had the palsy. He might suffer an apoplexy at any moment, she thought. If the Almighty summoned him home in the next few seconds, it would postpone the wedding. She wouldn't have to marry the marquis . . . but the bishop still lived. He still prattled onward about "men's carnal lusts and appetites."

She glanced at the gold pillars that framed the quire, the breathtaking stained glass looming in the apse. At almost two hundred feet, the holy structure's impressive height seemed so ominous; she sensed its weight bearing down on her, crushing her . . .

"First, it was ordained for the procreation of children . . ."

Amy looked sidelong at her father. The duke was positioned between her and the groom, holding her right hand in a firm and proper manner, keeping her caged, his eyes directed at the bishop. A thin smile touched his otherwise dour mouth. At least he was cheerful about the union.

"Secondly, it was ordained for a remedy against sin, and to avoid fornication . . ."

She peeked at the marquis askance. He was stiff as stone, his expression inscrutable, but she was privy to his innermost thoughts, his wickedness, and as the wedded vows unfolded, her heartbeats increased, her skull teemed with the knowledge: she would soon belong to the vicious man.

If the devil wasn't so fit and robust, she might wish him an apoplexy instead, but he was filled with a dark energy that maintained his formidable physique, his miserable existence—and soon he'd set that deep-rooted rancor upon her.

"Thirdly, it was ordained for the mutual society, help, and comfort, that the one ought to have of the other, both in prosperity and adversity . . ."

Comfort in adversity.

Amy's lips quivered. She glanced from one side of the nave to the other, searching for comfort, but the stone walls, the religious monuments offered her poor succor. She was sinking, drowning in an indefinable heaviness—and she hadn't the wherewithal to save herself.

"I require and charge you both, as you will answer at the dreadful day of judgment when the secrets of all hearts shall be disclosed, that if either of you know any impediment, why you may not be lawfully joined together in Matrimony, you do now confess it."

Within the structure's vast space, the bishop's voice boomed, resounded in her head. She swallowed, her throat tightening. There was a smarting in her breast. Perhaps *she* was going to have an apoplexy. Perhaps the Almighty was going to strike her dead for the dishonesty in her heart.

"For be you well assured, that so many as are coupled together otherwise than God's Word doth allow are not joined by God; neither is their Matrimony lawful."

Amy was feeling ill, a churning movement in her belly. The marquis looked at her in an oblique manner, communicated with her using his eyes: *You belong to me.*

She pinched her lips. It was too late to voice her objections now, to break the engagement. She was trapped. The congregation was seated behind her; the legion of society members had swarmed the cathedral to witness the union. It would be a scandal, a shame beyond words if she grabbed her skirts and dashed from the holy dwelling.

Besides, where would she go? Home? The Duke and Duchess of Estabrooke would disown her, surely. And she wouldn't go to St. James, to Edmund. Never again. She would never again beseech the scoundrel for help. The bloody bastard had already abandoned her.

She inhaled a deep breath at the recollection, so cutting. After she'd reached the front entranceway of the town house, slipped through the door, her heart beating with vim . . . she'd found the street deserted, filled with mist.

The coward!

He'd changed his mind about wedding her; he'd surrendered to his misgivings, his perceived shortfalls, and had slipped away, into the darkness, dooming her to a marriage with the mad marquis.

"Samuel, wilt thou have this Woman to thy wedded Wife, to live together after God's ordinance in the holy estate of Matrimony? Wilt thou love her, comfort her, honor, and keep her in sickness and in health; and, forsaking all others, keep only unto her, so long as you both shall live?"

A set of icy gold eyes pegged her. "I will."

She shuddered. She had to go through with the wedding, even if her heart was bleeding, her pulses screaming.

"Amy, wilt thou have this Man to thy wedded Husband, to live together after God's ordinance in the holy estate of Matrimony? Wilt thou obey him, and serve him, love, honor, and keep him in sickness and in health; and, forsaking all others, keep thee only unto him, so long as you both shall live?"

She blinked, feeling woozy. A sound pressure at her hand and a stern, reproaching look from her father rustled her voice, so weak, and she said, "I will."

The bishop looked at the duke. "Who gives this Woman to be married to this Man?"

"I do," said the duke.

The bishop stepped forward.

Amy prayed he'd stumble over his ecclesiastical vestments, but he maintained his poise. He clasped her right hand between his freckled fingers, breaking the bond between her and her father. The duke walked off to the side.

Bullocks!

With trembling muscles, the bishop then guided the marquis's right hand over the bride's. "Say after me as followeth . . ."

Amy stared into the pair of wicked eyes, sparkling with warning. She was covered in a cold sweat. She had contracted the clergyman's palsy, it seemed, for her own fingers started quaking; her toes, too.

After the instruction, the marquis followed with the recitation, his voice low:

"I, Samuel, take thee, Amy, to my wedded Wife, to have and to hold from this day forward . . ."

He squeezed her hand.

She winced.

". . . for better for worse, for richer for poorer, in sickness and in health, to love and to cherish, till death us do part . . ."

Amy was about to vomit.

". . . according to God's holy ordinance; and thereto I plight thee my troth."

The bishop loosened their hands, and for a moment,

Amy breathed without restraint, but just as swiftly, the old minister set her fingers over the marquis's right hand.

"Say after me as followeth . . ."

Amy fingers twitched as the groom glowered at her with silent promises of pain—everlasting pain. Weakened, she let the hot tears form in her eyes as she recited:

"I, Amy, take thee, Samuel, to my wedded Husband . . ."

She choked. After a short pause, she recommenced in a shaky voice:

". . . to have and to hold from this day forward, for better for worse, for richer for poorer, in sickness and in health . . ."

Slowly her voice withered, her last vow a mere whisper:

". . . to love, cherish, and to obey, till death us do part, according to God's holy ordinance; and thereto I give thee my troth."

The bishop disentangled their hands.

Amy's head was pounding with blood, making her dizzy. The vertigo threatened to immerse her in darkness, and she welcomed the thought of that darkness. It was a far better fate than wedded matrimony to the mad marquis.

The bishop placed a gold wedding band on the Holy Bible, assisted by his clerk, blessing the ring. He then handed the band to the marquis.

"Say after me as followeth . . ."

His expression black, the marquis captured her left hand; his eyes narrowed on her until the gold orbs peered at her through dark slits. He repeated:

"With this Ring I thee wed . . ."

The marquis slipped the cold, smooth band over her fourth finger, claiming her as his wife.

". . . with my Body I thee worship, and with all my worldly Goods I thee endow: In the Name of the Father, and of the Son, and of the Holy Ghost. Amen."

"Amen," she whispered weakly.

The bishop opened his arms. "Let us pray."

The newlywed couple knelt at the altar.

"O eternal God, Creator and Preserver of all mankind, Giver of spiritual grace, the Author of everlasting life; Send thy blessing upon these thy servants, this Man and this Woman, whom we bless in thy Name . . ."

The tears poured from her eyes; she sobbed. The congregation likely believed them tears of joy, but she ached in her breast . . . ached for another, worthless man who'd devastated her heart.

"It's too late, Lady Gravenhurst," her husband whispered into her ear. "You're mine."

Edmund sat on the dank floor in the dark cell with his legs raised and his bruised hands folded between his knees. He'd pounded on the iron door, groped through the chinking between the blocks in the wall, screamed himself hoarse . . . and still he was trapped.

The fire had fizzled from his soul; he had lost all sense of time and orientation. He was weak with hunger, his only salvation the cool water that trickled into the compartment through the stone slabs.

Was she safe?

The thought hounded him. In the stillness, it tormented him. He had waited for her at the town house's entrance, but the blackness had smothered him before he'd reunited with her. He had stirred from his dreamless sleep to find himself in the small room, his head in pain. But the injury had passed. The zeal in his breast had sustained him, pushed him to struggle against his captivity . . . but his gaolers consisted of cold stones. Invincible. Impenetrable. Not a sound penetrated the room. Not even a sliver of light. And he suspected *his* woeful cries went unheeded, too.

He assumed the attackers at fault. The rogues, desperate for their fortune, had likely incapacitated him in the hopes of getting to Amy.

He stiffened at the pain that welled in his belly. Was the lass hurt? Was she even alive? Or had the queen had her revenge? The very thought crippled him; he refused to believe Amy was dead. He dwelled on another matter, sighing with a heaviness in his breast. How many days had passed? Was Amy wed?

He imagined her, frightened. A marchioness. Or had she escaped her fiancé? He suspected the former. She had a loyal heart. She'd not disgrace her parents with a scandalous disappearance; she'd not be welcomed home from Gretna Green without a husband.

"Arrgh!"

He slammed his fists into the floor, his knuckles

smeared with dried blood from the previous fruitless poundings. How long would he remain imprisoned in the interminable darkness? It niggled at him, small bites. Was she furious with him? Did she think he'd abandoned her? Forsaken her? It cut his heart, the idea that she believed ill of him.

An iron key rustled in the lock.

Slowly he lifted his head, listened, but there was someone at the door; he wasn't imagining the noise.

He bounded to his feet in a burst of energy, his heart palpitating, strengthening him. As he fisted his fingers, he meshed his lips together in hunger; he yearned for revenge.

The door creaked.

He grabbed the iron entrapment and yanked it; it pounded the adjacent stone wall with trembling force.

"You miserable son of a—"

The boy paled. He stood, unmoving, the key still secured between his grimy fingers and poking toward the door.

The blood in Edmund's brain burned with ungratified violence. He squinted, his eyes sore even in the weak light, and spied the grubby lad in quick assessment.

"Who sent you?"

At the terse demand, the chap stuttered, "I-I dunno." He shrugged. "I was given a coin, told to come 'ere at midnight and unlock the door. But I'll not come to the cemetery at night."

Cemetery?

"Where am I?"

Edmund scanned the rest of the chamber, identified the sarcophagi. He was in a wretched crypt! His footfalls rapid, he dismissed the boy and scaled the winding stone steps, seeking freedom.

At last, in the sunlight, he stumbled, the warm rays piercing. He made his way through the empty church, into the courtyard. The quiet countryside stretched before him, the eerie gravestones.

It was familiar, the grounds . . . the parish church on the outskirts of Town! What the devil was he doing *here*? Why had the attackers dragged him here, where they'd hounded Amy?

But he'd not the wherewithal to dwell on the matter. He had to get to London. He had to get to Amy.

Chapter 24

During the wedding luncheon, Amy sat at the head of the reception table, next to her surly husband. She fidgeted with the fare spread out across her willow-patterned plate, pushing the roasted ham from one end of the dish to the other, staring at the carved morsel with apathy.

"Eat something, Lady Gravenhurst," the marquis whispered into her ear. "I won't have you faint at our reception."

"I'm not hungry," she gritted, keeping her eyes fixed firmly on the blue-and-white earthenware, ill at ease with her new title.

He murmured, "You'll need your strength . . . for tonight."

Amy cringed.

The foul cur! He had promised her a lifetime of pain—and he intended to keep his word. He intended to torment her with thoughts of their distasteful wedding night.

She tightened her fingers around the silver fork as

vile images entered her head, polluted her soul. She then remembered Edmund's sweet touch . . . and the recollection compounded the gloom in her breast, for she wouldn't know such passion and tenderness again, not from her wicked husband.

Her belly empty, she still sensed the queasiness in her innards. She stabbed her food with the cutlery, imagined the meat Edmund's fickle heart. He had abandoned her, the bounder, and the truth of it still curdled her spirit.

"A toast." The Duke of Estabrooke lifted to his feet and hoisted a sparkling glass. "To Lord and Lady Gravenhurst."

The myriad guests in attendance raised their glasses, too. The room was filled with luscious floral arrangements, cascading from stone urns. White linen covered the tables, the furniture forming an elongated U-shape, with the newlyweds at the head of the proceedings.

Amy smiled in a polite manner at the gathered company. She scanned the amassed crowd and spotted James and Sophia Hawkins, and the Duke and Duchess of Wembury. As she eyed the scoundrel's odd yet loving family, there was sound pressure building within her skull. They might have been *her* family if the blackguard hadn't run off, deserting her.

Her father resumed the blessing: "The scripture tells us: if we suffer, we shall also reign with Him."

Amy's heart cramped at the biblical words. She would suffer, she thought. She would suffer greatly for keeping her parents content, for keeping the Estabrooke name unsullied. As harrowing as the circumstances seemed to her now, she comforted herself with the knowledge that she had protected her family from scandal.

"The duchess and I have suffered these many years, but our suffering is at an end; our daughter restored to us and to her rightful husband."

Amy looked at her husband—for better for worse. Might they form a truce? Might they come to terms with their wedded union and find civil ground?

But she quickly dismissed the fanciful thought, for her spouse clutched his table knife and glared at the duke with such icy regard, she shivered.

"From the beginning of creation God made them male and female. For this cause shall a man leave his father and mother, and cleave to his wife; and they twain shall be one flesh."

The words "one flesh" had goaded the marquis, for he stiffened, firmed his jaw bones. He was likewise put off by their joining, it seemed.

"What therefore God hath joined together, let not a man put asunder." The duke smiled, ending the toast with "To the Marquis and Marchioness of Gravenhurst. Love is eternal."

The glasses clashed all around them, a chiming symphony of well wishes, but the last remark about eternity, coupled with the snarling expression across her husband's lips, tossed Amy's spirits even deeper into the doldrums.

She was married.

Forever.

She dropped her fork and napkin on the table, her breastbone smarting. She had performed her duty as an obedient daughter. She was now a suffering wife.

She needed air.

Her husband reached for her, but she snatched her wrist away before he yanked her back to his side. He offered her a cutting glance as she bustled off, but she ignored his darkening expression. The cursed devil owned her. There was plenty of opportunity for him to heap more misery upon her. She would take one last breath of freedom before she confronted her doom.

She bunched her fingers into fists, burrowed her fingernails into her palms. As she hastened through the room, she passed the row of tall windows, the sunlight piercing. She moved quickly through the patches of warm rays, disregarding the whispers and curious looks that followed her silk-slippered steps.

The Duchess of Wembury intercepted her hustling footfalls, offering her a small smile, her lips uneven as her umber eyes revealed an uneasiness.

"Are you well, Amy?"

"I'm fine," she said succinctly, a storm of feeling in her breast, for it was the woman's wretched brother who'd condemned her to a miserable companionship with the marquis.

Mirabelle cupped her hands in a gentle embrace. "I had a talk with Quincy. He seems to think . . . Oh, this isn't the right time." She huffed. "Hell's fire! Do you have feelings for my brother Edmund?"

Amy was curt: "I assure you, I do not!"

"Good." She sighed. "I'd hate to think . . . Congratulations, Amy."

"Thank you, Your Grace," she returned stiffly.

The duchess squeezed her fingers with firmer pressure. "You and I are friends, my dear. If you ever need an ear . . ."

Amy winced at the kind offer of friendship, the balm stinging the wound on her heart, for the woman's compassion contrasted with her brother's indifference and the marquis's brutality, making her woeful situation all the more unpleasant.

"If you will excuse me, Your Grace."

She pulled her hands away and dashed off again, the looming doors so alluring, but her flight was stymied once more as the Duchess of Estabrooke stepped beside her, pale green eyes glossy with tears.

She simpered, "Oh, my dear, you're wed!"

Aye, Amy was wed. It was a foul, wretched truth. She needn't hear about it at every opportunity. She needn't be reminded she was the Marchioness of Gravenhurst.

Ugh! Even the title sounded abysmal. She munched on her bottom lip, seeking escape, peering at the doors over her mother's head.

"I want you to enjoy yourself on your wedding tour; visit all the best shops in Paris . . . and I need to talk with you about the wedding night."

Amy hardened as more unpleasant images settled in her head, making her sweat.

"A wife has certain duties she must perform . . ."

The conversation stalled as the duchess stuttered, and Amy gazed at the doors with longing, her toes restless.

"Yes, Mother," she said brusquely after a few minutes, her ears burning. "I understand. If you will excuse me."

Once more, she hurried for the doors.

Once more, she faltered.

The Duke of Estabrooke stepped between her and the exit. The man's tall figure eclipsed the doors, snuffing her hopes. She gnashed her teeth.

"I am well pleased in you, my dear."

She shifted. "Thank you, Father."

"You have made me very happy. The years of anguish I endured at your loss are naught more than a dream."

He embraced her.

She stiffened.

He had not hugged her since her return from the underworld, and at such an inconsolable moment in her life, the gesture wasn't welcome.

"If you will excuse me, Father. I must prepare for the wedding tour."

He bowed. "Yes, of course, Lady Gravenhurst."

Amy almost tripped; the title ringing in her ears. She scuttled through the doors at last and breathed with more gusto, her corset pinching. In the cool passageway, she fanned her features with her fingers, rubbed her clinched midriff.

She moved off a little more, one step . . . two, her eyes fixed on the next set of doors in the offing. Air.

She needed air. Space, too. The road wasn't too far from the front entranceway. If she slipped through it surreptitiously—

"I'd like a word with you, my lady."

She cringed as she sensed the rough pressure on her arm, the man's clipped words. Slowly she turned around and glared at her husband.

He offered her a scornful smirk. "Do not scowl at me, Lady Gravenhurst."

As his fingers burrowed into her arm, she girded her muscles.

"I'd like a moment alone, my lord."

The man's stormy eyes pegged her. "I don't think so, wife. Fetch your bags. We have a ship to catch in the morning . . . and a long night ahead of us."

The town house doors opened wide as the cheerful wedding guests streamed from the belly of the prominent estate.

Edmund, unobserved, regarded the party of merry-makers from across the street, sheltered by his anonymity. He spotted his sister, Mirabelle, and her husband. His brother, James, and sister-in-law, Sophia, appeared next to the Duke and Duchess of Wembury, sporting their finest attire. Although not of the peerage, the couple had "saved" Amy from destitution, hence their inclusion in the nuptial affair as a show of gratitude.

A crescendo of cheers and applause filled the air; as did a swarm of white rose petals, showering the newlywed couple.

He stood, transfixed, like a condemned convict standing at the chopping block, watching the executioner sharpen his axe blade. In a shimmering, pale blue pool of fine linen, with flaxen curls and bejeweled headdress, Amy radiated in the sunlight—and severed the veins in his heart.

A darkness rolled over him as he watched her slim figure descend the grand house steps, her hand intertwined with her husband's, the Marquis of Gravenhurst. At least, Edmund assumed she'd married the marquis. It was unlikely she'd found another man to marry her in such a short period of time.

He swallowed deep mouthfuls of air, expanded his breastbone in savage gluttony, taking in every bit of breath that filled his lungs, and still he starved for oxygen, drowned in a thick, murky mire that filled his soul and squelched his dreams.

"She looks beautiful."

Quincy stepped beside him, his expression somber, his eyes thoughtful.

"Aye," he said in a strangled voice. "She's beautiful."

In an idle gesture, Quincy kicked a pebble, sending it skipping across the stone pavement. "I thought I'd find you here. Where have you been these past few days?"

Imprisoned, he thought bitterly.

"I figured you'd gone off to get foxed." He shrugged. "I wasn't sure, though. I wanted to look for you, but James insisted we leave you alone, that we stay out of your affairs."

Edmund raked his molars together, for the one time the pirate captain had listened to him, obeyed his wants, Edmund wished to the devil he hadn't. If his brothers had searched for him, found him in the crypt, he'd have escaped sooner . . . and saved Amy.

"I had a talk with Belle." After a short pause, Quincy said, "Amy will be taking her wedding tour in Paris; she'll stay the night at the Montgomery Inn in Dover before setting sail for the continent." Quincy folded his arms across his chest. "She doesn't look like a blushing bride, though. She looks forlorn, don't you think?"

Edmund's heart twisted. He looked at her from across the street; she had not perceived his presence as she entered the gilded carriage with the Gravenhurst coat of arms, but he'd noted the frown that had touched her brow, her lips before she'd settled inside the vehicle.

It knotted his innards to witness her in a sorrowful frame of mind, and he gathered his breath, his wits. "I'm too late."

He observed the splendid vehicle as it set off down the street amid a hail of flickering white kerchiefs.

Quincy patted him across the back. "It's why I prefer the opium dens; the smoke helps. Come. Let's have a drink." He sniffed. "And a bath."

An hour later, Edmund stared at the glass of rum; ignored the hecklers, the foul scents that filled the flash house. The seedy patrons caroused; their guffaws and tasteless antics permeated the atmosphere, deepening his frown.

"And you think this queen sent the attackers after you?" said Quincy as he twirled an empty glass between his fingers, frowning.

"Yes."

Edmund glowered at the dark drink in his hand. At least Amy was alive. Unharmed. Perhaps she'd offered the rogues payment, ceasing the harassment. She was a resourceful lass; she'd have found some way of obtaining the necessary funds.

"Were you really going to marry her, Eddie?"

He fisted the cup. "Yes."

The word resounded in Edmund's skull, making him disoriented with vertigo. A heaviness pressed on his breast, his lungs. He breathed deep, easing the pressure, the dizziness.

"I'm too late, though."

He swigged the last of the rum, strummed his finger across the glass lip. He needed to forget that he had lost Amy, that she belonged to another man. The blood in his skull pounded like bare-knuckled pugilists. As another haunting reflection wedged itself in his head, he imagined smashing the glass against the table and taking the lacerated edge, carving out the marquis's throat.

"If the swine makes her unhappy, I'll kill him."

Quincy eyed him thoughtfully. "The marquis's a respectable gentleman; I've never heard a lick of gossip about him. I'm sure he'll take good care of her."

Edmund glared at his brother, his vision starting to turn hazy. "He frightens her."

"How?"

"He's a lout, apparently."

Quincy set his elbows on the table. "The couple might live apart after the wedding tour; it's not uncommon. If she keeps her own house, you can still be together."

He pinched the throbbing bridge of his nose between his fingers. "I won't live as her lover."

"You can't live apart from her, either."

The sage truth gripped him with such gusto, he was breathless. "I think I'll put a bullet in my head."

"It'll end your suffering, but what about Amy's pain?"

He growled, "What would you have me do? Poison her husband?"

"Swallow your pride and take care of the girl; give her whatever she needs to make it through her miserable marriage to the marquis."

Edmund burrowed his fingers into his burning eyes. A bleak sentiment possessed him. Without Amy at his side, he hadn't the desire to even breathe. He would for her sake, though. He would live in torment alongside her. Together. In hell.

Disoriented, he said, "I've seen him before."

"Who?" said Quincy.

"The marquis."

"At the house today?"

"No, before."

"At a ball?"

"I'm not sure." He shrugged, groggy with drink. "But I remember his face from somewhere . . ."

A shadowy figure formed in his foxed mind; a circle of smoke whirled around a cigar and a strange fellow's head.

"It won't help you, you know."

Edmund took a swig of the gin. "What won't help me?"

"The drink." He nursed the cigar in his bejeweled hand. "It won't help you to forget."

"It's all worthless, is it?" He chuckled at the theatrics. "The club? The drink? Is there no escape from one's 'tired' life?"

"There is escape."

"Oh?"

"In death."

"The Pleasure Palace!"

Quincy frowned. "What?"

"That's where I've met him."

Edmund grabbed his head, spinning; he delved through the murky memories, searching for the truth. He remembered the man's penetrating gaze, his enigmatic manner.

There is no salvation for me.

"I met Amy for the first time that night, too." He sifted through the lush sounds and sensuous sights in his head. "We *both* saw her that night."

This is my first visit to the club, too.

"It was the night the attacks started . . ."

Edmund lost his voice as his thoughts gathered and knotted. He remembered his friend's advice: *What about another suspect? Can the clues point to a different villain?* The investigator's officious suggestion sparked a flurry of ideas . . . and hinted at a new culprit in the attacks against Amy.

Edmund jumped to his feet.

"Where are you going?"

He stormed from the flash house, inebriated, his steps fuzzy. He had found himself at the crypt today, at the grave of the lord's former lover. Did the marquis mean to tell him . . . ?

"I have to go to Amy!"

Quincy followed him into the dark street. "Why?"

"She's in danger." He flagged a hackney coach. "It's the marquis who sent the attackers after her." He entered the vehicle, poked his head through the opened door. "After me!"

Quincy paled. "Are you sure he means her harm? What if he wanted to keep you two apart until after the wedding? He might have suspected your plans to elope."

"No!" Edmund grabbed his brother by the scruff of the shirt, twisted the fabric between his pulsing fingers. "She's in danger, I know it! I need you to go to Anne Street. Fetch John Dunbar; he's a friend. If he's not at home, go to the Bow Street Magistrates' Office. Tell him to meet me at the Montgomery Inn in Dover."

Edmund pushed Quincy away from the vehicle and pounded on the roof, urging the driver to the coast, promising him ridiculous riches if he dismissed every bit of common sense and careered toward the inn on the bustling shoreline.

Chapter 25

Amy eyed the large bed through the looking glass. In the darkened room, she spied the flickering firelight as it danced with verve across the quilted coverlet, folded and pressed neatly at the foot of the structure.

Her fingers trembled as she raked the boar bristles through her smooth tresses. The hair glistened and shined; it needed no more primping, yet she stroked the long locks in an even manner, averting her eyes from the bed, gazing into the mirror at the ruby necklace circling her throat. In the low light, the gems seemed black, like stones, weighty and pinching her airway.

"I don't want to make this more difficult than it need be, Amy."

She stiffened at the scratchy sound of the moniker, for he had never used her first name without the accompanying title, always so distant and formal, even ruthless, in his conduct, but she belonged to him now. Their wedded bond fostered an intimacy she wasn't able to ignore any longer. She had her wifely duty to perform.

Amy peered at the devil through the reflective glass. He was positioned in a wide wing chair. He had already divested his shirt. Dressed in his trousers, he brooded in the seat, his hands gripping the armrests, his long legs spread apart in a lazy manner as the firelight glowed in his eyes, like burning coals.

"Come here," he said softly.

Slowly she lowered the silver-plated hairbrush, set it atop the vanity. She listened to the hard, heavy thrusts of her heart, knocking against her breastbone. In the mirror, she detected her left breast, the muscles throbbing. Draped in a thin white night rail, the organ clearly pulsed under the light material.

She pushed away from the padded stool and approached the marquis, her every footfall a grueling effort. He followed her movements with scrutiny, moved his steely gaze across her toes, thighs, and midriff. He looked at her breasts, her bustline before he connected with her eyes.

She paused between his legs, her pulses spiking.

"Dance for me," he whispered.

She bristled. "What?"

"Dance for me, Zarsitti."

Amy fisted her fingers, her palms sweating. "Y-you know? But how?"

She had never confessed her tainted past to the marquis. How had he unearthed her wicked secret?

He touched the night rail, rubbed the soft fabric between his fingers without touching her flesh. "I saw you at the Pleasure Palace."

As he caressed the flimsy dress, she cringed. "How did you know it was me?"

"Your birthmark," he murmured. "Only I and your parents know of the kiss between your breasts . . . and your lover, of course."

She stopped breathing as he lifted his fingers and stroked the hollow between her breasts. He smiled at her stiffness, twisted his lips into a grimace.

"I'd like you to dance for me, Zarsitti." He dropped his fingers. "One last time. We will then put the past behind us and begin anew."

She breathed deep again, her muscles tingling with sensitivity. Dance for the devil? Arouse his carnal senses before he bedded her?

The nausea teemed in her belly.

She stepped away from him, firmed her lips. She thought about denying him the request—the demand!—and slamming her heel between his brows in a high kick. She imagined him toppling out of the chair, senseless. It warmed her blood, the thought.

But the man was her husband, her life partner. If she walloped him, she'd surely endure years of misery at his brutal hands. He possessed a deep-rooted darkness; she had confronted it on the riverside terrace at Mortlake. She wasn't too keen to witness such savagery again. If he was offering her a truce, if he truly desired to begin anew, she thought it wise to accept the proposal—for her own well-being.

Amy stepped nearer the hearth, chilled. She remembered the exotic dances well, but her feet seemed encased in clay. Under the marquis's critical glare, she was transfixed.

"Dance for me as if you were dancing for him . . . Imagine I was him."

She stiffened at the unseemly suggestion, for she'd no more desire to dance for the seaman than the marquis, her heart still sore from the pirate's desertion.

As the darkness thickened in her soul, she closed her eyes and steadied her breathing, meditated on more pleasant memories . . . like her first kiss with the scoundrel.

The music. The torchlight. The flora. The images filled her head as she slowly rolled her hips and undulated her waist. She moved her fingers in an artful manner as she dreamed about the dark, wooded path at Chiswick . . . and Edmund's heady voice murmuring into her ear, encouraging her to be spontaneous, to enjoy life.

Stop trying to fight Fate, Amy.

The words strangled her, wrenched the hope from her soul. She remembered the sweet kiss, so full of passion and life. She remembered the profound feelings surging through her breast, urging her to take his advice and seek contentment . . . but a cold, watery darkness now resided in her soul, for she knew she would never be cheerful again.

Amy twirled in front of the firelight, reflecting on her wretched circumstances. As her limbs twisted and her spine arched, she allowed the fresh torment to fill her veins and smother her spirit, for she had no need for hope anymore.

After a few minutes, she was spent and the dance ended. She slowly opened her eyes, disoriented. As she adjusted her distorted vision in the dim room, she made out the large chair and the dark figure ensconced within it.

"You dance beautifully, Zarsitti."

"I dance with pain," she qualified stiffly.

"I know."

He lifted from the chair and approached her in laggardly strides, his large body moving toward her like an ominous storm.

He cupped her cheek in his palm, steered her toward the bed. "I won't make this more painful than it need be, Amy."

She bumped into the bed. She was warm, her muscles loose after the vigorous stretches and movements, but she hardened as soon as he bussed her mouth, the kiss cold, like death.

"You can run to your lover in the weeks ahead." He pushed her onto the bed, glowered at her. "Every time I'm with you, you can wash away my touch by being with him; you have that comfort. I envy you that, Amy."

She scooted to the head of the bed, but he followed her, crawled over the coverlet until he had caged her between his legs, the flames in the hearth at his backside, casting his features in darkness.

"I have no lover," she whispered, bones rigid.

She winced as he stroked her cheek. Her nerves thrummed with energy as he settled his weight overtop her, pinning her to the feather tick.

"Aye, you do. And he'll come to you, even if you're my wife. Do you think he has pride?" He moved his thumb across her brow. "There is no pride when it comes to love, Amy."

She struggled for air, for distance as he swallowed her with his robust presence. He covered her like the night—a frosty winter night.

She squirmed. "I can't do this!"

"Shhh." He bussed her lips again. "It'll hurt less if you're still."

She shuddered at the forced intimacy, her muscles taut. "Can we . . . ?"

"Postpone the wedding night?" He lowered his arms, flanked her head. "I don't think so, Amy." He breathed hard, brushed her hair away from her face, her throat. "I've waited for this night for a very long time."

She opened her eyes wide as he circled her throat, pinned his thumb and forefinger across her airway, applying pressure.

Her senses screamed as a visceral strength welled in her blood, pounded in her veins. She gasped for breath and thrashed under his weight, but he paralyzed her with his bulk.

"I don't want to hurt you, Amy." His mouth quivered. "I have to, though."

He's going to kill me!

She grabbed his wrist, wheezing. She scraped her fingernails across his demented hold in frantic movements, drawing blood, but he gripped her firmly.

"Why?" she rasped.

She bucked her hips, her efforts unfruitful. It might be a ghastly fate, marriage to the marquis, but she wasn't ready to give up her life to avoid it!

He loosened his fierce fingers. "Because I hate your father . . . he killed Ruby."

Amy's heart throbbed with vim. He had parted his strong fingers, clutching her like a vise, yet still, a little air flowed into her starving lungs. He pinched her airway with just enough force, she was rendered breathless yet still conscious, and listening: listening to the dreadful unfolding tale.

"I loved Ruby," he said hoarsely. "I loved her more than my wealth, my title, my respectability. She was a country girl without an education, but she possessed spirit." He trembled. "I wanted to marry her. I wanted to break the betrothal contract I had made with your father six years earlier, but he refused; he wanted a bloody noble heritage. And he didn't want society to think his precious offspring was flawed in some way, that I'd prefer a peasant girl to you, a duke's daughter.

"I was going to end the agreement anyway; I didn't care about the scandal, but your father intervened before I could make Ruby my wife." He revealed his teeth as he gritted, "He told Ruby lies; he told her I'd never loved her, that I'd used her for sex and nothing

more, that I would never wed her, a country wench, for
I was promised to you!"

Amy sensed the tears in her eyes. The hot, briny
moisture soaked her lashes and slipped across her
cheekbones at the madman's savage words.

"Yes, your father's a monster . . . and he made me
into a fiend, too." His eyes flashed. "I found Ruby.
Dead. She had taken poison. She was pregnant with
my child and she knew the disgrace that would befall
her if she didn't marry soon. She thought I didn't care
for her." The man's voice cracked. "She died thinking
I had used her." He then seethed, "I want your father to
pay sorely for that sin."

Amy grappled with her wits, keeping her thoughts
afloat, her eyes and fingers searching for freedom.

"The kidnappers?" she said raggedly.

"Aye, the kidnappers. Hired at my behest. Fifteen
years ago, I sent the men to take you away from your
father and kill you. I wanted him to lose his only child
as I had lost mine. I wanted him to suffer with the
knowledge that his dream of a noble lineage would be
shattered at your loss, for you were his only child; your
mother wasn't able to conceive again."

She grappled with his hardy fingers as her heart
pulsed with painful exertion, keeping her alive. "But
I escaped."

"Aye, you did. You were a spirited child; you fled
into the rookeries. I thought I'd never see you again.
It wasn't the revenge I had planned; I'd wanted your
father to weep over your grave, to weep over his lost

dream, but your disappearance sufficed for a time." He seized her hair with his other hand. "I watched it torment your father for years."

She gasped, "Isn't that enough?"

"I'm afraid not, Amy." He frowned. "As soon as I saw you at the Pleasure Palace, as soon as I saw the kiss between your breasts, I knew I had found you again. I hired two cutthroats to fetch you, to bring you to me, but you evaded them." He shushed her, rubbing his thumb across her jawbone, her lips. "It doesn't matter now. The cutthroats still proved useful, spiriting your lover away."

Her eyes widened.

"No, Amy, he didn't abandon you; I'll give you that comfort. I suspected your desire to cry off, so I had the men follow you; I suspected you might run away with your lover. I couldn't let that happen, though."

She gasped, "Edmund's . . ."

"Alive," he assured her. "I'm afraid he'll mourn your loss, too. Unfortunate, really. I've no desire to hurt anyone other than your father."

As she slowly withered under the mad marquis's vicious hold, she ruminated about the pirate scoundrel. He had not abandoned her! All his tender words, his promises had remained true. He'd intended to take her away, to marry her.

She remembered everything she had shared with him over the past few months and a warmth strengthened her; she grasped at the comforting sentiment as she battled the darkness threatening to overtake her.

"I don't hate you, Amy. Not like I hate your father. I wish it didn't have to be this way." He burrowed his fingers deep into her hair. "But I have to do this, for Ruby."

"Samuel, please!"

The darkness washed over her eyes for a brief moment, then receded as he loosened his fingers, breathing thickly.

"I wish it could be different, Amy, but I can't let you live as my wife or bear your lover's child: a child I'd have to claim as my own. I can't let your father's dream of a noble legacy come to pass. I can't do that to Ruby. She's suffered enough at your father's hands."

As the pressure increased at her throat, she uttered weakly, "You're doing to me . . . what . . . my father did to Ruby."

"An eye for an eye, Amy." He growled, "I want your father to find your body with the ruby necklace. I want him to know *I* ended his dream, like he ended mine."

The darkness was slowly creeping over her eyes again. The pain, the heaviness at her throat was unbearable and she clutched the marquis's hard fingers in desperation.

"Do you remember our night together on the terrace, after the ball?" he whispered. "Do you remember our talk about the stars? They prophesied your contentment, Amy. I didn't tell you that, then . . . but I'm about to prove the damn heavens wrong."

The pounding in her head intensified. Hard, knocking sounds. Strange cries. Shouts. Shadows.

Amy gasped as the stress at her throat abated; she choked. She reached for her tender muscles, mouth agape, drawing in air, but the darkness was stronger . . .

Love is eternal.

Edmund grabbed the marquis and tossed him across the room; the wall shuddered with the fierce impact. The devil rolled and Edmund pounced on him, pounded him with his fists, slammed the side of his tightly furled hand into the fiend's shoulder, snapping his collarbone.

As the blood seeped through Edmund's veins, it pooled in his head and ravaged his senses, making him blind with vertigo, bleeding his wits. He was gripped with a feral need to tear the marquis apart—and he pummeled him with enough force to fracture his own wrist.

Yet the devil lived.

The men struggled like baited bears in a pen, pressing their weights upon each other, striking with wild passion. The commotion triggered a stirring rebellion among the inn's patrons, who gathered at the door, gawking in dismay.

Edmund crashed his knuckles into the devil's face, his features already stained with thick, hot blood. The last blow rendered the villain dead or senseless.

With loud and raspy breaths, Edmund looked at the bed . . . and the lifeless figure prostrated across the feather tick, her lovely green eyes open—and unblinking.

He groaned in a low, wounded whimper at the fragile sight of her. He was already on his knees and he crawled beside the bed, his heart beating with savage blows.

"Amy?" he rasped.

He stroked her soft, pale cheek, stained with tears. As his fingers trembled, he rubbed her bruised flesh, cupped her listless head, shaking her.

"Wake up, Amy," he whispered in a broken voice.

But her eyes remained quiet, vacant.

A dark howl welled in his belly; it burned in the bowel of his soul.

"No. No. No! *Amy!*"

He snatched her off the bed and settled her limp body on the hard wood floor. He quickly rustled her limbs and attempted artificial respiration.

He had witnessed his brother Quincy perform the procedure aboard ship after an intense sea battle . . . but as he stared into Amy's blank expression, as he imagined her gruesome final moments, alone and frightened, hope withered in his breast, and he sobbed with a bitterness that curled his heart and hardened his soul.

Forgive me, Amy.

Chapter 26

Amy was huddled in the window seat, wrapped in a warm, woolly shawl, watching the snow flurries. The first flakes of the winter season, the tiny puffs dropped quietly onto the earth; there was no wind disturbing their long journey from the heavens. The white dots slowly covered the sleeping ground, and the atmosphere changed from murky mud puddles and shriveled shrubs to a blank and pristine slate.

At the sound of sharp footfalls, she turned her head away from the frosty glass. She observed her father as he entered the sitting room, looking grave.

"How long will you stay with us in the country?"

She peered through the window once more. She eyed the ice crystals that had formed across the pane of glass in intricate patterns.

"Am I unwelcome, Father? If you prefer it, I can gather my possessions and live with friends. The Duke and Duchess of Wembury have issued me an invitation, as have Captain and Mrs. Hawkins."

Amy wasn't so bothered about her unfixed living arrangements anymore. A few months ago, she would have panicked at the uncertainty of her situation, at losing control of her surroundings, but she had found a peace that brooked insecurity, and she wasn't feeling stressed about her ambiguous circumstances. She had grounded her heart and soul in an unshakable foundation: love.

"I didn't think he would hurt you," said the duke in a stiff manner. "It's been fifteen years since the incident."

The incident. Ruby's death. Her father had no feeling; he assumed the marquis without a heart, too. But the marquis had a heart. A dark and twisted heart. An unforgiving heart.

"Yes, I'm sure you didn't know he'd hurt me." She looked back at her father with pointed regard. "But he did. And if it was legal, I'd divorce the devil on the grounds of cruelty. However, I've retained a solicitor. He will inquire into the prospect of my obtaining a divorce on the grounds of insanity."

The duke's lips firmed at the dreaded, scandalous word "divorce."

"I won't pay for it." He hissed, "It's shameful."

"You needn't pay for it, Father," she said in a steady voice. "I've other monetary means."

He stiffened at the implication, for without a generous husband or father, a married woman had no other recourse for obtaining funds except through a friend . . . or a lover.

"There are only *two* instances where a woman has successfully divorced her husband."

"Yes, I know." She maintained a cool countenance, undaunted. "I suspect my defense will fail in the end, for wickedness isn't akin to insanity. However, I will still hunt the blackguard down and see him presented in court for the attempt on my life."

The duke paled. "He is your husband."

"A pity, that, but it will not prevent me from seeking justice. I will not rest until I see *his* neck in a noose."

The court wasn't likely to be very sympathetic toward a battered wife; justice smirked at a woman's pleas in most instances, but in the rarest of circumstances, the cruelest of deeds, a legal separation was granted to a couple—if not a hanging.

The duke glowered at her with burning gray eyes, but Amy shrugged at his wrath, indifferent. He had calculated and conspired with enough innocent lives over the years. She wasn't going to let him contort a single soul more.

A footman appeared in the doorway and announced, "Mr. Hawkins to see Lady Gravenhurst."

Amy smiled. "Show him into the sitting room, please."

The servant bobbed his head and stepped away from the door.

The duke scowled. "I will *not* tolerate indecency in my own house."

"I've invited a friend to tea, Father." She returned tautly, "And I don't answer to you anymore."

The old man pressed his lips together tightly, the pink flesh turning white.

Edmund Hawkins soon entered the room and bowed.

The duke snorted and departed from the sitting room in brisk strides. As soon as he had vacated the space, Amy's stiff features softened and she smiled again.

A tingling heat moved through her veins as she gazed into the scoundrel's smoldering eyes, the dark blue pools shadowed even more by his low brow. He was dashing in his greatcoat and tall leather boots, and he warmed the chilled room with his virile presence.

She slipped away from the window seat and treaded softly across the wool runner, keeping her eyes fixed firmly on the handsome man standing in the middle of the room, unmoving, his dark, wavy hair moist with melted snowflakes.

She stopped in front of him. She sensed his increased breathing; her own heart pattered with vim. He didn't touch her. For a moment, he stared into her eyes without speaking a word or making a movement, and then he removed his fine leather gloves, lifted his fingers, and stroked her cheek, making her sigh.

He said in a tender voice, "You look well, my love."

"I am well."

She nuzzled his large palm, caressed his wrist, the fractured bone having healed after his brawl with the marquis.

Amy remembered the final black moments at the inn. She had feared the darkness, but it had transformed into brilliant light, and a peace had come over her: a peace she still carried with her in her heart.

She rubbed her fingers slowly over the man's wrist, feeling his hastened pulse. "I've missed you."

His breathing deepened, his touch strengthened. "I've missed you, too."

She relished the intimacy, however limited. The slightest contact, the softest word filled her with intense warmth.

"I can escort you into Town, if you'd like. To the orphanage."

Amy had adopted her mother's charitable inclinations, patronizing a foundling asylum alongside the woman, who quietly supported her daughter's efforts to free herself from her wicked husband.

"Yes, I'd like that," she said in a low voice. "And how are you enjoying your new employment?"

He stroked her cheek with his thumb. "I'm growing used to being on the right side of the law. I think I've found my place in the world at last."

She smiled. "Are you sure you can live without the sea?"

"I can live without anything—but for you, Amy."

She kissed his palm, still nestled at her cheek. "You're a scoundrel at heart, Edmund Hawkins."

"I know." He bussed her mouth, making her sigh again. "There's talk about forming a metropolitan police force."

"Really?"

He nodded. "It won't happen for a few more years, though."

"And James?"

"He's talking to me again. Growling, really."

She grinned. "That's good news."

"I wasn't sure if he'd ever speak to me again after I'd joined the Bow Street Runners. He's still convinced I'll bring *him* to trial for his past crimes."

"He's your brother; he'll forgive you for the treachery, I'm sure."

He humphed at that. "Quincy sends his regards."

"How is he?" she wondered in a soft voice.

"The same. Worse." He shrugged. "I'm not really sure."

She was thoughtful. "He'll find his way out of the darkness . . . you did."

Amy sensed the turmoil in her lover's soul and stepped into his arms, resting her cheek against his shoulder.

"How's William?"

He embraced her, bussed the crown of her head. "He might set sail in the spring again."

"I'm glad to hear it."

The Hawkins brothers were doing well for the most part; that was really all that mattered, for with each day that passed, there was hope for a stronger future. She had learned that lesson, as well.

As Edmund's muscles stiffened, she lifted her chin and looked into his ruminating eyes. "What is it?"

He stroked her spine. "I have news about Graven-hurst."

After he'd joined the Bow Street Runners, Edmund and his fellow comrades had searched for the pusillanimous marquis, who had vanished from the inn at Dover. The devil had regained his wits after the fracas and, in the tumult, had slunk off into the night. He had likely boarded a vessel for the continent, although Amy wasn't entirely sure of his whereabouts.

She wasn't disconcerted at the remark about the marquis either, for the villain possessed no hold over her senses or her heart . . . however, he prevented her from realizing one important dream: marrying Edmund. Unless a divorce was granted—or she was widowed—she'd never have the pleasure of calling the handsome scoundrel "husband" or keeping a home with him, a family.

There was a twinge in her breast at the gloomy thought. "You've located the marquis?"

"No . . . but his wife found me."

Amy blinked. "What?"

He steered her toward the divan and settled beside her in the comfortable seat. "A woman approached me at the magistrates' office, claiming to be the marquis's lawful wife. She carried papers to prove it; there are church witnesses, too."

She gaped, breathless. "But how?"

"After Ruby's death, the marquis delved into a debauched existence. He traveled as far as Scotland and immersed himself in the habit of drink. Apparently he wed a Scottish bride in a drunken stupor." He caressed her fingers, the appendages trembling. "The marriage laws in Scotland are more lax than those in England, though still legal. As soon as he sobered, the marquis paid the wench to keep away from him, and she was happy to accept the terms; she was a common barmaid and she desired to remain in her homeland with her family. The throat-cutting ways of the *ton* didn't appeal to her, it seemed. As soon as she had heard of the marquis's wedding to you, though, she feared the monthly stipend would end, and she came to London, seeking her rightful place as the marchioness."

Amy munched on her bottom lip. She clasped Edmund's hand and squeezed it tight between her fingers as a stirring energy welled in her belly, threatening her composure. "Th-that means . . ."

"That means, with the proper evidence, the Consistory Courts in the Doctors' Commons will have to grant you an annulment on the grounds of bigamy; your marriage to the marquis isn't legal."

She shuddered as the last gloomy thought pinching her heart was snuffed out.

She was free.

"It's over," she whispered, weakened with joy.

"The legal proceedings might take some time, Amy."

"But there's hope."

She was filled with the blessed sentiment; it touched her every pore.

"But I still don't understand," she said in a quiet manner. "Why did the marquis marry me if he was already wed to another woman?"

"Revenge," he returned succinctly. "He wanted the duke to think he'd achieved all his dreams, his goals . . . before he took them away."

Amy sniffed. She hadn't even sensed the tears. The briny drops washed away so many months of hardship. A new dream sprouted in her soul: a dream for a better life . . . with Edmund.

He rubbed her hands between his palms in methodic strokes, silent, brooding.

"What's the matter, Edmund?"

He eyed her with intent. "When the annulment is settled, will you be my—?"

"Yes!"

She threw her arms around his neck and kissed him with the desire that had been building within her heart for months.

He chuckled, his eyes bright, but then he steadied his merry features. "Are you sure you want to marry me, Amy? There will be unhappy folks at our wedding."

"Like my father?" She scoffed. "I'm not going to let our fate mirror that of Gravenhurst and Ruby. I'm not going to let convention dictate the truth in my heart."

He looked away from her.

"Do you still think you're not good enough to be my husband?"

"I'm *not* good enough for you, lass." He looked back at her with passion, his words shaking. "But I love you with a fierceness in my soul that takes away every bit of good sense I own."

"I love you, too." She grinned, cupping his hands. "And I've decided to take your advice: I'm going to have more fun in life."

He laughed; the rumbling sound warmed her ears. "I guess that means I'm going to have to be more responsible."

He kissed her, then; the gesture singed her right down to her toes.

"You've seduced me, Amy," he murmured into her mouth.

She snuggled with him on the divan, cherished the closeness. "And I'll keep seducing you for the rest of our years together, you notorious scoundrel."

Next month, don't miss these exciting new love stories only from Avon Books

Seven Secrets of Seduction by Anne Mallory
She might not be part of society, but Miranda Chase is just as captivated as everyone else by the salacious book that has the *ton* atwitter. When she writes an editorial about it that draws a debaucherous viscount to her uncle's bookshop, Miranda's quiet life will never again be the same.

Sugar Creek by Toni Blake
Rachel Farris returned to Destiny with one mission: protect her family's apple orchard from the grasping Romo clan. But hard-nosed, sexy Mike Romo is the law in town, and he won't back down until his family gets what's rightfully theirs. This longtime feud is about to heat up with electricity that neither anticipated.

Tempting a Proper Lady by Debra Mullins
Captain Samuel Breedlove needs to stop Annabelle Bailey's wedding. Priscilla Burke is desperate for it to go on. As the proper lady and questionable gentleman meet head to head, it seems a seduction—with unforeseen consequences—might be in order.

When Marrying a Scoundrel by Kathryn Smith
When her dashing husband left to seek his fortune, heart-broken Sadie Moon made a new start for herself. A successful businessman, Jack Friday has everything he ever wanted... except Sadie. But when their paths cross under most unexpected circumstances, will their undeniable attraction rekindle a love once lost?

At Avon Books, we know your passion for romance—once you finish one of our novels, you find yourself wanting more.

May we tempt you with . . .

- **Excerpts** from our upcoming releases.

- Entertaining **extras**, including authors' personal photo albums and book lists.

- Behind-the-scenes **scoop** on your favorite characters and series.

- **Sweepstakes** for the chance to win free books, romantic getaways, and other fun prizes.

- Writing **tips** from our authors and editors.

- **Blog** with our authors and find out why they love to write romance.

- **Exclusive content** that's not contained within the pages of our novels.

Join us at
www.avonbooks.com

AVON

An Imprint of HarperCollins*Publishers*
www.avonromance.com